The Cross and the Badge

From the case files of Detective Will Diaz (ret.)

Book 1 of the Lawman series

By William R. Ablan

"For I know the plans I have for you," *declares the* LORD, *"plans to prosper you and not to harm you, plans to give you hope and a future."*

Jeremiah 29:11 New International Version (NIV)

Dedicated to the Love of my life who believed in me from the very beginning . . .

. . . And to the boys and girls who wear the badge. May God keep you safe every day!

CHAPTER ONE

IRAQ

The blood was long gone.

But then what did I expect. After all, it had happened on this very spot of ground almost thirty years before.

I still crouched down, looking closely on the spot of bare ground as if some fleck of evidence of what had happened here might remain.

"This is the place?" my wife, Jewell asked.

I nodded. "This is where Max died."

Jewell and I had ridden up to this remote location on horseback. The nice sunny day, with clouds moving slowly across the sky, had made for a pleasant ride.

"What are you thinking?"

"I think it's time."

"To tell the story?"

"Yes. He was one of us, and his story needs to be told. And it's time to close that chapter on my life."

Always the counselor, she said, "So that's why we're here. To find closure."

I didn't say anything for a second but stared at the patch of ground. I'd have expected it to be barren, or maybe the grass just a little taller. Anything to mark the place a friend died.

But it was a patch of ground like any other. A little grass, a few small rocks, and dirt.

I reached into my pocket and pulled out the piece of collar brass from my old Army uniform. I studied the small disk with the two old crossed pistols on it. It was the symbol of the U.S. Army Military Police Corps.

I dug down with my bare hand on the spot and dropped the brass into it. Then I pushed the dirt over it.

Now the patch was barren. In a few days, grass would sprout back up, but it would forever hide the small token I'd placed there.

Maybe someone would find it years from now. Maybe they'd wonder what MPs were doing up here in the middle of nowhere. Would they'd guess it was done as a means of forgiveness for a friend.

It was time that I gave Max his honor back, and that's why I buried the piece of collar brass.

I leaned back and remembered where it all started. And when I got home that evening, I began writing.

The first words went on the screen, and I found myself hearing Max's voice again.

"Jesus, Will. Have you ever seen anything like this?" Max asked.

I looked out at the storm. The rain falling on the metal roof of the HUMVEE sounded like someone furiously tapping their fingers against it. It splashed off the roof and ran in rivers down through the open turret. Max and I were soaked despite our rain gear.

I'd put a black trash bag over the radio to keep the water off. The radio was supposed to be waterproof. Being deep inside Iraq in the middle of the Gulf War was not the place to find out.

I looked up at the turret, and all I could see of my gunner was his legs. He was covered by a poncho. While it kept him sort of dry, the water ran off him and in with us.

I'd been cold and wet before, but this was plain misery.

I shook my head in disbelief. The slight motion caused a small trickle of water down an open area in my raincoat. Cold rainwater ran down my back, wetting my MOPP gear and chilling me even more than I already was.

"I've never seen rain like this," SP4 Max Laurie whispered.

"We don't get rain like this."

One of the definitions of a desert is a dry, arid region that receives less than ten inches of rain a year. The desert of Iraq qualified as such, but it looked like it got all its rain in a matter of hours. The heavy rain just swallowed up what little light there was, and the night was just darker because of it.

Years later, I would think there was an almost supernatural quality to the darkness.

There was a flash on the horizon, followed by another and then a third. They must have been intensely bright for the light to pierce the heavy rain.

Someplace, not far away, there was a battle being fought. American M1 Abram tanks were engaging Russian built T series tanks in one of the last tank battles of the 20th century.

The majority of what the M1s were fighting would be the newer T-72s, the so-called "Lion of Babylon." There would also be T-62s, and some older creaking T-55s tossed into the mix. The Russian tanks were formidable tanks, but the engagements were terribly one-sided. The T series tanks couldn't be mentioned in the same breath with the M-1.

The M1 had all the advantages. It could shoot further, had better armor, could see in the dark, and the computer-assisted gunnery was lethal. In the rainy Iraqi night, it was War of the Worlds, and we were the Martians.

Another bright flash momentarily lit up the night, and in that lightning flash, I saw the rest of our convoy. Our MP Platoon was one-quarter of a parameter of armed vehicles. Our job was to help protect the Battle Central, which was a collection of expandable vans that held maps, radios, and workspaces. Battle Central ran everything an armored division needed to fight a battle.

Currently, our formation was like an old-time wagon train. The Battle Central sat clustered inside a defensive ring. We (the MPs) held one-quarter of that ring. Another quarter was manned by a team of engineers, with another held the First Armored Division Band. The fourth quarter was kept secure by soldiers assigned to the Division HQ. They were the cooks, clerks, and so on that supported Battle Central.

"Wow!" Max exclaimed as another bright flash split the night. "Somebody just got their bell rung!"

Max was my driver and had been for the almost two years I'd been with the MP Company. He was a farm boy from Montana, and I'd known him longer than I'd known most people. We'd gone through basic training and AIT together. We were both assigned to Ft. Riley, worked narcotics there, and investigations, and we both went across the street to 1st MPs. Now we were both with the 501st MPs and deep in Iraqi territory. Like most young men and women who desired a career in Law Enforcement, he'd joined the Military Police to get a notch on the old resume. Max discovered that law enforcement wasn't what he wanted and spoke about starting a guide service when he got out. Maybe that was part of the problem. While the rest of us had climbed in rank, he played yo-yo with his. He'd been promoted, busted, promoted, and busted again. This last time I'd asked that he'd be assigned to be my driver.

The Captain did that, hoping I could turn him around. Max was a good soldier, and one hates to see a good soldier go bad.

I unzipped my raincoat and the MOPP gear top under it and reached into my BDU shirt pocket. I kept pieces of bubble gum there. I passed one over to Max and then handed one up to our gunner. I had to tell him I had some gum for him. It was so dark that he almost couldn't see my hand reaching up to him.

At 34, I was the oldest man in the platoon.

As I sat there in the dark, listening to the thunder of the rain, and watching the flash of tank guns, I thought about how I'd ended up here.

My name is Will Diaz, and if you'd told me four years before that I'd be in a place I knew little about, fighting a war, I'd have told you that you're crazy.

But here I was.

I'd been raised as a cowboy in Colorado. The real kind that can ride, rope, and do all the cowboy stuff but not before an audience, but for a living. But my real passion had been the stars. I'd gone to college and taken a degree in Astronomy and Physics, only to find I'd gone into a field where it was difficult to get a job.

Needing to make a living and pay off student loans, I'd applied to my local police department. I tested, interviewed, and figured it would be a cold day in hell before they hired me.

That cold day must have arrived because they hired me. Somebody teased me that I was hired because I fit into the uniform of the guy who left.

There are times I believe them.

I rose through the various ranks and went to different departments. I'd been Undersheriff for one sheriff's office and a Chief of Police for a small town. But when that little town went broke, things went wrong. Every other department was either laying off or not hiring. I could only watch as the bank took away almost everything I owned. I soon found us living in low-income housing and the prospects for a job slim.

One day, while job hunting, I passed the Army Recruiters office. There was a sign in the window that announced Army opportunities. I walked in. The Staff-Sargent behind the desk looked up from his work and asked if he could help me. I told him that he'd probably throw me out when he found out how old I was. He asked my age. I told him. He said, "Sit down."

Two weeks later, I found myself the senior citizen among a bunch of children in an Army Basic Training company.

Being a civilian cop paid off. After MP school, I worked undercover narcotics for two years, and another year as a Military Police Investigator before I realized that I needed to get some troop time. My request to go to 1st MPs was quickly greenlighted

A year later, I was transferred overseas to another MP company. And now, here I was shivering in the dark in the middle of Iraq. I wondered if my life insurance policy was going to be up for grabs before the end of the week.

We'd crossed the Saudi/Iraq border the night before. I was expecting a fight when we did that, but we crossed with all the ease of a man driving from one side of town to another.

The most significant danger was from our own traffic. The engineers had bulldozed some small roadways through the berm that marked the border between the two countries. That night, it seemed that all the traffic in the world was converging on those roadways.

We crossed in the middle of the night. All I could see of the Humvee ahead of us was the small red blackout tail lights. I told Max to keep an eye on that vehicle and hoped he knew which one he was supposed to be watching. Max had NVGs (Night Vision Googles) on and said he had us covered.

We passed through the berm, and when we got to the other side, Max muttered: "We're in Indian country." He's half Cherokee, so I figured he could get away with the comment.

We stopped at about 4 AM. I caught forty-five minutes of sleep that night.

We were up before sunrise and ate a quick meal of cold MREs. Then we were moving again.

As we drove, I began to get worried. So far, there had been no resistance. Someplace out there, the much-vaunted Republican Guard had to be waiting. Maybe they were planning on going for our supply train, get us encircled, and from there wage a war of attrition. As our ammo and fuel ran out, we'd soon be in a serious pickle.

It wasn't until well after dawn that we began seeing evidence of the Iraqi Army. There were multitudes of small underground bunkers. Helmets and gear were strewn about. We stopped and checked some of the bunkers out. Soldiers had lived here and then left in one big hurry. Blankets, boots, eating utensils, and personal effects were left behind. I crouched by the entrance of one bunker. I was leery of going in. I'd had an uncle who lost a hand in WW II by going into an "abandoned bunker." This empty bunker would be the perfect place for a booby trap. Along comes some slap-happy GI and blows himself up because he wanted a trinket. I settled for a red beret minus a flash I found tossed on the ground and a spoon.

Other more adventurous souls went into the bunkers. One of the soldiers came out with a spiral notebook like a kid would use in school. The cover had a picture of Saddam printed on it.

About an hour later, we saw our first Iraqi soldier. That is if you can call a man dressed in Bermuda shorts and a Chicago Bears t-shirt a soldier. He's was standing and waving his arms over his head. My team and the LT's team rolled towards him to check him out. He kept his hands raised as we drove up.

"Keep your eyes open, guys," I said. I didn't need to say anything. My boys knew their jobs. As we got within fifty yards of him, and with his hands still held high, he dropped to his knees.

Max and I both exited the hummer. Our gunner covered us from his perch with the M-60 machine gun. I had my rifle pointed at the Chicago Bears guy as the LT, and his driver approached him from another direction. I approached him slowly. He looked at me and smiled, his hands still high

"What kept you guys?" he asked in perfect English

"Anyone else here?" I asked. It didn't surprise me that he spoke English. People all over the world speak it. What surprised me was his dress and manner. He wasn't afraid of us.

"Yes, there are seven of us. The rest are in the bunker." The Chicago Bears Guy motioned with his thumb to a small berm of dirt. "They don't speak English, and they don't know Americans. They're afraid you'll kill them."

The LT said, "Tell them to leave their weapons behind and come out with their hands up. We won't hurt them."

Max and the LTs driver ran over near the entrance.

The Chicago Bears T-shirt guy shouted something. A hoarse answer came back, and a few seconds later, the first set of hands appeared at the entrance to the underground bunker. The hands were followed quickly by a man wearing an ill-fitting uniform, and then another, and a third. Before long, we had six men kneeling next to the first on the warm afternoon sand.

One of the drivers jumped down into the small trench by the entrance, looked in, and announced it was clear.

With the LT keeping our POWs covered, I searched the seven men. The most dangerous thing any of them had was a nail clipper. I pocketed that.

Max had pulled out his flashlight and had crouched down to look into the bunker. I saw him go in and came out a moment later with an ammo bandoleer and an AK-47. "Sir," he called to the LT. The LT motioned for him to wait while he kept me covered. After I'd finished zip-tying their hands behind their backs, I stepped away. Only then did the LT relax his weapon and go over to see what Max had found so fascinating. After talking for a few minutes, he came back and asked the English speaking soldier, "Where's your ammunition? Your bullets?'

"What ammunition? They picked me up in the marketplace, handed me a uniform, a blanket, and a rifle that didn't work. We've been out here for a month with almost no food or water. Bullets? They didn't give us any."

"How do you speak English so well," the LT asked.

"I'm a student. The University of Chicago. I'm studying Anthropology. I came home to visit my parents and got caught up in this."

The LT nodded and called for a couple of more Humvees, this time from Fourth Platoon. Fourth Platoon was setting up a POW camp, and some of them had a fulltime job just picking up prisoners. They picked up our POWs and took them away.

That was almost twenty-four hours and a lifetime ago. I wondered where the POWs might be now. Surely they weren't being rained on.

A new trickle of water seemed to open, and the rainwater was splashing onto my rain jacket, running down my arm, and soaking into the already drenched sandbags at my feet. Despite a metal roof, the Hummer leaked. The open gun turret didn't help, but I saw leaks where you wouldn't think there would be.

I moved a little. My feet were cold and wet, and the sandbags on the floor took valuable space from the already cramped Humvee. There was no way to shift around much.

We'd put the sandbags down as extra protection against landmines. They'd saved at least one life. That afternoon, while crossing a minefield (one of our own that we'd used to push the Iraqis through), the Chief of Staff's vehicle had struck one of those juice can size mines. It blew off the back tire and put a hole in the fuel tank. Shrapnel had gone through the bottom of the vehicle, the sandbags, and the back of the driver's seat. The flak jacket that his driver had been wearing saved her from serious injury. The impact slammed her into the steering wheel, knocking the breath out of her and busting her nose. She'd later complain about the Purple Heart she received. She didn't think she deserved it.

Another flash illuminated the horizon. Almost instantly, the light was sucked into the darkness. I tried to see what was going on around us in that split second of light. All I could see was the rain-soaked landscape.

There was a tap on my window. I looked over to see the vague shape of Sgt. Michael Jones. He wore a parka under the rain jacket and NVGs. I dropped the window, and more rain came in.

"Jonesy, what are you doing out here?" I asked.

He sucked in a breath. He didn't much like stomping around in the rain, either. "The LORAN's on the blink again."

"I'll be right over."

Historians have called the Gulf War, the first GPS (Global Positioning System) war. The Iraqi's certainly didn't expect the attack we pulled off. It was almost impossible to cross the trackless desert and for not one, but several divisions to do so was unthinkable. Without GPS, the Iraqi military was pretty much road-bound. They had underestimated us. GPS made it possible to navigate the desert as easily as a man might find his way around downtown Manhattan.

What few people realize was that the GPS devices weren't that common in the line outfits. Artillery units had them, and some of the Armor units, but the rest of us made do with LORAN (Long Range Navigation) devices.

LORAN has been around for a long time, and the principal is amazingly simple. Around the world is a network of radio transmitters separated by hundreds of miles. By timing the intervals between the pulses of these transmitters as well as their position, the device could figure your location pretty well. Small ships and even airliners had used LORANs for years to find their way around the globe.

Finding your way across the desert was much like sailing a boat. There were few, if any landmarks, and if you weren't on a roadway, and without help, the chances of being able to go from point A and arrive bang on target at point B were slim.

I'd done it once, and it had blown everyone's mind when I did it. It was nighttime, and our LORAN had gone down. I'd quickly confirmed that we'd blown a fuse, and without a spare, there was little hope of getting it up. I looked up into the sky, spotted a star on the horizon, and said, "Steer straight for that star, and we'll find our way back to the company."

Navigators call this "Dead Reckoning." You find a star, and you know where it lies in the sky, and by heading towards it, you find land. In our case, we were aiming for our company area, which was a series of tents and a berm. My target was less than a hundred yards across. Dead reckoning works best when aiming for a much larger target (like a continent). I was counting on getting within a quarter-mile of our base, hear the generators, and then get home that way. The fact we came bang on it was more luck than skill. But it still blew everyone's mind.

We'd received our LORAN devices in January. I was the only one in the company who understood such high and mighty terms as "Right Ascension" and" Declination" or had any knowledge of computers. At last, that Astronomy degree was actually doing me some good. I helped the mechanics install them into the platoon leader's vehicles.

Then I programmed them all. But the things were always going down. They also weren't the best way to find your way around a desert. In the sky or on the ocean, you can steer a straight course. But on land, you had to go around hills, and holes, and ravines, and getting back on course was often challenging.

I grabbed the night vision goggles, put them on, and pulled the rain hood up over my head. With the night vision goggles turned on, the world was all black, white, and green. I could see the rain-soaked desert and the vehicles around me. But most of my surroundings was swallowed up by the rain.

I wasn't in love with the NVGs. They screwed up your depth perception, something awful. The first time I'd put them on and looked out over the hood of my Humvee, it seemed I was looking over the edge of a cliff. I took my time, trying to be careful of where I walked. My boots made sucking, sloshing sounds in the mud. I got into the driver's seat of the LTs Hummer and put my M-16 on the console between us.

Getting the LORAN device back online followed a time-honored tradition that hadn't been invented yet. As many a Tech Support Engineer would employ with computers, I simply rebooted the system. I didn't know why no one else had caught onto this little trick. Maybe they were afraid of the tiny buttons. As I waited for it to come back up, I sat listening to the rain splash on the Humvee and the mud outside. I remembered an episode of MASH where Hawkeye had said that rain sounded like steaks sizzling on a grill. It did.

I've seen rainstorms before, but nothing like the rain this desert received. What had been a dust bowl yesterday was a lake today.

I liked the rain during the summer back on the ranch. It always rained during the haying season, and that would mean a rare day off. Instead of loading the heavy bales onto trucks, we'd have to turn them so that they dried. If you put the bales wet into the stack, you were risking a fire.

The LORAN came back up, and I checked to make sure it was receiving information from the stations I'd selected. I was using a couple of different transmitters.

Most were in Saudi Arabia, and one in Turkey. I could have used a couple in Iraq, but for whatever reason, Saddam had left those up and going. I expected that he'd wise up and shut them down, so I stayed away from using them.

Satisfied, I sat back and waited for the rain to slow down. The LT was sitting shotgun, wrapped in a woolen blanket. In the faint light of the LORANs screen, I could see his breath. Behind me, his driver shivered, and Bill, his gunner, was up in the turret.

Being from the high mountains, I know all about cold. But cold in the desert is a different thing. We always think of the desert as hot, and it is. But at night, with nothing to hold the heat, the sand gives up whatever heat it sucked up during the day. During the day, we'd be running about in our shirt sleeves. After sundown, jackets and gloves came out.

After a few minutes, I decided that the rain wasn't easing up anytime soon.

"Yell if it goes down again, Sir," I said, and put my night vision goggles back on. I turned the power knob on and waited till they came up.

And I was looking at a man. About twenty yards away stood a soldier. What the heck, I thought. It looked like someone from our convoy had been going between vehicles, or had needed the bathroom and gotten a little lost. He stood just outside the perimeter like he was trying to decide which way to go.

Then I realized I wasn't looking at an American soldier. The uniform was wrong. He had no helmet and was carrying an AK-47. It was an Iraqi soldier.

"Bill," I cried up to the LT's gunner. "Target, 11 O'clock, twenty yards out!"

"Where?" Without NVGs, he couldn't see him.

The Iraqi was reacting to my shout, and he was turning, looking. I knew any second he'd start shooting. I had no idea just how bulletproof the HUMVEEs were.

I'm not dying in here without trying to pitch back, I thought.

I broke the first rule of combat. I left my cover. With one hand, I hit the door release, and with the other, I grabbed my M-16, which I'd placed on the center console. But as I rolled out, the M-16 didn't come with me. It got hung up on the gears and backrest of the driver's seat, and I fell into the mud with a splash, and without my rifle.

I glanced up. The Iraqi had decided where the shout came from. Any second, his finger would squeeze that trigger.

My hand went to my right hip. In one smooth move, I drew the Colt 45, which was the standard sidearm of an MP at the time. I felt absolutely no fear as I rolled to one knee and came up with the pistol level, my hand automatically supporting it in classic pistol fighting position. I'd been training for pistol gunfights for almost 15 years now. Pistol qualifications at the Police Academy had been tough but thorough. And for years, I practiced scenarios of my own, all of them based on real-life incidents. Toss military training in, and all of it had prepared me for just this moment. In that instant, everything came together, and before I even squeezed the trigger, I knew that the shot would be a center mass kill.

Without even thinking about it, I squeezed the trigger, and like countless times before, the hammer on the pistol fell. With an explosion of sound and light, the weapon discharged. The flash caused my view of the world in the NVGs to go from black/white/green to a blazing white as the discharge overwhelmed the sensors.

In an instant, I was blind. And in the next, the perimeter went nuts. Everyone opened fire, and I dropped face-first into the mud. I heard cries of "Cease Fire, Cease fire!" No one knew why they were shooting. They were just shooting. But it was still several seconds before the last shots were swallowed up in the pounding rain.

I got up from the mud as the world once again became white/green/black. I turned the NVGs off and removed them from my face. The LT was out of his HUMVEE now. He had his flashlight on. The filtered red light barely lighted the rain in its path. I still held the pistol in my hand, but glancing at it, I had to wonder if it was functional right then and there. It had been in the mud. I was sure there was at least mud in the barrel. But as trained, I still kept my target covered.

My target was on his back and lying in the mud. He looked less like a man and more a broken toy. One leg crossed over the other, and one arm slung out. The AK lay in the mud where he'd dropped it.

"Target is down," I heard the LT call.

I approached, holstering my weapon. By this time, most of my platoon had gathered around. They looked at me and then the dead Iraqi and back again. There was a single bullet wound in the soldier's body. It was an "O" ring hit, just below the heart.

"Right in the kill zone," someone said.

The LT played his light on him and nodded. "Good shooting."

He picked up the fallen AK and handed it to one of the guys standing next to him. The soldier he'd given the weapon to finally managed to drop the magazine. It fell into the mud. I looked at it in the faint light of the flashlight. It was empty. Then I heard the bolt on the AK drawn back to eject the live round.

I Looked.

Nothing ejected. The weapon was empty.

I felt my hand start shaking, and there was spasm in my stomach.

"Are you OK," I heard Jonesy ask.

I was too busy throwing up to answer.

CHAPTER TWO

IN THE CHAIR

"Iraq is thousands of miles and almost a year in the past, Will," Pastor Morgan said.

I was sitting in his comfortable office at the church we attended in Waverly, Colorado. There was a small table between us. I had a cup of coffee on it, and I wanted a coaster because when I picked it up, the cup left a ring behind.

Pastor Robert Morgan sat across from me. I'd known Robert since First Grade. He was a year older than me but had been held back a year in school. It seems he was too busy having fun instead of concentrating on his studies. His dad had set him straight. As it was, he and his two twin sisters were in my class. I'd taken one of the Morgan girls to the prom.

He'd always been a nice enough guy, and there was a bright gleam of intelligence in his eyes. Robert wore cowboy boots, Levis, and a plaid shirt. A battered Stetson hung on a hook. He looked like he's just wandered in from the barn, only he was cleaner. The diploma on the wall was in direct contrast to the image the man projected. It read Stanford on it. It looked out of place next to the military awards and pictures, the Russell print, the cowboy bronze, and rodeo buckles.

My biggest surprise was that he didn't seem surprised when I called for the appointment.

"Will," he said, "Why are you here today?"

Why, indeed, I thought. "Pastor, I've got a bit of a problem. I've been in some rather intense jobs in the last fifteen years, and I'm starting to fall apart a little."

"I know. I've followed your adventures. But tell me about them anyway. What kind of jobs?"

"I've been a cop for almost 15 years. Some of that was most recently in the Army."

"Gulf War?"

I nodded. "Anyway, I've got so much stuff going on in my life, and I've shoved so much stuff onto the back burner to deal with later that a lot of it is starting to fall off the stove. I think I've forgotten where I put half of it, to be honest."

"Well, let me get to know you a little again, Will. You were a soldier?"

He already knew that answer, but he was trying to get me to talk, something I seemed to have forgotten how to do much of recently.

"First Armored Division, five-oh first MPs," I answered.

"See much action? What was it like?"

I wasn't ready to talk about that yet.

"Driving hundreds of miles. Minefields. Artillery strikes."

"And now?"

"I'm with the Conejos Sheriff's Office. My title is Detective."

"You're married to Jewell?" he asked. "She's been attending church here for some time."

"Yes. We'll be going on one year real soon. I've custody of my kids, and we're busy trying to form Waverly's version of the Brady Bunch."

"How's that going?"

"Rather well, I think." I paused, thinking about her, a smile on my face that quickly faded. "She's the reasons I'm here."

"I know. Jewell works as a counselor for us, remember? But I want to hear you say it."

I didn't want to admit that one, but I had to. "I'm shutting Jewell out. I've got so much junk bottled up, it's getting in the way, and I'm shutting her out." I smiled again. Just saying it was like planting boots on top of Everest. "And I don't want to do that."

He looked at the paper I'd filled out again. "As a detective, what are your duties?"

"I'm a detective slash Crime Prevention Manager. I wear a lot of hats because my pay comes from a lot of different sources."

He looked again at the paperwork I'd already filled out. "You said you've been a cop for almost twenty years now, counting your MP time. You've been a detective, even a Chief of Police. Where do you see yourself going?"

From the look on my face, he knew he'd hit a sore spot.

"From where I sit . . ." I paused. "It could be a blessing or a curse. I get to do a lot of things I've never done before. I get to build a new division right. Of course, if I fall on my face, it's all on me. In about five years, I'll be able to retire."

"And you're not ready to be put out to pasture."

I thought about one of the incidents that had brought me here. "I don't want to be. I think there's still plenty of life left in this old mule." I paused before going on. "Well, let's say that I don't know. I'm wondering. Maybe."

"Maybe?" he asked. "That sounds like a pretty big word there."

It was a few seconds before I spoke. Admitting this was tantamount to saying I was losing my mind.

"We had an incident a week ago. One of the PDs needed help arresting this guy. Anyway, he gets a little out of hand, and all of a sudden . . ."

Seconds crawled by.

"Yes," he finally prompted.

I stared at the wall, trying to relive what had happened. "The guy got a little out of hand, and all of a sudden . . ." I paused and swallowed hard. "All of sudden, I was there, but I was also somewhere else. An incident I'd been part of almost two years ago."

Pastor Morgan leaned forward. This time I looked at him.

"You know," I said. "I've heard of people having flashbacks in stressful situations." I looked at his face, wondering what he was thinking. "I never thought it would happen to me."

"What happened two years ago?"

I let my mind drift back.

"It was after midnight in Germany, and I was on routine MP patrol. There were three of us watching over the Ansbach Military Community that night. We were all NCOs and were looking forward to a quiet shift. Wednesday nights usually were.

"I'd driven around between the different Kassernes (German for barracks, or so I think), and was looking forward to getting off duty at six AM. We let the privates run the gate guard that night. Running patrol that night was my buddies Jonesy, Max, and myself.

"And then the night went to hell." I let myself relive it, and the memories flooded back. I closed my eyes, remembering the MP van I drove, the quiet German night, and then the call on the radio.

"Four Oh One, Four Oh Two," the radio squawked. "We have a report of a disturbance at Shipton Kasserne! Main parking lot. Reports are of a man with a knife."

I picked up the radio and answered. "Four Oh Two, en route."

Shipton was a small barracks just outside of Ansbach. I was already driving in that direction and was minutes out. At one of the intersections, I saw the other MP Patrol. It was Jonesy and Max. They fell in behind me. I drove up to the main gate where a very excited gate guard was pointing and yelling, "He's over there. In the parking lot."

I nodded, and drove to the parking lot and turned in, calling over the radio that I was on the scene.

I've rolled up an all manners of messes in my years in Law Enforcement, wrecks, riots, fires, but this was a first. As I turned into the parking lot, in my headlights stood a man. He had no shirt on and held a hunting knife in one hand. Blood dripped from his arms and chest, where he'd cut himself. He stood squarely on to me, anger burned in his face, and he hunched over slightly, his legs spread like he intended to fight.

He stood next to a Ford F150 pickup. He'd broken every window on it, the tires were flat, and the truck body looked as if it had driven through a hail storm.

Oh, man, I thought. Here we go. I stopped the van and got out, my hand on the butt of my 45. "OK, let's make nice. Put the knife down!"

He looked at me, a smile on his face, and yelled back, "Just shoot me!"

I had to smile. "OK," I muttered. "That isn't going to work."

I'd taken my hand off the pistol now, and I was walking towards him. "Come on, soldier. Put it down. We don't need anyone getting hurt. And we sure don't need this worse than it already is."

That's right, I thought. Try to reason with him.

"Leave me alone, and it won't be!"

Jonesy and Max had joined me as I approached him. Between the three of us, we made a cordon with each of us about three meters apart. He backed slowly away until he was standing with his back against a brick wall.

I kept trying to talk to him. "Come on, man. There's been enough trouble tonight. Let's stop this."

"It's over anyway! My wife's gone! My career is gone! Just shoot me."

"You got kids?" I asked.

"That's none of your business," he shouted, which in street-smart cop talk meant, "Yes, I've got kids."

"Look. You're not helping your children or yourself. Put the knife down, please. Let me help you!"

"I'm never going to see them again anyways. My wife took the kids, and I don't even know where she went." For a second, I saw his rage crack, but in the next, it was back. "Want to help me? Shoot me! I'm in Hell. Just shoot me!"

"We don't want to shoot you. And we can stay here all night if we have to. I want to help you."

I was frantically looking for options on how to end this. If I'd had pepper spray, this standoff would have been over. But the Army hadn't allowed us to carry it. That left my hands, my nightstick, or the gun. I'd already decided the gun was out. I was not about to kill this man. I'd managed to avoid that in almost twenty years of law enforcement. Someplace, there was a way out. I just had to find it for him and us.

I played the only card I had with the guy. "What happened? Tell me what happened so we can help you."

"She took off," he yelled. "She ran off with my best friend. She wrote to me. Told me I'd never see her or the kids again!" A sob wracked his body. "Sweet Jesus, I want to die!"

My mind was going a thousand miles an hour. I was trying to find that one thing I could use to calm him. I wasn't there. I briefly considered charging him with the nightstick, but I was trying to de-escalate the situation, not make it worse.

By now, the ruckus had drawn soldiers out of the barracks, and a crowd was the last thing I needed. I saw the CQ out of the corner of my eye, and Jonesy said to him, "Sargent, get all these people back inside. Right now!"

He started yelling to get inside, some listened, and some didn't. There was still a sizable crowd.

I was slowly inching my way towards the soldier, still trying to get him to talk. "Listen, we've got resources. We can help you find them," I said. It wasn't a lie. Give us a name and a DOB, and finding someone becomes a simple exercise.

"You're lying, man!"

He moved towards me with the knife, not close enough to do anything about it, but more a feint. I held my ground. He tried the same with Jonesy and Max, and they'd back up a step. I used it to my advantage and closed a little bit more. I was watching, waiting, confident that once I saw the right opening, I could disarm and subdue him. I know about knives, and I know how to take down someone who has one.

I got my opening. The soldier looked right at me and said, "Jesus, forgive me."

I was ready for his charge, but that's not what he did. He turned the knife to his stomach and started to fall on it.

I hit him like a tackle sacking a quarterback in an NFL game. He hadn't even made it halfway to the ground before I connected. His breath exploded from his body as we collided. We tumbled a couple of times, ending up in a tangled pile, one half of the pile wanting to die, the other trying to keep that from happening. In the lights, I saw a glint of steel. He still had the knife, and I slammed his hand against the pavement. He howled in pain. I'd broken his hand.

The man was sobbing, begging us to kill him and saying that if we didn't, he would. Max spoke briefly into his handheld while Jonesy, and I wrestled the handcuffs onto him.

"Ambulance is inbound," Max said.

Now the soldier was trying to pound his head into the pavement. I put one hand under his head and the other on his head so he couldn't hurt himself. I was still trying to reason with him, but it's somewhat tricky when you're trying to get control of a maniac.

After what seemed hours, the ambulance showed up. The EMTs administered something to him, and a few minutes later, he went slack.

We helped the medics load him in the ambulance, and in a few minutes, he on his way to the psych ward at the Army hospital in Nuremberg. They'd keep an eye on him and hopefully help him sort it all out.

I stood up and started flexing my hands. After restraining him for so long, they hurt. While I worked the pain out, I turned to the CQ and asked, "OK, what the hell happened."

It seems this young Sergeant had gone after his Platoon Sergeant with the knife.

I spoke with his Platoon Sergeant, and in a written statement, he told us that the soldier had received a bad EER (Enlisted Evaluation Report). A bad EER is something you want to avoid because it can affect future advancement and your overall career. Rather than appeal it through channels, he decided to plead his case with a knife. When the E7 ran and locked himself in his room, the soldier took it out on the E7s truck.

We got everything we needed and left the compound. I went to the Provost Marshals office to write up the incident report.

Only I couldn't.

I sat and tried to write the report. I got my name on the paperwork, and that's as far as I got. I walked around, tried again, and still couldn't.

The Desk Sargent looked up and asked how it was coming,

"It isn't," I replied.

I had to calm down, and that wasn't happening.

I finally walked into the Polezi Liaison Officers office and bummed a couple of smokes from her. I went out the back door where we had a bench. I sat down in the early German dawn, and I lite up a cigarette. I smoked it down to the butt. I had lite up number two when Jonesy came outside.

"You OK?"

I nodded, taking a drag from the smoke. Jonesy was hiding his emotions rather well. I hadn't smoked in years, and never while I'd known him. He knew I was in trouble but didn't know what to do about it.

"I just need to calm down a little so that I can write that report."

"Yell if you need help."

"I know where you're at." I spent a few more minutes smoking and looking up at the stars. I felt I could finally do something with the report.

Only I didn't have to. Agent Smith of the CID was leaning against the counter, talking to the Desk Sargent. CID was taking over the investigation. It was a simple matter of relating to him what had happened and giving him my statement. An hour later, we were finished and went off duty.

Word had circulated that we'd had some action. We had to retell the story to those going on shift, and I finally got to bed about seven-thirty.

I couldn't go to sleep. I was still too keyed up. I said to heck with it, got up, got dressed, and grabbed my camera. There's always something interesting to take pictures of in Germany, and it was my day off anyway.

I could sleep later.

I wandered about downtown for a bit and took pictures of the beautiful historic city. Eventually, I found my way over to Main Post. The MPs at the gate told me that SFC Carter was asking for me. We were friends, so I said I'd wander over and visit with her.

I was walking to the door of the Provost Marshals Office when she and the Colonel came out.

SFC Carter was the NCOIC at the Provost Marshals office. In short, the ranking enlisted soldier there. If the Colonel were the Chief of Police, she'd be considered a Deputy Chief.

"Sargent," she said.

Despite being in civilian clothing, I still snapped the Colonel a salute.

The colonel returned it, smiled, and let SFC Carter handle it. "Saw what you, Jonesy, and Laurie did last night. Good work."

"It was . . ." I took a breath. "Interesting," I decided was the word.

She chuckled, and this time, the Colonel spoke. "It was more than interesting, Sargent. You guys handled it well. No one got hurt, and the perpetrator was apprehended with minimum force. You guys made good calls all around."

"Thank you, Sir."

" We've put the three of you in for the Meritorious Service Award."

The puzzled look on my face prompted SFC Carter to say, "It's the highest award you'll get in peacetime."

I chuckled, "And I'm sure they'll downgrade it to an ARCOM or an Army Service Medal."

"Probably," she answered with a laugh, and then both she and the Colonel shook my hand.

I had a burger at the rec center if you can call eating half of it, and leaving the rest behind "eating." I left Main Post shortly afterward, wandered around town, and took more pictures. Finally, I went back to my barracks.

I was exhausted but still couldn't sleep. I got into PTs and went to the gym. Even after lifting weights, my nerves were too raw to rest. I checked out a pair of boxing gloves and headgear. There were a couple of guys from the Field Artillery unit who enjoyed boxing and would never pass up the chance to beat up on an MP.

After half an hour of boxing, I felt tired enough to sleep. I finally did.

I was patrol sup the following day. As I got ready, I heard the sound of my Specialists and Privates up and about. Usually, I'd see them in the bathroom, but not this morning. I knocked on one door to see if they were up. They had the TV on, and I could hear the voice of a news commentator.

They were up and watching the news. Their eyes were wide as they watched T-72s rolling into some city somewhere in the Middle East.

"What's going on?" I asked, looking at the television.

"Iraq invaded Kuwait."

I watched the coverage. The TV showed Kuwaiti tanks fleeing before the Iraqi assault into Saudi Arabia.

"You think we're going?" one asked.

I watched it for a second. "Oh, yeah. We'll be going."

I stopped talking. Pastor Morgan looked up from his notes and said, "You didn't catch much of a break, did you. One bad situation and then another."

"The Army pulled us off Law Enforcement duty and gave it to the other MP Company so we could focus on getting ready to go. You'd think we'd have a chance to rest up some. We didn't."

"So, let me ask you a question. How did you feel?'

"Feel?"

"I mean, you were a cop a long time before this. You were going through a divorce at the time. You were alone in a faraway land. And now you're headed for war. How did that make you feel?"

"Like I wanted to run and hide. I took one look at that stupid fool from the night before and thought I'm one step away from becoming that guy. All I need is a nudge."

"And you got that nudge, didn't you."

I looked at him with surprise. "How did you know?"

"John 10:10," he answered. He handed me a Bible and told me, "look it up."

I found the passage and read it out loud. *"The thief comes only to steal and kill and destroy. I came that they may have life and have it abundantly."*

"What does that mean to you?"

"I don't follow. What does this have to do with me?"

"Everything," he answered. "The thief is the Devil. Jeremiah 29:11 says that God has a plan for each of us, a plan not to harm us, but a plan to prosper us. I'm paraphrasing it, of course. But if God has a plan for us, then the Devil has a plan to take us down."

I thought about it. "You mean the Devil has me in his sights? He's gunning for me."

He nodded. "Think about what you'd gone through. He'd already robbed you. He took your property, your family, your career, and unless I misread what God is telling me, he did a pretty good job of robbing you of your self-respect. All that was left was to kill you. All he needed to do was give you a nudge."

"Kill me?"

"Think about it. You said it yourself. You were one step away from becoming that guy. You've already hinted you almost did become him." Pastor Morgan leaned forward. "He begged you to kill him. Sounds to me like a man who the Devil has you in his crosshairs."

It was like someone had yanked the rug out from me. Here all along, I thought that was just life. That every once in a while, everyone gets dealt a bad hand. And now he was saying all this was the result of a conspiracy. There was a manhunt going on, and I was at the top of the most wanted list.

"Jesus," I said. It was a prayer, not a curse. "So, what do I do about this?"

"You're not going to like what I'm about to say."

I was sure I wasn't. "Go on."

"Will, we've known each other since what? First grade?" he asked.

"That's about right," I answered.

"Well, I've been watching you for a while now. And I think I've got your number. You've been in the middle for a long time."

"Middle? Middle of what?"

"A desert. Middle of the road. Take your choice. The point is, you're in the middle. And you're about to get run over."

"Pastor, you better start making some sense. Did you get thrown from a horse one time too many?"

Pastor Robert Morgan wasn't backing down. "What religion were you raised in?"

"I was raised a Catholic."

"Are you still one?"

"I need something bigger."

"And have you found it?" He asked.

"I think so . . ."

"I think so," he said. He doodled something on his notes. "Interesting choice of words. If you've found it, why aren't you there?" He leaned forward. "You're still in the middle."

I read my Bible. I go to church. What more did he expect out of me?

"Something is holding you back from going forward. I think it's one or all of three things.

"First, what will people think if tough guy William Diaz got turned on by God. I mean, he was bad enough to go off and get a Bronze Star, but he couldn't face life on his own two feet. And yes, that's the term I want to use, get turned on by God. God is all or nothing. There's no in-between."

I was hearing, but I was trying not to listen.

"What happens to a man who walks down the middle of the road?" he asked.

"He gets run over."

"And that's your problem. You've walked down the middle of the road so long that I have to ask why? You always have. Even in school. It was like you were afraid to ruffle people's feathers."

"If memory serves," I said with a smile, "that was what you did best."

He chuckled. "Guilty as charged." Then he leaned forward. "The only thing I can come up with is you're afraid of what people will think of you. At this stage of the game, you'd make one heck of a politician, but a lousy man of God."

"What else is keeping me in the middle?"

"Mistrust," he said. "Would it surprise you to learn I used to be a SEAL team medic?"

"It would." Pastor Morgan was a tough guy's tough guy. Most cowboys are. He'd ridden bulls when he was a teenager. I'd never have pegged him as a SEAL. But then it never has been about the size of the dog in the fight but the size of the fight in the dog. I knew he had plenty of fight, so it shouldn't have surprised me.

That he ever became a preacher did. I'd always expected he'd grow up and be guest of honor in some prison someplace.

"I've seen what you're doing, Will. It's a typical reaction. When you burn yourself on a stove, you stop touching stoves. We pull back from getting hurt.

"But when people do it, we fall back. We put up berms and wire to keep the world out. The trouble is, all it does is make you lonesome and keeps God out too. You've got to learn to trust, if not in people, then at least in God."

"And the third thing?"

"It's associated with the trust issue. You don't want to look like an idiot," he said. "People have let you down. Organizations have let you down. But I'm here to tell you that God will never let you down. You have to learn that trust isn't a dirty word."

"So, start moving forward."

"Get out of the middle of the road!" He picked up a Bible that was on his desk. "Pick up that Bible and ask God to open it to you. And take down the wire and the barriers. Too many people do that and let God in only on Sunday or when things are at their worst. He has to be in your camp always. Through the good and the bad. And you need to let him be in charge. Not you."

"Why not me?" I knew it was a stupid question.

"That answer is too easy. If you're so good at running your life, then why are you here?"

I blinked. If I'd needed a spiritual kick in the pants, Pastor Morgan had just delivered it. "So, what do I do?"

"John 3:3. You know it?"

I nodded, but he said it anyway. "Jesus replied, *'Very truly I tell you, no one can see the kingdom of God unless they are born again.'*"

"What exactly does that mean?"

He looked at me and said, "That means stop trying to run your own life. Give all your hurts and sins to God, and let him dispose of them. And learn to trust him. He'll never let you down."

I nodded. I didn't like having that mirror held up to me. I didn't care for what I saw in it. I knew that there was such a thing as a gift of discernment and prophecy. Was God showing him things about me that I'd hidden from myself? Or was I just that transparent? Either way, I knew he was right.

"You're right," I said. "Jewell has told me that I need to have God reveal himself to me."

"I agree. Ask God to reveal himself. Then we can get to work." He smiled. "Now, tell me some good stuff."

"Well, I have some. My buddy Max from my old platoon is coming out. He's talking about opening up a guide business here?"

"You mean, like a hunting guide?"

"That. Fishing, hiking, all that."

"It's nice to have an old war buddy around." He stopped talking for a second, and his eyes went oddly vacant. "You need to be ready for the challenges that will come your way."

I didn't know what he meant by that, but I nodded anyway.

I looked up at the clock on his wall and said, "Same time next week, Pastor?"

"Let's close in prayer," he said, and we did.

When I got home, I found a message from the Sheriff. He was asking me to cover a dispatch slot that evening. The flu was going around, and there was no one to cover for a sick dispatcher. I figured if he was asking for help to cover such a small slot, then the flu epidemic must be getting worse.

So I put on one of the many other hats I wore and went in. Besides, I figured, I can do some NCIC checks and get caught up on some cases.

But before I'd left home, I had a talk with Jewell about the session I'd had with Pastor Morgan.

"Could he be right?" I asked her. "I mean, he outlined those three things."

"Baby," she said, putting her hand on my shoulder. "You know I love you, but I have to agree on at least one of them." I looked into those beautiful brown eyes I'd come to treasure so much and waited for it. "You have pulled back. You have put up wire. You have put up barriers. The only thing you haven't done is put landmines out, but you'll do that. And you're keeping everyone out."

I thought if I heard it from her, then it had to be true.

"So, what do I do about it?"

She thought about it for a second and then said, "Like he said, part of your problem is you don't trust God. You're not even sure he's even real. So try this. Take your Bible with you tonight. I told you, and now he's told you what I'm saying again. Before you start reading it, ask God to reveal himself to you."

"Sounds like a triple dog dare play to me."

"Well, my God is a triple dog dare kind of God."

I chuckled and took my Bible with me.

Once there, I relieved the dispatcher on duty and quickly reviewed what was going on. There wasn't much, so I pulled my cases and ran the searches I needed. That took a few hours. When done, I still had almost six-hours ahead of me.

It looked like a lot of folks had the flu tonight. The phones were quiet, the radio was silent, and aside from routine traffic, nothing was going on.

I took out my Bible and just opened it. Before I dived in, I did what Jewell and Pastor Morgan had suggested. I folded my hands on the dispatch desk and said, "God. I've been going down a new trail of exploration. I have areas in my life that seem to be keeping me from getting where you want me to be. I think part of it is I'm not entirely sure you even exist. And if you do, we live in a Universe so vast that I'm having a lot of trouble believing you'd be worried about me.

"So here's the deal. Convince me you're real. Convince me you care enough to even listen to my prayer. Jewell says you're a triple dog dare kind of God. I triple dog dare you to show up and convince me."

I didn't know what to expect. I didn't anticipate a burning bush. I certainly didn't expect some sage looking guy to walk through the door, or angels proclaiming this, that, or the other thing. I didn't know what to expect.

And then I had to kick myself. You challenged God to show up! Just who do you think you are?

"Will," I muttered, "You're pretty full of yourself if you think you can boss God around."

Time passed. I got me some coffee and ate the sandwich and chips Jewell had packed me. I smiled, noticing she'd tossed a small bag of Hershey Kisses into the bag. I ate them while I drank my coffee and read my Bible.

It was around 2:30 AM, and the patrol deputy had just gone home for the night. I still had a little over three hours looking at me.

I was still reading the Bible and praying.

And then, God showed up.

CHAPTER THREE

THE CASE OF THE 7-11 BANDIT

I got home at 6:30 AM.

The kids were already up and heading to school. It was a fascinating process to watch. The younger kids wanted to go a million different directions, but somehow they managed to make it to the bus on time. They did that mostly through the efforts of the oldest, Tanya, or "Chica Girl" as I like to call her. She was the self-appointed Chief Wrangler of the younger kids. Somehow this young girl kept them in line. Each kid ran by and gave me a quick kiss. Tanya would make a decent NCO.

After they got on the bus, and it drove off, I stretched. A yawn escaped my mouth. My eyes felt sandy and itchy from the long night. I was tired, but my spirit was jubilant. I was going to go into the office for a couple of hours today, but first, a good morning cup of coffee and some breakfast with my beautiful wife.

"Good morning, Love of my life." Jewell had seen me drive up and handed me a freshly poured cup of coffee. I needed it.

"Good morning, mine." I gave her a big hug and a kiss.

"How were things last night?"

"Quiet," I answered. "But I've got one to tell you about."

"Tell me after you get comfortable. I'll have some breakfast for you in five minutes."

"Sounds good." I headed for our bedroom.

I hung my jacket up in the closet and took my shoulder holster off. Pulling the forty-five from the holster, I dropped the magazine and ejected the round from the chamber. I was always careful to make sure I cleared the weapon. Finally, I put it away in my bedside drawer. I changed into the gray PTs that had ARMY printed on the chest, and went into the kitchen.

I sipped my coffee as I came back in. People find it strange that I can sleep after coffee. But a cup before bedtime relaxes me, and I always sleep well. In Germany, I'd drink a pot of Turkish coffee before retiring. It put me right out every time.

Jewell was frying up a couple of eggs and bacon. I caught the warm smell of toasted bread wafting through as well. Sitting down, I sipped my coffee and waited. The tiredness was starting to hit me. I'm getting too old for graveyard shifts, I thought.

The bacon smelled heavenly, and my mouth watered. I was hungry, and when Jewell served me a moment later, I was ready to dig in. She sat down next to me. I took her hand, and we prayed.

"Father, we thank you for this food. We ask your blessing on it, and this wonderful woman who made it. And Father, there are those who are doing without today. Somehow, meet their needs. We ask and pray this in the Holy Name of Jesus, our Lord, and Savior. Amen."

I picked up a slice of toast, broke the egg yolks with it, and began eating.

"You were going to tell me about something that happened last night."

I nodded. I wondered how many men had this kind of conversation with their wives. "Well, I did what we discussed. I triple dog dared God to show up."

"Did He?"

I chuckled. "He sure did."

"OK, what happened here. Are we talking an acid flashback, UFOs landing, burning bushes, what?"

I chuckled. "Nothing like that, I assure you. God showed up in His Word. He showed me something no one knew when it was written down."

"That's a relief," she said with a laugh. She knew how God talked to people, and speaking through the Word is a common way of doing that. "It's nice to know that I'm in no danger of having those nice young men in their clean white coats showing up to take my husband away. What happened?"

I picked up my fork, cut a piece of egg, and placed it and a slice of bacon onto some toast. It made a sort of sandwich. I continued eating as I spoke. "It was about two-thirty, and I was in the Book of Job. I was in chapter twenty-six, and I have to tell you Job is one cool book. But his buddies needed to be slapped around."

"That's why Job calls them miserable counselors," she said, being familiar with the book. Later I realized people tend to go through their own Job experiences in life. Unfortunately, not all come out on the other side as well as Job.

"Anyway, I was reading verse seven. Here I am reading along and all of a sudden, I had to stop, back up, and reread it. What I read was, '*He stretcheth out the north over the empty place, and hangeth the earth upon nothing.*' I had to reread it, and then again. I couldn't believe what I'd just read."

Jewell leaned closer, studying my face. She knew God had shown me something, and she knew I'd gotten the message right between the eyes. "And?"

"Well, when I read that piece, I couldn't help but think of that picture of the Earth taken from the window of Apollo 8 as it came tearing around the corner of the Moon on Christmas Day. Here's the Earth rising above the lunar surface like some incredible work of art.

"And nothing is holding it up. There are no strings. Nothing! It was just there, floating serenely in the cosmic night. Just like it was said it would be.

"And at that moment it was like a voice said, 'Didn't I tell you. See. There are no strings involved. Now is that good enough for you?' "

I paused, ate some more egg and bacon, and thought how that second seemed like an hour when God became a lot more than just a noun in my little world.

I went on. "And I had to stop and think about how people understood the Cosmos back in Job's day. There were several ideas. The best being the Earth was being carried around on the back of a giant turtle. That turtle was being carried around on the back of a bigger turtle and so on. The point is it was turtles all the way down.

"And I remembered you telling me that Job is the oldest book of the Bible. Anyway, right there, in a book thousands of years old, something is said that had to wait for 20th-century men to see with their own eyes and cameras. I had to stop and ask where Job got that knowledge. After all, Moon Ships were in short supply back then, and I've never been a big believer in the Ancient Aliens idea. So if Job and his buddies hadn't seen it, and there were no little green men to tell them, where did this information come from?" I paused and smiled. "I don't know if you've ever read that piece, but it's almost a casual throwaway of an idea. Well, cut out the middleman and say it came from God."

I shook my head in amazement and laughed. "All I could do was look at the far wall and mutter. 'It's true. Every word of it is true!' "

Jewell nodded. "And what do you think?"

"You want my conclusions? How's this. If God who makes galaxies, stars, and worlds can be bothered enough to meet me like a friend, then I need to get up out of the Command Chair and let him take a seat."

I stopped, thought a second, and then went on, "And since Jesus could beat death, PTSD is nothing. I'm going to get over this with Him on my side. And I'm going to be the man and husband you need me to be."

Jewell smiled. "Is it safe to say the wire and barricades are coming down?"

"Down, and hauled to the dump."

When I laid down for a quick nap, I realized that for the first time in a very long time, the ghosts of the past weren't there to haunt my sleep.

I got up at 1 PM. Jewell had made some tuna salad and left some in the fridge for me. She'd gone to counsel a woman at the church. I ate, got dressed, and drove into the office.

I found plenty of work waiting for me. The patrol deputies had been busy.

In the evidence safe was an evidence bag, all sealed up, signed, and ready for me. It held a single piece of yellow and green paper and identified itself as a money order purchased at 7-11. The face value was for $300.00, but according to the report, 7-11 had rejected it, saying it was worth only $3.00. Someone had altered it. I looked carefully and could see where some of the numbers didn't line up with others. It was a fair job, but it just wasn't good enough. It was a numbered item, and the 7-11 computers knew its actual value.

I'd learned about counterfeiting from one of the best, and that's from someone who did it. Considering that he got caught, well, maybe he wasn't that good.

When I went to the Police Academy, I didn't go to the Golden Academy. I went to the new Western Slopes Academy, located in Delta, Colorado. The facility was a two-story building, used to house the seasonal workers who came in for the crops. The place was vacant when they weren't in town. It was a low rent school because it proved that schools didn't have to look like a school. We slept downstairs in cubicles and took our meals at picnic tables in a central common area. After hours, the picnic tables served as a study hall for us. The actual classroom was upstairs, with small desks cast off from a local school.

Our cook was a convict from the honors farm. It was a low-security prison where prisoners came to get ready to go back into the world. He was an older man, quiet and interested in just doing his job. Every night after the meal was served and the dishes done, a van would show up to take him and his assistants back to the facility.

One night, their ride was running late, and it wouldn't be there for another hour.

We were at the table studying when he came up to the table and asked if we'd like to learn something useful from the criminal element. I have a feeling that he might have come to Jesus, and he'd been prompted to share this. He told us he was doing time for forging documents, and he took a piece of chalk and began giving us a mini-seminar on how to alter documents such as checks, money orders, and such. What I learned from him was information most cops get only from experience. I'd used what he'd taught me over the years.

I read the report associated with the evidence. A few weeks before, an unknown subject had stopped at the local Texaco Station in Antonito and cashed it. He'd used it to purchase a tankful of gas, a couple of candy bars, chips, and soda pop. They gave him the rest in cash.

They never questioned it. After all, a money order was money in the bank. But this money order was worth only three dollars, not three hundred. They were out three-hundred in cash and inventory.

The clerk who took the money order remembered the guy who passed it. He'd stood and flirted with her while she cashed it. I knew the clerk, and I could understand his flirting with her. She was a pretty girl, but the tactic might have been less about her being a pretty girl and more about keeping her from looking at the money order. He was trying to distract her. If that was the case, it didn't work. She remembered him.

I placed a call up to Adams State and left a message for Officer Niles Thompson to call me back.

I have to laugh at TV detectives. It seems that they only have one case at any given time on their desk. They give it their undivided attention, and the evidence always gives them clues. It's a very true maxim that the evidence will describe the crime and give you clues as to who did it. But the TV detectives and their techniques are nothing short of a miracle. Of course, they only have an hour to do their magic, so they have to get help from scriptwriters and directors.

Fingerprints are one of those things that they use. The bad guy always left good prints. In the real world, you'd be lucky if you got anything usable at all. And if you did, they almost always turned out to be anyone except the suspect's prints. I'd investigated thousands of cases, and never once had fingerprints been useful in solving the case.

This money order had to be lousy with fingerprints. Some of the prints belonged to the deputy who took the report. Some belonged to Anna, the clerk from the Texaco station. Then there would be those of whoever made and sold the money order, and the owner of the Texaco, and a bank clerk or two, plus whoever handled it anywhere else along the line. But I would take fingerprints anyway. I might get lucky. One of the prints might belong to my perp

I'd send the money order to CBI (Colorado Bureau of Investigation) and see if they could get any prints from it.

I took some instant photos of the money order and then looked it over. "Pay to the order of Alan Hale, Jr.," it read. I chuckled. I wondered how many people caught that. Whoever this guy was, he has a sense of humor. Probably had a fake ID to back it up too!

The phone rang, and I answered it. "Conejos County Sheriff's Office, Detective Diaz speaking."

"Will," the voice on the other end said. "It's Niles up at Adams State."

"Hey, Niles. You still doing police sketches?"

"Sure do," he answered. I'd known Niles Thompson for years. During my stint with Adams State College Department of Public Safety, he'd been my training officer. "What do you have?"

"Fraud case. Guy's passing altered money orders, and the girl he passed it to thinks she can give a good enough description for you to draw the guy."

I heard him rummaging about and then say, "How's tomorrow at 2 pm looking for you?"

"I can make that work. Let me call her, and if it's OK, we'll drive up to your office. I'll let you know if it doesn't."

"Cool, I'll have some coffee ready."

Niles had been Navy, and Navy guys know how to make a good cup of coffee.

He hung up, and I called Anna. She was okay with the time, and I told her I'd pick her up and drive her there. She was okay with that, too.

I looked at the name on the money order and wondered what I'd get if I ran an NCIC/CCIC check on it. I went into the dispatch office.

"Can I use the terminal," I asked the dispatcher. She nodded towards it, and I sat down. Quickly I logged on and typed in Alan Hale Jr. Of course, I got about a billion possibilities to sort through. That was pretty much a dead end. I was sure he was in there someplace, but it would require a lot of effort to mine out a single person. The guy probably wasn't a local, so maybe he'd done this somewhere else.

I wrote up a general notification to see if it would generate a response. I included what had happened, details of the case, my name, number, and department. I posted it and wondered if I'd get a hit off it or not. If he did this on a regular basis, someone had to have an active case open. If I were able to work with another agency, we'd increase our chances of getting the guy.

Done with that, I went back into my office, updated the case notes, and then carefully cataloged the evidence away.

The phone rang again, and I went through my identification spill.

"So, how's the founding father of the Regulators," the voice on the other end said merrily.

"About as well as the worst rookie in the most hated police force in the world." Jonesy knew I hated being called the founding father. If anything, our little club was a group idea. I didn't hang the name on us.

"Yes, but I make in one month what it takes you six to make."

He had me there. "Jonesy, how you doing, man."

"Hey, spreading love and sunshine all over the beautiful City of Angels. So how's being a detective in a small town."

"Small county," I corrected him. "About what you'd expect. Trying to get them to take evidence and documentation seriously. Usual stuff, a stolen car, blown up mailboxes, and chasing some yahoo spreading altered money orders."

"No murders, huh." He sighed. "We get about one a day. Sometimes more, but all I get to do is stand around and look good."

"Well, if I ever get a good one, I'll give you a shout. Hey, guess who's moving up this way? Max!"

"Max and Eva! What's he doing moving out to the sticks?"

"Told me he's going to set up that guide service he was always talking about. He decided to come out and try it here. Jewell and I are having them over tonight."

"Cool, man!" Then his voice changed. It was that voice shared between NCOs when they had information concerning a soldier. "You know about Max?"

"Know what?" I asked. Whatever it was, it was something he felt strongly enough about it that he had to share it. Some people might call it "Gossip." NCOs call it a "heads up."

"Oh, that's right. You were gone by the time this happened. About a month before Max went Echo Tango Suitcase, we had to referee a domestic between him and Eva."

"Bad?" I asked. In the military, a domestic could be anything from a simple disagreement to World War III. Unfortunately, they happened rather often. Military life can put a lot of stress on a family.

"Bad enough! Eva spent a few days in the Krankenhaus (hospital for those of you who don't speak German). Max got confined to barracks for a week, and the CO made him a deal. Get his butt in counseling or get an article fifteen. It would have been a waste of good paperwork anyway. He was already heading out. He went to counseling, but I don't think it was enough."

"What was the problem?"

"Well, you weren't there long enough after we got back to see. Max was out drinking almost every night. My girl heard he had a girl downtown. She didn't know who it was. He became very removed from everyone, and except for work, we almost never saw him."

I sucked in a breath. If Max had been beating on his wife, drinking, and messing around, we might get some business from him. Not good.

"Jonesy. Why are you telling me this?"

"Eva said he pulled a gun. Max denied it, and later she changed her story and said there wasn't a gun involved. Now he sure didn't bring one from the states with him, and it's difficult to purchase a gun in Germany. That said, we never found a gun."

"I'll keep it in mind, and I'll make sure they're doing OK."

"Do that and say hello for me. Well, I just called to say Hi, and I miss that sorry white ass of yours."

"Hey man, don't put it that way. People might talk!" I responded with a laugh.

"Well, once you've had black . . . "

"Yea, I know. And definitely, don't talk like that!" We both laughed. "I miss you too. Hey, listen. When can the big city get by without you?"

"I can take some vacation in about six months."

"Great. You used to brag how great the fishing was down in the Carolinas. You get your hip waders and your flies, and we'll go fishing up here on the Conejos."

"I do like fried trout," he said. "We'll do it then. Hey, take care of yourself."

"You too, man." I hung up.

I double-checked that the evidence was good to go. I then filled out the processing form that I would send off to CBI (Colorado Bureau of Investigations). Their forensic lab would do the fuming for me and photograph any latent prints they developed. There was a knock on the door, and I looked up.

"Howdy, Sheriff."

Sheriff Tony Madril came in and sat down. He had a cup of coffee. I saw him so much with a cup of coffee that I was half-convinced that it was surgically grafted to his hand. He was never, ever without it.

"How're things running?" he asked.

I briefed him on where we were on some cases and where we weren't on others.

He nodded as I went through each. "So, the bad news is I'm nowhere on who's blowing up those mailboxes. Pretty sure it's some local kids in Sanford. I even think I know who they are, but no one is fessing up."

He put his coffee on the desk. "That's too bad. Guess we'll find out who it is when one of them comes in missing a couple of fingers."

"Let's hope it doesn't come to that."

"What else. What do you think of the case situation vs. the old days?"

He meant my first tour with the Sheriff's Office before I left to go to New Mexico and run my own small department. "Things have changed, and not for the better."

"How do you mean?"

"The people have changed. Back then, we'd managed to build our efforts as part of the community overall. Today, that's not happening. The guys between your previous and current administration sure did a good job of alienating us from the community."

"I don't understand."

"We're the bad guys now. People have zero faith in the local cops. We've got to change that." I looked around the room like it would reveal what I was about to say next. "And the people have changed. Rather than teaching their kids integrity, they're teaching them that's a bad word. For instance, the mailbox cases. I interviewed a kid, read him his rights, and his dad said you aren't talking to my boy. He's within his rights, but this guy is an elder in the church there. Back then, he'd have told his boy to fess up, he'd have paid for the mailboxes, and probably made the kid put them up." I paused. "Guess it boils down to people don't care about right and wrong anymore. I know he thinks he's protecting the kid, but when he blows his hand off . . ."

The Sheriff chuckled. "The world changes, Will. You and I are dinosaurs when it comes to ideas of right and wrong, integrity, and the like."

"Well, I'm not about to become extinct just yet. Last time I checked, there's zero wrong with right and wrong or having some backbone."

"I'm with you on that. We might be a little old school, but we're not finished yet."

"Yep," I answered. "Not by a long shot."

CHAPTER FOUR

DINNER WITH MAX

There was one thing that caused some heartburn between the county commissioners and me. I had married a lady who lived outside the county. Home was only about five miles (as the crow flies) outside the county line, but because I was living outside the county, money wasn't staying in the county.

Jewell owned her own home. It was on a county road right smack in the middle of the farming community of Waverly. Waverly district is a beautiful place to raise kids and live. There are farms and ranches, old homes mixed with a few new, a school/youth center, our church, and good, hard-working people on every side that watched out for each other. About the only downside was there wasn't any place to buy groceries or even a late-night coffee. But there also weren't any bars and very little traffic to mention. If you wanted a movie, shopping, or whatever, you went into Alamosa, which was minutes away.

I pulled into the driveway and smiled. The black and white frame house had been new in the late 1800s, and Jewell had been working hard to make it home even before I met her. Yellow roses were in bloom around the porch, and the lawn was neatly trimmed. The picket fence needed a paint job, but we were getting things together to make that happen. There was a garage in the back that I was working on to make an actual garage to park and work on cars in. There was another building that was leaning to one side. I would be tearing it down in a couple of weeks. While it had been leaning for several years, sooner or later, it just might lean over onto someone. I wasn't inclined to let that happen.

I got out of my cruiser. One of the perks of being a detective was I had a squad car assigned to me. Ironically, it was the same cruiser I'd driven almost ten years before.

"You're going to like this," the Sheriff had said when he brought me aboard.

"What's that?"

"You get your own cruiser."

"Cool." That wasn't a big deal. I'd had patrol cars assigned to me before.

"You and Trigger are together again."

I'd looked at him with my mouth wide open. I was amazed the old beast was still running. Trigger was an old Plymouth Fury that we'd purchased surplus from the State Patrol. They'd ran her into the ground long before I got it. I'd put another two hundred thousand miles on the odometer.

The name "Trigger" came from Roy Roger's horse. One of the city cops had gotten in a chase only to have the guy leave him behind like he was standing still.

My comment when he told me the guy would try to do the same to me was "Outrun Trigger? Never!"

And he didn't.

The intervening administrations had added even more mileage to it. Trigger had almost a half a million miles on it, and it was still running.

I smiled, thinking about how that car and I were reunited. How had RJ described it? It's like Captain Kirk getting the Enterprise one more time.

The warm spicy smell of enchilada casserole welcomed me as I entered the house. Jewell was at the counter, cutting squares out of dough.

"Hello Love of my life," I said. I went up behind her, putting my arms around her. "Sopillas?"

She nodded. "I thought they'd be great for dessert."

Sopillas is a South Western tradition. Its fried bread and you can stuff it with meat, beans, or whatever. When it's cooked, it puffs up, leaving an open empty cavity. As Jewell mentioned, it's a great dessert. Put some honey inside, sprinkle some powdered sugar on it, and it's a slice of Heaven.

I smiled. When I was a kid, I'd always wanted a Norman Rockwell life. Somehow, I'd gotten it. "Hmm," I said, my mouth already watering. "That will be perfect."

I let her go. I took off my jacket and hung it on the chair. It would be going to the closet in a minute.

"How was your day?"

"Got an interesting case. Some guy is altering money orders. I don't think this is the first time he's done that. Anyway, my witness says she can do a police sketch."

"Taking her to see Niles?" She put some of the raw dough into a pan filled with hot oil. There was a sizzle, and if by magic, the dough swelled and turned brown.

"Tomorrow. I think this guy has been doing this a lot, and that I can crack this one. I'm playing every lead I can on it."

I looked around. The house was quiet.

"Where are the kids?"

"They're playing up at the youth center," she answered. One thing I was pleased about was that her girls got along just fine with Gerry. We were becoming Waverly's version of the Brady Bunch.

"And how was your day?" I asked.

"Counseling," she answered. "Had two cases this morning. Both marriages in trouble. Usual story. The husband's out drinking, and then comes home and takes out life's problems on her."

"Did she call the cops?"

"No." She placed one more square of dough in the hot grease, and it made a hot sizzling sound. Within a matter of seconds, it too puffed up. She turned it over quickly with a fork, and the bread cooked a delicate golden brown. Quickly she placed it on a tray lined with paper towels. "I tried to talk her into it, but she didn't want to get him into any trouble. Says he hasn't hit her yet."

"When it gets to that point, it's too late."

"That's what I told her. She's going to have to sooner or later. It's just going to get worse and worse for her."

"We had a case at Ft. Riley. Every Saturday, 4 PM, we just showed up at this one house, and he'd be beating her up. It was almost like a standing appointment with us. I'm surprised we didn't call to make sure we were still on every week. We'd arrest him, take her to the hospital, and his chain of command would come and get him and confine him to barracks for a bit. And a couple of days later, she'd be calling his Captain or First Shirt and telling them she needed him home and so on. He was calling her, and making her call them."

"Scared of him?" She already knew the answer to that one.

"Try terrified. Anyway, it's driving us and his command crazy, and she's getting beat up every week." I took off my shoulder holster and felt the weight of the forty-five pull the shoulder rig towards the floor.

"What happened?"Jewell asked, placing more of the fried bread on the tray.

"Well, one Saturday, we went over to referee the incident, got there, and it was all quiet. We find her sitting at the table, drinking a cup of coffee. She has a black eye, a split lip, and he's lying on the floor with a butcher knife through his heart."

"She walked?"

I nodded. "With all the reports and medical records of past abuse? Oh yeah. The jury called it self-defense."

Jewell had no sympathy for him. "Good for her."

I took advantage of the lull in the conversation to put my pistol and coat away. When I came back in, I said, "Need you to play counselor tonight."

"Max and Eva?"

I nodded. "I got a call from Jonesy today."

She smiled, knowing that Jonesy was one of my best friends. "How's he doing?"

"Looking forward to getting out of LA and coming out and doing some fishing."

"You'll enjoy that. That will be a week of war stories," Jewell said in mock horror. "And I can't wait to meet him."

"Heck, some of those stories might even be true. Jonesy gave me the heads up about an incident that happened after I left Germany. It seems there was a huge fight between him and Eva."

"Bad?"

"He put her in the hospital for a couple of days."

"What did command do?"

"Not much. Max was leaving within a month. Doing anything official was a waste of good paperwork. They babysat him through counseling.

She nodded, thinking about it. "Drinking?"

"He was supposed to have a girlfriend downtown, too."

"Was he always like that?"

I thought about it for a moment before answering. "No, when I first meet Max, he was a solid farm kid. Good morals and wouldn't touch a drop."

"It's strange how so many people changed after that war."

"It's called PTSD," I explained. "Despite our doing a lot of it, killing and watching people killed isn't a natural act. It changes you."

We were both thinking about the day she told me I needed to get some help. When I told my folks that I was going into counseling, they tried to talk me out of it. They said that they would label me as crazy. Well, crazy or not, I was already in it, and it was doing me some good.

"Not everyone does that," I said, answering her unspoken thought. "Real men don't go to counseling."

"Well, I think you working it out just makes you more of a man." She glanced at the clock. "You need to get ready."

I got up from the table. I had to pass through the dining room on the way to our bedroom. Jewell had set the dining room table with four settings, silverware, and glasses. She was pulling out all the stops for our guests.

I changed, carefully putting my pistol away. I timed that one pretty close because as I came into the kitchen, I saw a red and white Ford pickup pull into the driveway.

"They're here," I said.

I waited until they had gotten out and came to the door. As I watched, I noted that Max didn't open the door for Eva. I remembered when he used to. They knocked, and I let them in.

"Sgt. Diaz!" he exclaimed, a big grin on his face.

"Max!" I responded with equal enthusiasm. There was no shaking of hands here. Not when you'd walked through Hell and then some with someone. It binds you in ways most can't understand. Instead, I threw my arms around him and hugged him like a long-lost brother.

"It's good to see you." I hugged Eva wondering what reaction that might spark from Max. If they were indeed having issues, I might see something, but he acted like it didn't matter. Of course, we'd all known each other for years, and I certainly wasn't a threat to his relationship. "Eva, welcome to America."

"Thank you," she said as I ushered them into the house. I studied them as I introduced them to Jewell. She hugged Eva and shook hands with Max, and then said. "Eva, want to come into the kitchen while the men go into the living room and catch-up."

She paused, looked at Max, and he smiled. It seemed permission had been given.

"Yes." Her Bavarian accent was still noticeable. "I would like that very much."

"Something to drink, Max?"

"Do you still drink beer?"

"Not so much anymore. I can offer you a soda.

"Got a Dr. Pepper?"

I handed one to him and grabbed a Diet Coke for myself. I popped the top on mine, and we went into the living room and sat down. I motioned for him to do likewise.

"You're looking good. Civilian life agrees with you." I said.

"It does. Well, I never thought of myself as a soldier. More a misassigned civilian. "

"Well, for a civilian, you sure saw your piece of the road."

"We all did."

"And Colorado?"

"Well, I bought a place."

I noted and filed away that he used the pronoun "I" instead of "we."

"Where?"

"It's more a cabin than anything else. Sanchez's old place. I think you know where it's at."

I thought for a second and then placed it. "You purchased Candy's cabin? I never thought he'd sell."

"Probably for more than what it was worth, I'm sure. But it's got everything I need for a guide service. We've got a house, and there's a bunkhouse where the hunters can stay. There's a good road, a couple of sheds, and a barn. It's a stone's throw away from the mountains, and there's plenty of pasture for the horses and a corral."

"Got any horses yet?" I knew Candy didn't own any.

"Not yet. I don't know much about horses beyond riding them. We never owned any back home. You, Jonesy, and Terri were the real cowboys in the outfit. I just worked a ranch, wore jeans, boots, and the hat."

"I can put you in touch with some folks I know who specialize in horses. And Terri was a cowgirl," I said, then taking a sip of Coke. "At least you can two-step. I still can't."

"Well, there was only one place to do that anyway." He shook his head. "Besides, Terri sure could fill out a pair of Levi's."

I paused, thinking, that's an odd thing to say, even if it were true, especially with your wife sitting in the next room! I began to understand why Jonesy gave me the heads up. So far, I'd confirmed in my mind that he and Eva weren't a team anymore and that he most certainly had a wandering eye.

"Got an application in for your permits and all that?"

"Working on all that. Takes time," Max answered.

"And money. How you guys fixed for cash?"

"Got a couple of months squirreled away. I got a little extra out of the loan, so I have operating capital to get what I need. It will keep bills paid till it starts picking up.

"I'm looking for something to help tide us over, so I don't have to dip into that too much."

I thought it over. "There's nothing at the county I can think of. We sometimes have stuff for reservists, but that's far and in between. I know a couple of ranchers in your area that can use a good hand."

"I'd appreciate that. Start making a cowboy out of me for real."

Jewell and Eva came into the dining room. Each was carrying food that they placed on the table. "Come on, My Baby. Max. Dinner is up."

I smiled, looked at Jewell, and then Eva. Something passed over Eva's face. Something I almost missed. Eva was in her early twenties, and like so many girls from Germany, rather pretty. But she seemed older somehow, and the animation she had in her voice earlier while talking to Jewell seemed to evaporate like a fog.

"Let's say grace," I said. It was a heads up to Max that my life had changed in one huge way. We all took hands, and I prayed, "Thank you, Father, for this food, and bless the hands that made it. Thank you for Max and Eva at the table, and bless them. And Father, please meet the needs of those that go hungry this day. Amen."

Jewell began dishing up the food. It smelled full of chili and warm spices. Jewell said to Eva, "This is going to be a little different from what you're used to."

Eva smiled, but the smile was only on her mouth, not her eyes. "We have Taco Bell in Germany. I think I can handle it."

Good luck, I thought. Eva took a spoonful of Spanish rice, put it in her mouth and started to chew.

Her eyes widened a bit as the spices hit, but to her credit, she didn't choke on it. She looked at Jewell, and for the first time since we'd sat down, I saw some animation on her face. "This is delicious. How do you make it?"

"I'd have to show you. What I do is take the rice, fry it up, then stir in my spices, some tomato sauce, add onion, garlic, water, and cook it down. Come over one of these days. I'll teach you."

"And I'll teach you how to make some German food."

"I'm sure Will would like that. Honey, what was your favorite thing to eat over there?" Jewell asked.

I chewed on a mouthful of enchilada and thought about it for a second. "Absolute favorite? Schnitzel sandwich, pomme frits, and a cola. You guys had a drink over there that was a like Dr. Pepper with a twist of lemon. I loved that. The best sandwich place was right outside the main gate into Old City."

"I remember that place," Max said. "It was one of those stand-up and eat places."

I nodded. All three of us knew the place well. For a few minutes, it was like old times back in Germany. We sat, laughing and talking, and then Jewell asked Eva, "Do you miss Germany?"

She nodded. "I miss it terribly . . . ," and she looked at Max, and her face clouded over. The pretty, talkative girl was gone, replaced by an Ice Princess.

"She'll be flying back in October," Max said, firmly.

That's almost a year away, I thought.

Eva stayed quiet for a while, and Max and I told war stories.

"So, how did you two meet," Jewell, asked, indicating Max and me with her fork.

"On the bus to Ft. McMuffin," Max said. "We were all at the Atlanta Airport, and the bus came by and picked us up to take us to the training center. Will sat right down next to me and just started talking. Everyone else was very quiet, and he's there telling stories, finding out who everyone is, that kind of stuff. I remember Jonesy and Terri were on the bus with us. Greg and Eric were there too."

"Yep. And we all went through Basic, AIT, and then we all went to Ft. Riley."

"Almost never happens," Max explained, between mouthfuls of Spanish rice. "But the six of us were on that bus. The six of us went through MP school together, and then the same six ended up at Ft. Riley. And all six of us ended up working DST."

"DST?" Jewell asked.

"Drug Suppression Team," I said. "We'd all been assigned to 977th MP Co. When I got there, we had a lady captain. I remember when we first met, she asked me what I wanted to do while I was in the military. I answered investigations. I'd been a civilian cop for over ten years, and I felt I could be an asset. Anyway, I figured it was something that would have to wait. We were getting ready to head to Honduras for about six months."

I took a mouthful of food and then continued my story. "Anyway, about a month later, we were getting ready for afternoon formation when the Captain came up to me and told me I had a 1300 appointment at CID. I swear, the first words out of my mouth were, 'What did I do that I don't know about.' She said to show up. Then I noticed her approaching the others.

"Well, I go over to CID, told the receptionist I was there for an appointment. I had to show her my ID. She told me to sit down. While I'm waiting, Terri walks in, goes through the same process, and she sits down. We sat there looking at each other, wondering what the heck's going on, but not saying anything.

"A few minutes later, a couple of agents came out and got me. They took me into the Colonel's office. Right away, I knew what was going on. This was a job interview. I saluted, and he returned it. He told me to sit down.

"Colonel North was an old-time soldier and had probably been in since they rode horses in the Army. Anyway, he asks, 'Son, what do you know about illegal drugs?'

"I start rattling off a chemical formula and a lab procedure. He stops me and asks what that was, and I explained that was how you made LSD. He asked how I knew it, and I told him we'd made it in chem lab. He asked me a few more questions and then asked if I had any. I said, 'Yes, Sir. What's this all about?'

"He explained that they were rotating out the team members on the Drug Suppression Team, and they were lining up their replacements. I didn't even have to hear more. I smiled and said, 'Hell, yes, I'm interested.' He smiled and dismissed me, and the agents walked me out, telling me not to discuss this with anyone. I left, and about a half a block away, I run into Max headed that way."

Max twirled his water glass a bit. "I was a little lost myself about it, and when I saw Will, I asked if he'd just come from CID. He nodded, and I asked, 'What's going on?' He smiles and says, 'I can't tell you, but trust me. You're going to like it.' "

"And that how the Regulators were born," Jewell said.

"Yep," Max confirmed, attacking his food again. "We helped regulate drug trafficking in and around town. We stole it from Young Guns. Will here is the founding father."

Jewell looked at me. That was my cue to pick up the story.

"Since I was the oldest and the most experienced, they labeled me the founding father. It wasn't my idea. It just happened. The members are Max, Terri, Greg, Eric, Jonesy, and me. They put a Warrant Officer in charge of us; a CW2 named Bill Smaglinski. We were in this little out of the way corner of the post, and they gave us civilian looking cars."

"And we gave them Hell down there in Junk Town, didn't we," Max said.

"We sure did."

"So, where's everyone else at?" Jewell asked.

"Jonesy is LAPD, of course. Max is sitting here. Eric is a Texas Ranger. Greg is still in the army working CID. And Terri is FBI."

"So, what you're saying, Baby, is you're making the least amount of money."

"And don't think Jonesy didn't remind me of that." I laughed and picked up my drinking glass. "Ladies and Gentleman. A toast. To the Regulators." I raised my glass, as did everyone else. "Long may they ride."

There was a round of hearty, "Long may they ride." We drank, and then we all put our glasses down laughing.

The toast gave Jewell a chance for a different opening. "And how did you meet Max, Eva?"

"There's a place in Ansbach called Rancheros. The owners had tried for a country western theme and had stayed away from the disco atmosphere most of the other clubs had. Instead, they had a hardwood dance floor, country music, and my girlfriends and I used to go in there once in a while to talk and to hear a different kind of music.

"One night I went in, and my friends hadn't arrived yet. There were some guys and one girl at another table. They all wore jeans, boots, and had on cowboy hats. That's very unusual in Germany. And this one kept looking at me."

She paused and looked at Max and smiled at him. For just a moment, I caught a glimpse of the girl and the relationship between them I knew. It was heartbreaking.

"After a moment, he got up, came over, and asked, 'Have you ever two-stepped?' I'd never heard of it. He gave me his hand, took me out on the dance floor, and taught me how to two-step. When it came time to leave, he got my phone number and asked me out. I went home that night and told my roommate that I'd just met the man I was going to marry."

"That's a nice story."

After dessert, Eva offered to help Jewell with the dishes and   Max, and I went out and sat on the front porch, drinking our coffee and looking out at the stars.

"So," I asked. "How are things?"

Max sipped his coffee and said, "OK, Sarge. Where we headed? You've been looking at us all night."

We'd been buddies too long to fool one another. "Got a call from Jonesy today."

"Really? How's he doing?"

"Good. Might be coming down in a few months."

"That would be nice. What did he say?"

"You won't like it. When I told him you were moving up here, he got a little concerned that I might get some business from you. I told me you and Eva had a pretty good blow-up after I left. That they had to go in and referee it, and Eva spent some time in the Krankenhaus."

He was quiet for a moment and then said, "That wasn't my brightest moment."

"What happened?"

"Well, we got back, and I started noticing that she was a little distant from me. She wasn't talking or anything. So, I started hanging down at Rancheros a bit more than I should have. I came home drunk one night, she got in my face, and I slapped her around."

"Must have been some slapping around."

"I know what you're thinking," he said. "I'm fine. Really. It was a one-time thing. Besides, it was her fault. She got all bent. She shouldn't have gotten in my face like she did."

I took a sip of coffee, thinking through what to say next. "Max, how many times did we hear that exact statement when we had to go into a domestic?'

He seemed to fall back a little, regroup, and then said, "This time, it was true."

"Did you go to counseling?"

"I went and saw the Chaplin if that's what you mean."

"No, I mean, did you go through intense counseling? Jewell is a Christian Counselor, and I know the work she puts into her clients. Jonesy said that you were already short, and C of C just babysat you the last couple of weeks. That if you weren't already on the way out, things might have been done differently.

"What I'm asking, is did you get help for this?"

I watched my friend and saw something in his eyes I'd never seen before. It was anger, barely hidden, but still visible, like a flame behind a curtain. "What do you want from me?"

"Look," I said. "You and I have been through a lot together. Going through that changes you, and not always for the better. You need to get it out into the open and conquer this thing I just saw."

The flame went out. Or maybe Max had just hidden it better. "I know you're just watching my back."

"Always said I would. I don't want to have to see you in a professional capacity."

We sat for a moment, and finally, he said, "Sure is a beautiful night." And then, "You come to Jesus?"

"Matter of fact, I have. Does it show?"

He nodded and then shook his head. "Kind of. I'm glad you did. That stuff isn't for me. Too complicated."

"People make it complicated." I paused, looking out at the stars. "Remember that little white book we had to carry with us everywhere in basic training?"

"Yeah. The Smartbook." He chuckled. "Would you believe I've still got mine?"

"Yes, because I still have mine, too. It's duct-taped together and dog-eared, but I've still got it. Anyway, let me show you something I'm working on."

I got up and went into the house, got the book out of my ruck, and then came out.

"A Bible?" he asked. "Don't tell me you're adding to it. I thought it was a done deal."

"No, I'm not adding to it. I've got the wrong haircut to play prophet, and yes, it's a done deal. What I started doing is to pull the important stuff someone should absolutely know." I opened the Bible and showed him some handwritten pages I'd stapled into the back of the Bible.

"I'd like to think of this as a Smartbook for young Christians, and I certainly count myself among them. What I'm doing is going through and writing out the important stuff." I turned to one of the handwritten pages and handed it over to Max.

After a second, he said, "This is just one of the Ten Commandments!"

"Yep. Task Number one, or in this case, Commandment number one. You shall have no other gods before Me.' "

"There aren't a lot around these days," Max said.

"On the contrary, there's more today than there ever were back in the day of Moses and company. Maybe we're not bowing down to Zeus, and Thor is a guy in a comic book, but we've got more than enough to go around.

"Looks can easily become a god to people. Money, our careers, you name it." I pointed at the handwritten notes I'd started on the paper. The ink colors were all different, showing it was a work in progress. "I'd say the biggest issue we have today is ourselves. We're leaning on our education, our own experience, what the world and our friends expect of us. We end up being captains of our own life, and we become the most important thing in our own eyes."

I paused. "I got hit right between the eyes on that one last night."

"Oh?"

"I've been working on this for a long time," I said. "Maybe I'm trying to make sense of it on my own. Last night I ran right into God. He showed me something I'd never thought of. I wasn't trusting. I was trying to understand. You can't have the latter without the former. Either it works for you, or it doesn't. And it usually doesn't work because we don't let it."

Max read what I'd written and then said, "God's kind of full of himself."

I shook my head. "I don't see it that way. I see it as being said in love."

"What do you mean?"

"Follow my lead. All God is saying is, "Listen to what I have to say. Seek me, pray constantly, and life will be good. Try to walk in your power and doing what you think, and you'll have problems, and most of them you'll bring on yourself.' "

I watched his eyes. "People look at God and think he's a bunch of don't do this, that, or the other thing or else. I look at God, and I think it's the exact opposite. If I were to tell you, don't go tap dancing in a minefield, would you?"

"Of course not."

"Why not?"

"Well, mines tend to go bang, and when they do, you lose pieces of your body and possibly your life."

"That's all He's saying. You do this stuff, and you either hurt yourself or someone. Sometimes, there's a whole lot of someone's."

"I don't follow."

"Here's one people do all the time. 'Thou shall not commit adultery.' Who gets hurt?"

"No one if you don't get caught."

"Really?" I asked. "Well, let's look at that one. So you and some girl end up having an affair. What's the one thing that an affair requires?"

"I don't know where you're going with this?"

"OK, how about time. Even if all you last is three seconds, that's time that could have been spent with your spouse and children. At the very least, you're robbing them of that. And it just occurred to me there's another big casualty of an affair. Truth!"

"Truth? How do you get that?"

"You don't want anyone finding out, right. So you have to lie about it. The only real person you're lying to is yourself. Somebody, someplace, always knows about it. You might think you're getting away with it, that no one is the wiser, but someone always knows. And that almost always comes out when you don't expect it."

"I don't follow."

"How about my profession? I'm out messing around. One fine beautiful day, I end up having to arrest someone. The next thing I know, we're bargaining so that what he knows doesn't come out any further."

"Then that's between you and him," Max said.

"Maybe. But let's say the guy I arrested, well I did so for drunk driving. He knows what I've been up to. I let him off. I want my little secret kept. He keeps drinking and driving, and sooner or later, he gets into an accident and kills everyone in a mini-van. Now, who has my lie impacted?"

"That's kind of an extreme case."

"Stuff like that happens every day in the world." I paused. "Thou shall not go tap dancing in a minefield. If you and I are on patrol, and I step on a landmine, there's a good chance you'll get hurt, maybe even killed. Right?"

He agreed.

"So, I stepped on the mine, and you're also hurt or dead?" I took a sip of my coffee. "What we do impacts others."

I pointed at the paper. "That's why I made the first commandment the most important task in my Smartbook. If you fail at the one, if you fail to take God seriously, you fail at all of them."

"But why did you become a Christian? I mean, come on, Will," he said. "I know you, man. You like your booze. You like your babes. What's in it for you?"

"Because I finally figured out that me running on my own was a little like having Daffy Duck in charge of the Star Ship Enterprise. I wanted to be a better person, a better husband, a better man, and doing it on my own wasn't working. And after years of looking and ignoring it, I finally realized what I needed was right in front of me. I needed a ruler, I could measure my life against, and when I found that ruler, I realized I wasn't measuring up. God was just waiting for me to get out of the Captain's chair."

I could tell he didn't get it.

"OK, you've seen me at my worst. I admit I drank too much. I chased around too much. You saw me when I almost fell apart in Iraq. Heck, if it weren't for you, I wouldn't be here. I didn't want to be that person anymore. I was a victim, a loser, and almost less than zero kind of person."

He looked out at the stars and said, "But isn't the forgiveness of sins supposed to be found in Jesus?"

"That's true. But Jesus also said, 'Go and sin no more.' You see, Jesus knew one thing a lot of folks tend to ignore. He knew that every action has a reaction. He knew that if people went out and kept on the same path, things would happen. Jesus led people out of the minefield and warned them if they go right back into it, something is going to go bang.

"What Jesus did was balance the books in our lives. He got the red off our ledgers, paid our bills for us, and gave us the means to keep those books balanced. But if people won't take what he did for them and they keep doing what they're doing, the books remain out of balance. And that's where my problem was. My books need to be balanced. I like where they're at now. I can live with them. And I want them to stay balanced."

"Makes sense," he said, but his eyes said I'd lost him completely. He wasn't interested in what I'd found, and our conversation changed to more mundane matters. I was wondering if I'd just lost a friend.

They left about ten. I remember that I looked at Jewell as we both watched their truck go down the road. "What do you think?" I asked.

She nodded, and then said sadly, "I think Jonesy is right. You'll be getting some business out of them."

CHAPTER FIVE

SKETCHES

I got into the office early the next morning. As I was standing in the kitchen, pouring myself a cup of coffee, the dispatcher came over to me and handed me a message and a computer printout. Both were from a detective from the Routt County Sheriff's Office in Steamboat Springs, Colorado. The computer message read: *"I HAVE A TON OF INFORMATION ON THIS GUY. BEEN CHASING HIM FOR YEARS. CALL ME WITH A FAX NUMBER, AND I'LL BE HAPPY TO GIVE YOU WHAT I GOT."*

Been chasing this guy for years, I thought. How has he managed to avoid capture?

Of course, the guy has to be a drifter. The amounts were small, and the different police agencies probably had few, if any, leads. Eventually, the cases just got buried and then were closed unsolved. I expected he'd have fake IDs to back up who he said he was. Maybe he had a stolen license plate or three so he could throw investigators off a bit just in case someone did get a license plate number. He knew that he didn't want to draw too much attention, and was an expert at running under the radar.

The FBI had a specific monetary limit they'd be interested in, and since the amounts were small, he'd never drawn their attention. With leads sparse, it was left to people like Andy DeShong from Routt County to chase after him.

The phone message was from the same detective. It read, "Got info for you. Call me right away!"

I called him.

"Detective Andy DeShong, Routt County Sheriff's Office," the voice on the other end said.

I introduced myself and told him what had happened here.

"Yes, Alan Hale, Jr!" Andy laughed. "I wonder if he looks like the Skipper. Anyway, he has over a hundred different aliases. This guy has passed altered money orders in twenty-four states. Trouble is by the time we get the money order back; any surveillance tapes have been taped over. And no one seems to remember much about him."

"Well, Andy, I think his luck has run out. The girl who took the money order says she can describe him well enough that we should be able to do a police sketch."

He paused. "You're kidding. How does she remember him? He's supposed to be pretty unremarkable."

"She remembers him because he flirted with her."

"What?" he exclaimed, a little excitement creeping into his voice. "He's never done that before!"

"Well, this girl is one of those girls that guys just flirt with. Even gay guys flirt with her." And because pretty girls get flirted with a lot they remember faces. It's a survival mechanism.

I could almost hear him smiling on the other end of the phone. "When are you doing the sketch?"

"Today. I'm taking her up to Adams State. One of their officers is a police sketch artist. He helped me crack a rape case several years ago."

"Great! What's your fax number?" I gave it to him and then promised that once I had the sketch, I'd fax it to him.

"Make sure your fax machine has plenty of paper. I'll be sending you everything. And I'll make sure 7-11 security gets the sketch. I've been after this guy for five years."

"That's a long time."

"Call it a hobby," he explained. "This is the closest we've ever been to getting him."

"Let's hope we do. That way, you can get a real hobby, like stamp collecting." Before hanging up, I promised to get the sketch to him as soon as I had it.

A few minutes later, the fax machine began spitting out volumes of information. Andy wasn't kidding when he said he had a lot of information. There are books with fewer pages. I read the handwritten synopsis on the cover page. His handwriting was just slightly better than mine, so I had a lot of fun reading it.

The suspect had cashed money orders using over a hundred different names over eight years. Andy had broken down the number of money orders cashed per name, and I noted that Alan Hale, Jr. was one of his favorite aliases. I wondered if it was because it was easy to remember or if he was rubbing his victim's noses in it, betting they wouldn't snap. Jewell was the shrink in the family. I'd bounce the idea off her. He'd worked his scam all the way from Ohio, out to Nevada, south into Texas and up into Montana. All the money orders were small sums of money, never more than $300.00. But if you added it all up, the guy had written altered money orders to the tune of somewhere around two and half million dollars. And that's what we know about, I thought. For every money order we knew about, there had to be another we didn't.

Andy noted that there were few active cases out there on the guy. Chasing him was a hobby. He'd gotten a report here, a lead there, all carefully assembled over the years in a set of facts that would trap him.

And because of a pretty girl with a quick smile and a good memory, we might finally get this guy. The sketch would be the first massive piece added in years. Like Andy, I thought it just might be the break we needed.

I wrote up my case notes on the conversation and added the epic novel DeShong had faxed me into the case file. My case went from very thin to very thick in minutes. I then double-checked that Anna and I were still on to go for our ride up to Alamosa that afternoon. By nine-thirty, I was finally able to sit down and review what the deputies had brought in.

There had been a couple of thefts of gasoline from tractors in the fields, and a handful of tools from another. Unless we got fortunate, these were cases that probably wouldn't be solved. I made a note to put something out to the local farmers and ranchers that this had been happening. They would hopefully stop leaving their equipment out in the fields, and maybe somebody would see something and report it. I put a couple of pins on a map to record their location, wishing I had a computer with a mapping program like we had at Ft. Riley MPI. A lot of people banked on technology to solve crimes, and it does. But technology isn't magic, it's a tool, and you need to learn to use it. Most crimes still get solved with good old fashioned police work.

I drove out to Anna's house and picked her up. From there, it was a half-hour drive to Adams State.

I'd known Niles for years. He was with the Campus Police when I was a student at Adams State, and we met late one night when I was running the telescope as part of our observing program. He was checking doors, found the observatory open and me inside taking pictures through the telescope

Niles was an art student and was already doing sketches for local PDs. He'd helped me out more than once.

The Campus Police Department was still located in the old Casa del Sol complex, right next to the KASF-FM College radio station. The office complex looked like a two-story hacienda. There was an enclosed courtyard, and some apartments rented by students and instructors. But the majority was office space.

Most everyone I'd known was gone. Lee, who had been the Director when I was with them, had long since retired. He passed away a few years later. Page was gone, as were most of the younger officers. Only Jim and Niles were left. Jim was the director, and Niles was now second in command.

But some things hadn't changed. The uniforms were still the green shirts and tan pants, and they worked under the stigma of people thinking they were a bunch of Barney Fifes. It was an illusion they did little to dispel. It made it very easy to underestimate them because they were a highly professional, top-flight department.

Niles offered us a cup of coffee and then took us into a separate office. "I'm not making sketches like I used to," he explained. "We're using this now."

It was an identi-kit, something my department didn't have. I'd used them at MPI, and had I known they had one, I'd have just borrowed it. I made a mental note to see what I'd have to do to acquire one. I knew they weren't exactly cheap.

He opened it, and then asked Anna for a brief description of the guy and drew out a few templates. Creating a sketch of a suspect using an Identi-kit is like putting together a jigsaw puzzle. It has facial types, hair, eyes, nose, lips, and you put them together to create an image of a person. Sometimes, the results were spot on, but most of the time, they were more a ballpark.

"Is this him," Niles asked, the girl sitting next to him.

'No," she said. "It looks nothing like him"

Niles nodded, not expecting that it would. He handed her a catalog that had hair types, nose types, and so on.

"Let's start with the general face shape."

Anna flipped through it and pointed at a facial type, and Niles found that piece of plastic and replaced the face template with it.

"Closer?"

"Closer," she confirmed.

Niles smiled. He was heading in the right direction. "Good, now let's work on the mouth."

I got up and walked into the front office. Jim had come in, and we sat down in his office to get caught up.

"Glad you made it back from the Gulf," he said. "I didn't even know you were in the Army till I saw your name on the marquee at the 7-11, saying welcome back."

"The Gulf was interesting." With one sentence, I glossed over several months I could have done without. "With luck, I'll never have to do that again."

"Why did you enlist?"

"Needed a job," I explained, and told him how the tax base in our town vanished almost overnight, and no one else was hiring.

He shook his head. "You know, you were the last person I ever expected to become a cop."

"What do you mean?"

"I mean, you were studying all that highbrow math and stuff. And you chucked all that to put on the badge."

"Jim, I took my degree in Astronomy and Physics. Astrophysics majors don't go to the help wanted sections to get a job. They go to the obits. No one wanted to die the year I graduated."

He understood that. Jim wasn't a slouch in the education department. He had a Ph.D. in business management and was the equivalent of a Chief of Police.

"Remember my first arrest?" I asked.

He laughed. "Yeah! I've never heard a man hit such a high note!"

I chuckled, remembering that night. It had been a cold February night. It was a bone dry winter. There had been very little snow, and the local farmers were worried.

That night an Arctic cold front settled over Alamosa like a frosty blanket, chilling the town with subzero temperatures. My job was to walk the campus, check buildings, and generally help out where I could. It was quiet, Jim was bored, and I was cold. So he picked me up, and we were riding around just talking. They'd opened a 7-11 in town, one that stayed open 24/7, and we were going to get a cup of coffee. That's when I learned how a cop's night could go from boring to full speed ahead in a heartbeat.

Alamosa PD was on a chase, and they were calling for any assistance in stopping this guy. Jim and I happened to be almost right in the way. We were headed east on Main Street, and the guy they were chasing was headed west on sixth· Jim responded we could assist, and had just turned down 287 to block him. Sixth Street was less than a block away. We were already too late. The car APD was pursuing went shooting through the intersection. Two Alamosa Police cruisers were right behind him. Jim hit the overheads, gunned the patrol car, and we got around the corner just in time to see the guy wipe out.

At the time, Sixth Street was a two-way road, and it ended one block over from 287, right behind Safeways.

Railroad tracks blocked the way from there. I don't know if he tried to make the right between Safeways and the laundromat or not, but he was going too fast. The car kept going straight. He hit the rail bed, and then the tracks. He might as well have hit a wall. The slope of the rail bed had the effect of rocketing him up as if he'd hit a ramp. But his tires caught the rails, and that was like a jet fighter grabbing the arrestor cable on an aircraft carrier. All the momentum needed to go somewhere, and it threw the car onto its side. The vehicle spun crazily. For a split second, I saw a cloud of dust, the headlights twirl around, and then more dust as his momentum carried him off the tracks and down the other side.

The police cruisers slammed on their brakes, and the APD officers were jumping out. Jim stopped, told me to stay put, and then jumped out as well. A moment later, he came back.

"He's not in the car," he explained. "We're going over to the other side of the tracks and do a foot search."

We went down Tremont to some old, rarely used roads. Once, the roads had been busy with truck traffic from the produce warehouses that lined the tracks. But with the cutback in rail shipment, the warehouses were long since shut down and were falling into disrepair. Now the roads were little more than busted concrete with weeds growing through them. The area was dotted with sagebrush, affording easy concealment for a man on the run.

We got out and started our foot search. About a hundred yards away, I could see APD still clustered around the car. Except for street lights and the lights from the patrol cars, none of which did anything to provide much illumination, our search area was dark. We were utterly dependent upon our flashlights. The guy we were looking for had all the advantages. If he was smart and stayed low, he could easily elude us.

We made a full circle from where we'd parked, and soon we'd gotten back to the cruiser.

"He's gone," Jim said. I was in the process of agreeing with him but was making one final turn before we got back into the warmth of the patrol car. And right in the pool of light cast by my flashlight, I saw a man lying on the ground. For an instant, I couldn't believe it. Then I shouted. Jim was right. My voice went up several octaves. I'm pretty sure I went from baritone to soprano in half a second.

"Laird, over here."

Jim was approaching him and said, "Stay put, friend. You've already had a rough enough night." He had his cuffs out and quickly cuffed the suspect. I helped him get the guy up and walking to the car. The suspect had taken a beating from his rough ride across the tracks. He had a nose bleed, a nasty bump on his head, and there was blood on his shirt. We got him into the car, and Jim called APD, telling them we had their suspect in custody. We drove him to the county jail, where APD officers were waiting for him. We turned him over to them and got our coffee.

"I never heard a man's voice hit a high note like that!" Jim said, teasing me.

"That was a long time ago, Jim. I've never gone that high since. Close a couple of times, but not reaching it."

"Still, I never thought you'd be the one who stayed in law enforcement."

"I did hang up my guns more than once," I reminded him.

"And each time you swore to God that you'd never put them on again," Jim finished. "I think we've all done that at least once."

A knock on the door interrupted our reminiscing. Niles and Anna stood at the door. "We have a face," Niles announced.

He handed me the composite sketch. The guy was beyond ordinary looking. The sketch was of a middle-aged, white male, who was slightly bald. He was about as remarkable as vanilla ice cream. No wonder people didn't remember him. There was just nothing that stood out. You could have had a long conversation with the guy, had lunch with him, and then not remember what he looked like. He was forgettable.

Niles had made me a dozen copies of the composite sketch. On the sketch were the numbers for the templates he'd used in building it.

"I owe you, Brother," I said. "Buy you lunch next week?"

"Sure. Campus Café still serves a great patty melt."

"Good to know that at least some things haven't changed."

I drove my witness home and then went back to the Sheriff's Office. Once there, I composed what I wanted to put on the sketch, and typed in information onto the bottom of one of the composites concerning our suspect. I was careful to include contact info for both Andy and myself. Once done, I faxed it to Andy and then called him.

"Andy. I just faxed that sketch to you."

"Hang on. Let me look at it." He put me on hold, and I could almost envision him hustling to the fax machine and then back. "Got it," he said. "Got our contact info in there? Good. This looks really good."

"Good enough to put out?"

"Yes. Now, assuming we get lucky, we need to talk about how to hold him. I mean, if we get a call he's in a store right then and there, we'd like to be able to call the local cops and have him picked up."

I'd been thinking about that. "I've already talked to our DA about that. We've got a description of him, and his truck, and his MO. I'm asking for a John Doe warrant."

I could almost hear him cringe at that one, but sometimes you have to take the shot. "I wish we had something better to go on, but I agree. What does your DA say?"

"Well, he doesn't like it, but he'll give it to us."

He paused. "This is the closest we've ever been. Let's count on luck."

"I'll apply for the warrant and get it into the system. I'll let you know once it's out there."

"Sounds good, Will. You have a good night."

"You too." I hung up the phone.

I updated the case file and went home. It had been a good day.

CHAPTER SIX

BACK IN THE CHAIR

"What do you do for fun," Pastor Morgan asked. I was back at the church and in his office. A cup of coffee sat on the same coffee table.

"Lots of things. I read a lot. I take long walks. I still like to run. Hang with Jewell a lot,"

"Do you ever go out? Like to clubs and things like that?"

I shook my head. "They're too noisy for me."

"What do you mean?"

"I mean, it's hard to talk to someone when you can't hear what they say," I explained. "I'm not a big fan of clubs, bars, and the like. Way too crowded. I end up watching people too much. It's like stepping into a battlefield. And where's the fun in that?"

"And why's that."

I noticed he was writing some stuff down. "Well, I'm a cop. You never know when something's going to go down, or who might be gunning for you."

"You ever had something go down in front of you?"

"No. Can't say it has. But for all things, there is a first time," I answered. "Besides, I don't like those settings. One beer is my limit. And from what I've seen, people drink to excess, and they do things which usually mean problems for me."

"What kind of things have you seen people do?"

I thought about it. "Fights. Domestic violence. Kill people. The quickest way I can think of to become a murderer is to drive drunk. And it's a nice way to commit suicide, too."

"You've seen this?"

I shook my head as if I was trying to deny having seen it, I replied, "Too many times."

"What was the worse one?"

I thought about it, and then put my chin in my hand. "It was almost ten years ago, just a couple of days after Christmas." I let myself drift back to that night.

For such a cold winter, we hadn't had much snow yet. But you don't hear Bing Crosby singing about a Brown Christmas. It had just been cold. I was a patrol deputy with the Sheriff's Office, and I'd just come in to get a cup of coffee. It was the Saturday after Christmas day. The Christmas tree in dispatch was shimmering with lights, and the windows were frosted with spray-on snow spelling out "Season's Greetings."

In Antonito, Romeo, and Capulin, the bars were full. People were drinking, dancing, and partying. I'd made my presence known by doing walkthroughs, greeting people (especially those that were frequent flyers when it came to getting into trouble), and just generally keeping an eye on things. Christmas was often one of the few occasions where whole families got together, and everyone seemed to be making the most of it.

The night had been problem-free, and I hadn't had to arrest anyone yet. I didn't expect that to hold, but you can always hope.

I took a sip of my coffee and asked Little Joe, the dispatcher/jailer, how things were.

"Everything's quiet," he said. "I let them set up and watch television."

He meant the inmates and letting them watch Holiday Inn wasn't going to do any harm. I sipped the coffee and began heading for the squad room. I was thinking of a conversation my parents and I had a week before. They felt that my job was a cakewalk. They said all I did was ride around and look important. They couldn't understand that every time I left to work, there was a chance I wouldn't be coming back. I'd also tried to explain to them that my day could go to hell with the ringing of a telephone.

Like it was about to.

The phone rang, and I saw Little Joe straighten as he picked it up. A sudden serious look came over his face, and he quickly began writing stuff down into the log. He told whoever was on the other end, "Hold one, please." Then he looked over his shoulder at me and said, "There's a bad wreck right in front of the Rainbow. A semi hit a car."

I headed for the door, and getting into Trigger, I started her up and pulled out of the parking lot. The minute I was on the road, I hit the overheads. The nightclub was less than a mile away, and I had my foot in the carburetor. The big 440 was screaming with power. I was already on the radio, calling the Colorado

State Patrol (the wreck would be their jurisdiction). "Alamosa, Conejos 4, I have a report of a 10-50 at 285 near county road thirteen. Page out fire and EMS. A semi hit a passenger car."

"Copy that Conejos 4 Paging fire and EMS out now. Let us know what's going on when you get there."

I was already rolling up on the wreck. "Alamosa, Conejos 4. I've some info. Semi is jackknifed in the middle of the road . . ." And then I saw the car. "Oh, God! He didn't hit the car. He ran over it!"

The car, a blue and white two-door, had once been a cute little vehicle. Now the engine compartment and the front of the driver's compartment was crumpled down like a box an angry person had stomped on.

"I need Antonito PD to assist by blocking northbound traffic. This is going to be a mess. Show me out at that location."

"Roger that, Conejos 4."

I stopped Trigger broadside in the road and flipped on the spotlight on to give me extra illumination. My overheads were already on, warning oncoming traffic. I grabbed my flashlight and the handheld radio and ran to the car. Two girls were in the back of the vehicle. Both were scared out of their minds.

Already a crowd had gathered. People had spilled out of the nearby nightclub, attracted by the sight of something out of the ordinary. It was a chance to see chaos exemplified, with the chance of seeing someone die. I shook my head and reminded myself that I was dealing with a species that had tossed common sense into the trash can thousands of years before.

Then I saw Pat Wheat standing there. If there was one person who could help me, it was him.

"Pat! I need your help."

Calling his name changed him from a spectator to someone involved in the action. I didn't realize that I'd just changed his life.

The week before, Pat had been an inmate in my jail and was serving a month-long sentence for some minor offense. He had a rep for being a tough guy. It was a rep that didn't stand once you got to know him. He was one of the nicest guys in the world. Of course, we made him a trustee, and he'd helped keep the place cleaned up, prepared meals, and the like.

While he was doing his time, the Red Cross came in to get us all recertified on First Aid and CPR. He was watching and asked me, "Can I take this? It seems like something I should know."

"What the hell, I might need your help someday" I'd told him. "I'll pay for your class and testing."

And so the county inmate took First Aid and CPR alongside us. He tested, got his card, and thought that was pretty cool. I don't think he expected "someday" to arrive so quickly. But he stepped up to the plate when I yelled.

He ran up to me. "What's up, Will? What can I do?"

"You're going to help me. That's what." I held my flashlight up and peered into the car. I couldn't see the driver. The car was crumpled like a tin can around him, but the passenger was sitting in his seat, his head bowed. The passenger's chest and legs were drenched with blood. Blood was dripping from his nose and mouth and several wounds on his head. Every time he took a breath, his head would come up and then go down. I was very concerned about moving him. I could tell he'd suffered massive trauma to his head and neck. I'd move him only if I had to.

I turned the light towards the back seat. The girls seemed unharmed except for cuts from the glass. "Ladies, are you OK?"

"Get us out of here," one of them cried, her face twisted with shock. She knew something terrible had just happened but wasn't sure what.

"I think my leg's broken. I can't move it," cried the other. Pain at least gave her some focus in her world, though it was clear she didn't realize just how bad things were.

Getting the girl out would be challenging. I shone the light over her leg, and I realized that the seat had been shoved backward, pinning her in a bit.

"OK. Pat, let's get this door open. Let's get them out." I pushed the door release, felt it unclick, and then we both yanked on the door through the shattered window. It gave a little.

"One more time," I said. By now, a couple of guys had joined us. "On three! One. Two. Three," and we all pulled sharply on the door. With a groan, it gave way and opened, nearly toppling the injured passenger out. I stopped him with a quick, steadying hand.

I glanced around, and I could see the truck driver and a woman in the cab of the semi. They looked OK. I looked at one of the guys and said, "Run over there and ask him if I can have some blankets from his sleeper." He did and a moment later came back with a couple of thick quilts and a blanket

Pat quickly began pulling the broken glass from the back window. "Careful Pat. Don't need you losing a couple of fingers."

"Trust me. I'm careful." He'd gotten most of the glass out, and I used my nightstick to knock loose fragments down.

"OK, Ladies. Here's what we're going to do. We're going to get you out one at a time. OK," I said. "If it hurts a lot, tell me, and we'll stop. OK?"

I bent down and reached in, putting my arms around the first girl. "Put your arms around my neck. Ok, here we go. Somebody keep him steady (meaning the passenger in the front seat) and mind the glass." With a slight whimper, she came out, and one of the guys tossed a blanket around her.

The other girl was wedged in by the seat. I had to get some of the pressure off her leg if we were to get her out. I crawled into the car and sat next to her. Busted glass and blood made the vinyl seat slick.

"We need to get this pressure off your leg. I don't think it's broken, just pinned. Here's what we're going to do. I'm going to push as hard as I can against the back of the seat with my legs. Pat, you're going to have to help pull her out. Just pull her over me. Some of you guys help him!"

Pat said he was ready, and I asked the girl if she understood. She did. "OK, here we go. On Three! One. Two. Three!" I pushed with everything I had, and the front seat shifted forward a little. She felt it move and twisted her legs best she could. Pat had reached over me and had his arms under hers and was pulling slowly and steadily. She cried out in pain, and then she was loose. They drug her over me and out of the car.

Now what, I thought. "Pat, give them both a quick going over. Let me know what if anything's wrong."

I reached through the ruins of the car, trying to find the driver. I touched steel, fabric, and then something warm and wet. I felt around. I'd found the driver's neck. I could feel him breathing and a pulse. The car body was twisted around him, but he was still alive.

I glanced out, noticed that the girls were shivering with cold and shock, and tossed Pat my keys. "Pat put them in the back of the car and turn the heater on high."

I looked at my hand. It was wet with blood.

Pat hurried to comply, leaving me in the back seat of the car. Several of the guys hustled the girls over to the car.

A voice called to me through the broken window. "Diaz, what can we do to help?" I looked up and recognized the speaker. He was a local truck driver and had friends with him. You can always count on the modern cowboy to help out.

"Got flares?" I asked.

"Yes."

"Get me some traffic control going. Shut down the road, and start sending traffic down towards Conejos. If one of you wants to go down that way and direct them back towards Highway 17, I'd appreciate it."

"We'll get on it," said one.

I let State Patrol know that truckers were getting traffic control going and would be sending traffic down to Conejos and from there to 17.

With the initial response done, I shifted to just monitoring the situation. Getting the driver out without Jaws of Life was out of the question, and I'd move the passenger only if I had to. I was going from the driver to the passenger, just making sure they still had a pulse. I glanced at my watch. I'd been on scene five minutes. That put fire close, EMS maybe 10 minutes away.

"Will," Pat yelled. "I've got them in the car."

"Hang loose. I might need you." I'd just checked the driver and went back to the passenger. Nothing! I checked for it again. No pulse! "Pat, pull him out. His heart has stopped!"

Pat pulled the passenger out of the car, laying him out on the ground. I got out of the back of the car and looked at Pat. He was ready. "Just like we practiced," I said. "You compress, I'll breathe."

He nodded. I gave the passenger a couple of quick breaths, and Pat started compressions.

Want to find out what kind of shape you're in? Do CPR. We started and kept going. After a couple of minutes, we were both covered in sweat despite the cold December air.

"Switch," I cried. Now Pat gave a couple of quick breaths, and I took over compressions. We just kept on, switching every couple of minutes, the sweat dripping off us, our shoulders aching. Everyone stood and watched, enjoying the spectacle of two people doing everything in their power to keep someone from dying. I'd felt disgust and rage against people who could stand and watch someone die without lifting a hand.

"Switch!"

In the distance, I could hear the wail of a siren. I glanced up briefly. Fire and EMS were both coming in. Antonito fire was coming in from the south, and from the north, Romeo Fire and the Conejos EMS service. The Ambulance pulled up, and one of the EMTs jumped out. "Who's worse!"

"He is," I yelled back, pointing down at the passenger. The EMT knelt next to Pat and said, "Switch." I continued to push air into him. The EMT must have pushed too hard. Vomit flooded up into my mouth.

I gagged on it. It tasted of beer and cheeseburgers, and my stomach lurched. Turning my head, I vomited next to the man we were trying to save. I got control of myself. I had to continue breathing. Quickly I swept his airway to clear it of vomit and tried to keep breathing for him but couldn't. My stomach was heaving, and I started to gag. A fireman pushed me out of the way, taking over. I sat back on the cold pavement, my stomach heaving. Then I rolled on my knees to throw up again, my supper spreading out into a thick puddle of steaming vomit on the freezing road.

Pat hadn't seen me throw up the first time, but he saw the second time. When he saw me throw up, he began throwing up. Shaken, he leaned against the front of the ambulance, trying to use it for support. His legs and hands were shaking from cold and fatigue.

From the crowd, a man started laughing at him. "What's the matter, Wheat? Can't take it?"

It was the worst thing he could have said. Pat's head jerked, up, hurt, and pain in his eyes, and I saw it coming. Pat doubled up his fist. I don't know where he found the strength, maybe it was pure anger or pure frustration, but he punched the guy in the face, knocking him to the ground. In a second, I was up, pushing Pat away from the guy.

"Leave him alone, Pat. He's not worth it!"

Pat was looking me in the face, his eyes wide, and then he said calmly, "Jesus Christ! You look like hell!"

He didn't look any better. His face, hair, and clothing were wet with blood and sweat. Some of it was dry, some still glistening in the lights. It was as if he'd just done a forced march through a slaughterhouse.

I looked down at myself. My hands, arms, and uniform were slick with blood. My uniform was ruined because of the blood and vomit all over it.

And then the guy Pat had punched was on his feet. "He hit me! I want to press charges! I want to press charges!"

I glared at him. "Get the hell out of my face," I heard myself hiss. Then I found myself yelling at him. "Where the hell were you when I needed you? When he needed you," I demanded, pointing towards the man on the ground. The EMTs had moved away. He was gone. "Take a good look." He looked and went pale. "Get out of here before I finish you myself!" I growled.

Suddenly there was a hand on my shoulder. State Patrol Officer Al Henderson had arrived. "Will," he said quietly. "I've got the scene. Why don't you two put the girls in the ambulance and then go to the Sheriff's office? Get cleaned up a bit."

His suggestion made all kinds of sense. Pat and I did what he suggested. We got the girls transferred to the ambulance and then drove quietly to the Sheriff's office. When we got there and walked in, the dispatcher's eyes went wide at our appearance. "What the ... .," he gasped.

"Joe," I said. "Can you get us some towels and wash clothes."

"And soap," Pat added. We went into the kitchen and sat down at the table. For several long minutes, we just stared at each other, trying to come to grips with what had just happened.

"I'm hungry," Pat said, after a while. I realized I was too.

I stood up, washed the blood from my hands, and opened the fridge. I pulled out ham and cheese, mayo, and a loaf of bread. I put them on the table and grabbed us each of a bag of chips. So covered with blood, we made sandwiches and ate.

Joe brought in the towels and washcloths, and I told Pat to go ahead and get cleaned up.

"In a minute," he said. He made himself another sandwich and wolfed it down. After about ten minutes, he got up and washed in the squad room bathroom. He came out a few minutes later.

When I stood to go wash, I found my knees were shaking. "And I have a cake job," I muttered, remembering what my parents had said.

"Screw 'em," I said, then louder. "Joe, grab the Polaroid."

"What?"

"I want a picture of me," I said. "The next time someone tells me my job is easy, I can show them just how easy it is."

Joe got the Polaroid and took a picture as I'd requested. The photograph looked like it was torn from a slasher film. You aren't supposed to be wearing someone else's blood.

I went into the bathroom and washed the blood off my face. When I came out, Pat had made coffee and had poured us each a cup. We sat back down to drink it. About half an hour later, Al came in and got statements from us. "The fireman had to tear the car apart to get the driver out. He's in terrible shape," he told us. "Flight for life is on its way. The other guy didn't make it."

"How are the girls doing?" Pat asked.

"Cuts, bruises, sprains," he said, cataloging their injuries. "They're hurting but not hurt badly. They'll be in the hospital overnight."

Odd, I thought. A few hours ago, they were full of life. Now one was just so much dead flesh, the other fighting for his life. Our mortality never ceases to amaze me.

I nodded, and finally said, "What the hell happened, Al?"

"Well, you know kids. They've been dragging Main, and the Antonito cops have been writing a lot of tickets because the kids would get up to the city limits, do a U-turn, and come back down. So they just came a little further out into the county to do their turn. It looks like they didn't stop or notice there was a semi right behind them when they made their U-turn."

Pat leaned forward, his head resting on his hands. "I know those guys. To die that way . . ." I heard a sob escape his lips, and then another. A second later, he broke down and cried. After a few minutes, he got himself together. "I need to get home," he said. He looked at us. "I think I'm too shook up to drive." He seemed to have forgotten his pickup was at the Rainbow.

"I'll take you," Al offered.

Pat nodded, dried his tears, and stood up. "I'm ready," he said.

Al stood up, looked at me, and said, "Will. Can you get home?"

I nodded. "I'm leaving now."

As I drove home, I looked at the stars, trying to feel something beyond pure exhaustion. But nothing came. I was tired, and I felt like a wrung-out dishrag.

I got home, took a hot shower, and then threw my uniform in the washing machine on cold to soak the blood out. Maybe it would come out, perhaps not.

On impulse, I put the picture Joe had taken on the kitchen table. I was living at home at the time, and it was the best place to put it. I thought, let my folks tell me I've got an easy job.

I stopped telling the story and looked up. Pastor had his pencil in his mouth, nodding. He removed it to say, "But that wasn't the worse of it." Again, I wondered if I was just that transparent or if God was whispering something in his ear.

I smiled and shook my head. "No, it wasn't. The driver ended up dying two days later.

"But the worst happened a couple of weeks later. I had a chance to make some extra money by working a basketball game at one of the schools. I'd gone out to check the parking lot and had just stepped back in when suddenly this little cheerleader is standing in front of me. She sticks out her hand, introduces herself, and said, 'I want to thank you for trying to save my brother.' "

I wiped a tear away. "Pastor, to this day, I don't know what to say to her!"

He nodded, handing me a Kleenex. I wiped the tears away and then sat up straight in the seat, my hand banging the armrest. "A bunch of kids out there with no clue they'd just seen their last Christmas. Drinking, driving. They killed themselves in the name of having a good time!"

To his credit, Pastor Morgan didn't say anything right away. He just reached across, put a hand on my shoulder, and let me cry it out.

Finally, he spoke. "How did all this make you feel?"

"It tore me up!" I exclaimed. "How am I supposed to feel?"

"Tore me up isn't a feeling. It's a result of your feelings, your emotions. How do you feel?"

I had to stop and think about it for a bit.

"Lot of hurts," I said finally. "A lot of anger."

"Hurt and anger at what?" he asked.

"The people," I answered. I thought about that night. "They just stood there enjoying the show. Like it was all some pre-staged drama for their entertainment."

"And they just stood there?"

"They just stood there," I confirmed.

He nodded, then he said quietly, "What did you want them to do?"

I paused. "I don't know. Something! Instead, they just stood there. If I could have sold popcorn and peanuts, I'd have made money that night. Death was entertaining them!"

"And because they did nothing except watch, what do you think of them?" he asked calmly.

"That every one of them is nothing but a bunch of spineless, cold-blooded Son of a Bitches," I heard myself say to this man of God.

He smiled. "Do you think that's a fair assessment of the crowd?"

I'd walked right into his crosshairs. I knew he'd seen something and had to take the shot. I said, "I don't follow you."

"Let me put it another way. What's your name?"

"William Diaz," I answered. I didn't know where he was going with this.

"Anywhere in your name is God the Father, God the Son, or God the Holy Spirit mentioned?"

"No," I answered.

"Here," he said, flipping through the tattered Bible he used for these sessions. "Read this out loud to me, please. Matthew, Chapter 2, verse 1."

I took the Bible and read it to him. "Do not judge, or you too will be judged."

He nodded. "Now flip over to Luke 5, verse 37."

I turned to the Book of Luke, the pages rustling under my fingers like dry leaves. I found it and read it out loud. "Do not judge, and you will not be judged. Do not condemn, and you will not be condemned. Forgive, and you will be forgiven."

I knew where this one had just gone. "Steel on target, Pastor," I said, weakly.

"Do you see what was going on?" he asked. "You resented that the crowd didn't help."

I nodded.

"But that's not exactly true, either," he said. "Some people helped. There were the guys who helped you and Pat open the car and get the girls out. You had a guy who got blankets. You had truckers who stopped and got traffic control going for you. Isn't that true?"

"Yes," I answered.

"So not everyone just stood there. Some helped. Others didn't, and that's who your anger is directed towards."

I nodded, following what he was saying. "Go on."

"You're angry because they did nothing. Has it occurred to you that they didn't know what to do? The only two people in that crowd equipped to do anything were you and Pat. You at least had a starting point. You'd been there before. And Pat didn't even have that. He didn't know what to do. He didn't act until you told him to."

I blinked. I'd never thought of that way. "Gee," I heard myself say.

"And how about the fact they died. Are you angry at that? Was there someone in that crowd that could have done something to stop that?"

"I don't know,' I answered.

"Look at this way. You and Pat, a whole team of EMTs, and the resources of one of the most advanced trauma centers in the world couldn't save them. Is it logical to expect someone else could?

"It's not," I admitted quietly.

"Let it go, Will. No one except God could have done anything that night."

"Did he?" I asked. I realized there was some bitterness in my voice when I said that.

"We'll get to that in a second," he said, clearly one step ahead of me. I made a mental note not to play chess with this man. "But before we go there, I want to finish with you. Was there any hint of betrayal you felt that night?"

"From the crowd? How could I feel betrayed?" I asked.

"Betrayal can take a lot of forms," he said quietly. He leaned forward. "We've known each other for how long now, Will?

"Years," I answered.

"That's about right. We've drunk a lot of coffee together, ate at the same table, prayed together. We went to school together. You get to know someone pretty well when you do that."

"Agreed," I said, again wondering where he was going.

"Well, in all that time, I've noticed something interesting. You'd like to think that people are basically good, and they'll always do the right thing."

"I'd like to think they would," I answered.

"Well, the reason I bring up betrayal is that the crowd violated one of your most cherished beliefs. You think that people are good and will do the right thing. And I think that accounts for the anger more than anything else. They took something you want desperately to have proven to you, and they didn't."

"You've got to be kidding," I said. Because no one had taken action, I judged the whole crowd for violating my belief that people would always step up to the plate.

"The crowd isn't to blame. They didn't know what to do. They needed a leader, and you got them moving in the direction you needed. And don't sweat there being a few yahoos in the bunch. The world is well-stocked with them. But you already know that."

"I know," I said, still reeling from the anger and resentment I'd felt toward the crowd. It made sense. The crowd didn't know what to do. They couldn't have reacted any other way.

"There are a couple of other people you need to let off the hook here," he said.

"Who's that?"

"How about the driver of the car? You commented that it was just a bunch of kids out to have a good time. You also commented that drinking and driving were the same as murder if you killed someone. He didn't mean to get them killed. It was a moment of carelessness," he said. "I'm going to tell you something you already know. We live in a world where things happen. They don't always make sense, but you can be sure some good came out of it."

"What good came out of this?" I asked.

"Well, are you the leader today that you were before that night?"

I had to stop and think about what he'd said. "I sure wasn't," I answered.

"I'd say that was the night you became the person you are today. Could you have led soldiers in Iraq if that night had never happened?"

"Probably not," I answered.

"How about tackling that guy at Shipton. Could you have done it without that night?"

I had to admit I couldn't have.

"Because of that night, you became the man you are today. A take-charge, leader of men. God took something terrible and used it to remake you."

"I hadn't thought of that," I admitted after thinking about it.

"People learned that night that you were someone who they could count on. When the chips were down, you'd be in their corner fighting death itself if that's what it came to." Then he asked another question I hadn't considered.

"And how about Pat? What happened to him?"

I smiled. "Pat joined the Fire Department, and later became a councilman."

"He became a leader too. The town screw up became a man because of what happened."

I nodded. I hadn't thought about how God used the tragedy to change our lives.

"And before we pray about this, there's one last person you need add to the forgiveness list."

"And just who might that be?" I asked.

"Why did you react to the cheerleader like you did?" he asked, instead of telling me.

"I didn't know what to say," I answered.

"Did you think if you had been better trained, or had better equipment at the time, that you might have saved her brother?"

"No," I answered. "No one could have."

"Exactly. No one could have. And God used the incident to change you and Pat into the people you are today. And because of that night, there are people alive today who might not have been if it hadn't have been for that night.

"So, before we get going on praying, add yourself to a list of people to forgive. You did the very best you could have. Let yourself off the hook."

"I understand," I said. "I see I've looked at this thing through the wrong end of the telescope for a lot of years."

"One last thing, are you angry at God about this?"

"God? No. It wasn't his doing. Pastor, I'm very much a fatalist in that respect," I explained. "I look at the world as when it's your time to go, it's your time to go, and nothing can change that. It was simply their time. No, I can't hold God accountable for this one."

"Interesting," he said. I wondered what he found interesting about it. "You ready to pray?"

I nodded, and we prayed.

After we prayed, I wiped the tears that had flowed from my eyes and smiled at Pastor Morgan.

"Same time next week?" I asked.

"Same time next week," he confirmed.

CHAPTER SEVEN

WE GET LUCKY!

Gerry sat on a stump and watched as I swung the ax overhead into the log. It was a nice August day, and winter wasn't far away. It was time to make firewood.

The pine logs had all been cut into manageable blocks about a foot long. But each log was still almost two feet across and heavy with moisture. If we intended to have wood to burn to stay warm over the winter, we had to chop it down into manageable pieces that would fit into the stove. They also needed to dry out, and blocking would make sure that happened.

I was raising my son as I had been. I was teaching him that there's nothing wrong with getting your hands dirty. Learning to work hard at a young age was something every cowboy learned.

"Chopping wood is a bit of an art," I told him, between swings. "Most people will chop in the middle, and try to split these big logs. You'll never do it, especially if it's wet. If you have some wedges and a demolition hammer, you can, but without them, well, no one is that strong.

I held the ax and demonstrated it. "I start on the outside, splitting pieces off and work in."

I swung the ax, catching the block about five inches from the outside. A large piece of wood, split cleanly off. I picked that piece up, placed it on the block, and chopped it in two with one swing of the ax. Now that was useful firewood. It took about ten minutes to reduce the log into smaller pieces that would fit into the stove. Gary got up and moved the split wood and stacked it neatly against the shed.

"Better put your gloves on," I said, noticing he hadn't. "This stuff can give you a nasty splinter."

He slipped the leather work gloves on. "Did you do this when you were as old as I am now?" He kept moving wood.

I nodded. Gerry was only eight years old, but I'd known men who were younger. "Of course. I didn't get as strong as I am by sitting in front of the TV watching Bozo the Clown."

I pulled another log out of the pile and positioned it so I could chop it next. "It's easier and warmer to chop it now than it is in winter."

We'd been working steadily for almost two hours. What was a big pile of logs was still a big pile of logs. It would take a lot of work to reduce it down and make it into wood that would keep us all warm during the winter.

Jewell called me from the house. "Baby, you've got a phone call. It's the office."

"This can't be good," I muttered. It was Sunday, and if they were calling on a Sunday, It could only mean trouble. I swung the ax and buried the head in the middle of the log.

I went in and picked up the phone. "This is Will."

Patrick, one of our dispatchers, was on the line. "Will. Detective DeShong from Routt County called. Says he needs to talk to you right away."

Patrick gave me the number, and I made the phone call.

"Andy! Will from Conejos County. We got him?"

I could almost hear him grinning over the phone. "He just popped up on the radar," he said.

"Where," I asked.

"Raton, New Mexico. He went into a 7-11 there, bought some money orders, and the girl who waited on him called me after he left. She recognized him from the drawing. She got a good description of his pickup and the license plate."

"That is good news. The warrant is out there!" I said.

"I know. I already called the Raton cops, and they're looking for him. If we get him, you want to go with me. At least we can talk to him?"

"Heck, yes," I answered. "Let me know what's going on." I gave him my home number.

Jewell looked at me. I knew she was wondering what was going on.

"It was Andy DeShong from Routt County. We might have gotten our money order bandit," I explained. "He just left a 7-11 in Raton. Local cops are looking for him now."

She smiled and raised her cup of coffee. "Here's hoping they find him."

A few minutes later, the phone rang again. It was Andy.

"We got him," he said. "He'd already started altering the money orders. He had two done, and another he was working on. He's got a typewriter, everything he needs. Their detectives are collecting all the evidence now. They arrested him on that John Doe warrant."

I smiled, "Outstanding. When are you headed down?"

"I can leave tomorrow. Want me to pick you up?"

"Sure," I started to give him my address, but he stopped me and said, "No, the airport there in Alamosa. I've got a plane!"

"You own an airplane?" I gasped. Routt County must pay pretty well, I thought, but he shot that one down pretty quickly. "I'm retired, Air Force. I learned how to fly while I was in the Air Force."

Wow, I thought. His very own plane! I was impressed. "Sure. What kind of plane do you have?"

"A little Beechcraft TravelAir," he said. "Two engine job. It's great to get around the mountains. It has plenty of power and a good ceiling, which is important here in Colorado." I heard him flipping some pages and then said, "How about I meet you at nine. Pick you up right there at the big hanger next to the airline terminal. We can leave after I refuel."

"I'll be there," I answered. "SLV Regional Airport. That's only about fifteen minutes from my house."

"Perfect," he said. "See you tomorrow."

I hung up and smiled. "We got him! Damn, we got him!"

Jewell was smiling. "I knew you would. Once someone remembered his face, it was just a matter of time."

"Andy will be picking me up tomorrow morning, and we'll fly over to Raton. I want to talk to this guy."

I called the Sheriff and let him know that we'd caught the guy, and I'd be flying down to interview him with DeShong. The Sheriff was glad to hear it.

Gerry and I kept chopping wood. By evening, the big pile in need of chopping was a much smaller pile in need of chopping. It would be a couple of more weekends before it was all gone.

Jewell drove me to the airport the next morning. The SLV Regional Airport is a strange affair. The terminal that serviced the United Airlines Express flights was small. Of course, the aircraft were just small turboprop jobs that could hold a dozen people or so. You'd have thought the runway would also be a tiny thing. But it wasn't. The runway was long and wide. Jet fighters could land on it, and Malcolm Forbes's 707, "The Capitalist Tool," had been a frequent visitor. Rumor had it that a loaded B-52 could take off and land on it. I could easily believe that it could.

I gave Jewell a kiss and a hug and then grabbed my briefcase from the back seat.

"I'll be thinking about you," she said, a bit sadly.

I chuckled. "You do, and you'll have a long day. Be home tonight. Pick me up?"

"No, you can walk. You need the exercise." She was smiling when she said it. "Just call and let me know when you guys get in."

I walked to the door of the hanger, paused there, and turned. I smiled at her and then stepped through it and onto the tarmac.

A red and white twin-engine airplane had a fuel truck nestled up to it. A man wearing jeans, a leather jacket, and cowboy boots was walking around it. When he saw me, he waved and motioned me over.

"Andy DeShong," he said, sticking out his hand.

"Glad to meet you, Andy," I said. He had a good solid handshake. "Will Diaz." I nodded towards the airplane. "Nice plane."

"Not a lot of them around anymore," he said. "Beechcraft only built about seven hundred of them."

The fuel jockey finished filling that tanks and then put the caps back on. I noticed he was careful to make sure they were on securely.

"Where did you get it?"

"It was my Dad's. He was a B-25 pilot back in WWII. Flew a lot of missions in the Pacific, and then he became an instructor. He bought it after he got out. I think he missed flying. I got it since I'm the only one of his kids who ever learned to fly."

"You flew in the Air Force?"

He shook his head and indicated his eyes. "Eyes kept me out of fighters. Nope, I was a weather puke. Combat weatherman to be precise."

I whistled. I knew what a Combat Weatherman did. "That's a tough job."

"No, it wasn't really. The training was rough. Think regular weatherman mixed with combat infantry, and you get an idea what it was like. Other than that, it was like being back at home, working Dad's ranch."

"So, you're a cowboy, too!" I said. Funny how many of us were in law enforcement.

"Yep. From the top of my Stetson down to the toes of my Dingo boots."

The fuel jockey came over and handed Andy a clipboard. He signed it.

"Will, stow your bag behind the seat. Let me do a quick walk around, and then we'll get going."

I got up on the wing, and stowed my briefcase behind the left-hand seat as he'd instructed me, and then waited for him. Looking towards the fence, I saw Jewell was still watching. I smiled and waved to her. Then Andy bounded up the small step and gestured me in, saying, "Take the right-hand seat. The pilot sits on the left."

The plane had three-point safety harnesses like the ones aboard Air Force planes. Quickly, I strapped in. The cockpit was a little more crowded than I thought it would be. I was careful that I didn't hit the control wheel, the stirrups, or anything else.

Andy handed me a set of headphones and pointed at a plugin the dash where I could plugin. I did so and then put them on. "You hear me OK," he asked.

"Hear you fine," I answered. I made sure the microphone was near my mouth.

"We probably don't need these," he explained. "But I got used to them when I was learning. Besides, it makes talking back and forth easier. You don't have to yell over the engines."

He closed the door, made a final look around, and then announced, mostly to himself, "Turning one."

He snapped a few switches, pressed a couple of buttons, and the propeller began turning. The motor caught, and the prop blurred into almost invisibility. Glancing at his board, and satisfied with what he saw, Andy said, "Turning two," and went through the same process. Within a few minutes, both engines were humming loudly. With a glance towards it, Andy called the small control center and let them know he was taxing for takeoff. They acknowledged, and he released the brakes. Within a few minutes, we were turning out onto the runway.

"You're clear for takeoff," a voice said over the headphones.

Andy acknowledged it, advanced the throttles, and the plane started moving down the runway. I scarcely noticed when the airplane stopped rolling down the pavement and started up into the sky. He climbed the Beechcraft higher, spiraling up and away from the airport in a banking climb, the engines roaring with power. I looked out the window and caught a terrific view of the airport. I could see Jewell pulling away in her red jeep. Then the wings leveled out, and we were headed south.

"We'll fly over the mountains south of Taos," Andy said. "We've only got an eighteen thousand foot ceiling on this aircraft, and I don't want to waste that jumping over this piece of the Sangre de Cristos."

I nodded. "Can get a little wild, what with the updrafts and all," I said. "I flew across once on a Rocky Mountain Airlines Twin Otter. That's a ride I won't forget. And that was a nice day."

We were racing away from the airport. The floor of the San Luis Valley passed rapidly under the small plane. Within a few minutes, we had flown over the tiny, sleepy community of Las Sauces and the Rio Grande River.

Andy nodded down at a state highway and asked, "What county is that piece of highway in?"

I looked down. The Rio Grande River snaked lazily through roughly the middle of the Valley, cutting its way down towards Taos. There, along with help from plate tectonics, it had long ago carved out a magnificent gorge. The road he was indicating was Highway 142.

"That part of the highway is in Costilla County," I answered.

"Might want to keep an eye on that stretch of road. With all the stuff coming on the market these days, you could put a plane this size down on it real easy. Drug smugglers are looking for places like that. A set of NVGs, a couple of chem lights, and presto, you have an airport."

"I'll keep that in mind." I wondered if dope planes might account for some of the so-called UFOs that were reported from time to time in the Valley. By flying low, and using the hills and gorges for cover, a good pilot could fly in relatively unobserved.

He adjusted our heading a bit, and then said, "You said you were former military."

"Yes, Army. Military Police."

"In the Gulf?"

"Yes," I answered, and no sooner had I said and his eyes widened.

"Wait a minute. I know who you are. I saw a picture of six of you guys. They call you guys the Regulators!" He laughed. "That was a good job you guys did working that case."

"Just so you know," I responded, "our investigation results weren't that well received."

He nodded. "They rarely are. Still, it helped head off some huge problems. So, where's everyone now?"

"Jonesy is LAPD. Terri is FBI now. Greg went CID. Eric is with the Texas Rangers. And Max hung it up and opened a guide service right here in the Valley."

"Terri's the girl, right?"

"Yep."

He smiled. "Forgive me for saying this. I'm not into sisters, but she is one fine looking lady."

I smiled, wondering what the heck it was about her that caused grown men to go all gaga. To me, she was just Terri. "So, you know, she's not all black."

"No?"

"No. She's also Irish, Swede, a little Chinese, and Cherokee. Would you believe her and I are distantly related."

"Hmmm," he said. "How did you all meet?"

"We all met in Basic Training."

"Did you guys get any awards for what you did?"

"All we got was page two in Stars and Stripes. I'm sure that's where you saw us. Some folks would just have soon seen us all court-martialed. Either way, it's one hell of a story."

"You'll have to tell it one day."

"Only over a couple of beers!" And it would take a lot of beers to get the whole story. And since I rarely drank anymore, it made his chances of getting the full story almost zero.

After a few more minutes of flying, Taos stretched under us. It looked like it had grown since the last time I'd been there. To the west, I could see the gorge cut by the Rio Grande. Off in one corner, sheltered by the Holy Mountain, the ancient pueblo baked in the sun.

"Ever been to Taos?"I asked.

"Always wanted to? Have you been there?"

"I spent a lot of time there. There used to be a place called Michael's Kitchen. I'm not sure if it's still there or not. Served the best-stuffed sopapillas I've ever eaten."

"Good, huh."

"Past good. If you ever do get down there, try eating there. Also, try to visit the Old Mission at Rancho de Taos."

"Why's that?"

"History mostly. It's an old Spanish church. It's this big adobe structure with two bell towers. You walk in, and the ceiling is high over your head. I went to mass with my cousins there when I was a kid. Vatican Two had already happened, and every Catholic Church I'd ever been in had moved the altar so that the priest faced the congregation. You go to Mass there, and it was like walking through a time warp. They do it the old way. Service I went to was in Spanish, and I'm pretty sure the vestments were there when they opened the place back in the early 1800s."

"Old school."

"Very," I said. "There's a painting of Jesus in there. Under certain lighting conditions, a cross appears over his shoulder."

"That's cool."

We talked about history, and I thoroughly enjoyed the flight. Before too long, we were landing at the airport in Raton. A minute later, we were rolling up to our parking spot. A car was parked on the tarmac, and a young woman was leaning against it. She had a handheld radio in her hand and sunglasses on. That marked her as a cop. I shouldn't have been too terribly surprised someone was waiting. After all, they knew we were coming, and it was a professional courtesy to pick us up. But it was still nice that we had a ride.

Once Andy parked and shut the plane down, we got out. He put some wheel chocks under the tires and made sure it was closed up tightly before we walked over to the woman

"Detectives DeShong and Diaz, I presume," she said, putting out her hand. "Lt. Lana Pacheco, at your service."

"Are you taking us to the jail?" I asked.

She nodded, but said, "I thought you might want to look and see what we caught him with first."

A few minutes later, we were sitting in the detective office of the Raton City Police Department. Lana shared the office with a couple of other detectives. None of them were around right then.

"Ok," she said, pulling out a file. She opened it and went straight to the evidence custody document.

"My officers spotted his vehicle at the Motel 6. They got his room number and called me. I was the one who knocked on the door."

I nodded. A man knocking on the door might have raised alarm bells, but not a pretty Latina lady.

"Then what happened?" Andy asked.

"I had the officers standing about a door down. They came up as I Identified myself, and I asked if I could come in. Our perp chuckled, and said, 'I was wondering how long it was going to be before the cops caught up to me.' He stepped aside and said, 'you might as well come in.'

"We went in, and he had a Royal portable typewriter on the table in the room." She pointed to it on the inventory sheet, "and it had this money order," she pointed to it, "in the carriage. He'd already begun altering it. We got a picture of it in here." She indicated a couple of other money orders. "These two had been altered already, and this one in the process. I got his driver's license and then discovered he had a briefcase full of fake IDs. He assured us that this was his actual driver's license. We've verified that's true." She turned the page, and there was a photocopy of an Iowa State Driver's License. "Your suspect's name is Danny Kreps from Ottumwa, Iowa."

"Radar's hometown?" Andy asked.

She nodded, knowing the reference. "Kind of looks like him, too. Only older and going bald. Nice guy."

These kinds usually were, I thought. It was part of the game they played. Being a nice guy just caused folks to trust you a little more.

"Think we'll have any problems with a confession?"I asked.

"I doubt it. We questioned him a bit, and he answered all our questions without a problem. When we impounded and inventoried his pickup, we found several receipts that should be of interest to you, Will. He purchased twenty, fifty-pound sacks of potatoes from a La Jara Potato Coop in your county. The receipts are the same day he passed that money order, so you can place him in the area.

"He says he took the potatoes to Denver and sold them at the Flea Market off of I-76. I asked him how he'd purchased them, and he said with cash obtained from cashing the one money order at the Texaco and another at a Jack's Market. It would seem you've got another bad one floating around out there that you don't know about."

Andy leaned back and shook his head. "Gee, I guess we did get him. What am I going to do for a hobby now?"

"As I said, try stamp collecting," I answered with a chuckle. And then I said, "Lana, I don't know how to thank you guys."

"Well, after we talk to him, we can all go to lunch. I haven't eaten yet. And neither have the officers who helped with the takedown."

A small price to pay, I thought.

She made us both copies of the reports they had, and then let the county jail know we were on our way.

The Vigil-Maldanado Detention Center had been open for just a few years, Lt. Pacheco explained. It was named for both a long time sheriff and a longtime county commissioner. It was located on the edge of town on Hereford Ave, just down the street from the State Police Headquarters building.

Like most jails, there was a notable lack of windows, lots of wire, and block-like construction. It was also isolated. There was only a scattering of official-looking buildings and the prairie around it. We parked, went in, and after checking our weapons, we were escorted to a small room with a table and four chairs. A camera tucked up in one corner kept an eye on things.

A few minutes later, the door opened, and a guard brought in a small man dressed in an orange jumpsuit. Lana wasn't kidding. The guy looked like Radar, only a lot older with a receding hairline. He was also a bit taller and heavier. He smiled when he saw Lana.

"Ma'am," he said and extended his hand to her. She took it and then introduced us. "Danny Kreps," he said, extending his hand. Lana was right. He was a very nice guy.

I took the offered hand, as did Andy.

"Please sit down," Andy said. Kreps sat down, looked at us, and then cocked his head. "You're the two who tracked me down. I was wondering if anyone ever would."

"I've been chasing you for five years," Andy said. "Will here has only been on your trail for a few months."

"How did you figure me out?"

"You screwed up, Danny," I answered. "You flirted with a girl with an excellent memory."

He chuckled and then closed his eyes. "Ah, yes. That girl at the Texaco station?" He laughed again. "Yeah, she's a hot one. I couldn't help myself. But I reckon I'm not the first guy who's dropped the ball because of a pretty girl. Yep, just put me right up there with Samson and David."

"You know your Bible!"

"I do. I spend a lot of time in motel rooms. Those Gideon's sure get around."

I smiled. It was a Gideon that gave me the Bible I took to Iraq.

"Danny," I said. "Do you want to talk to us?"

"Actually," he said. "I want to play 'Let's Make a Deal.' "

"What's your deal?" Lana asked.

"You had a John Doe warrant chasing me around. Iowa has one also. I plead guilty to yours, confess as much as I can remember on other crimes, and I plead out to the one in Iowa. I do my time in Iowa. I know they'll want to come and get me. I have a good following up there. They'll do it to close the books on the case."

"Why Iowa," Andy asked.

"I've got family there," he replied, then paused. "Heck, I might get a chance to see them now."

I glanced at the other detectives. "We'll have to talk with our respective DAs," Andy said. "But I don't see any reason why they wouldn't go for it just to put this thing to bed."

"Fine, I'll take your word you'll do that then," he said. "OK, show me what you got. I'll try to tell you everything I've done and as much as I can remember."

"Fine," I said. "But first . . ." I pulled out a Miranda warning with his name typed on it.

Lana started a small tape recorder and spoke the date, time, and location and then said, "This statement is from Danny Kreps of Ottumwa, Iowa concerning a five-year career of purchasing and then altering money orders. I'm Lt. Lana Pacheco of the Raton Police Department. Present with me is Detective Andy DeShong of the Routt County Sheriff's office in Steamboat Springs, Colorado, and Detective Will Diaz of the Conejos County Sheriff's office. Gentlemen."

"Danny," I said. "I need to read your Miranda warning to you first."

"Go ahead."

"Thank you," I said, and began reading to him from the sheet. "On this date, Detective William Diaz of the

Conejos County Sheriff's Office, Conejos, Colorado, read me this Miranda Warning before questioning me. I understand that I have the right to remain silent and not answer any questions. I also understand that anything I say can and will be used against me in a court of law. I also understand that I have the right to speak with an attorney before questioning and to have one present with me during questioning. I further understand that if I can't afford an attorney, one will be appointed to me. I also understand that should I answer questions now, I can stop at any time and request an attorney.

"Danny, do you understand your rights?" I asked.

"I do."

"Do you want an attorney at this time?"

"No, I don't."

"And are you willing to talk with us at this time?"

"I am," he said. "Give me a pen. I'll sign the waiver." I gave him my pen, and he signed and dated the waiver.

"Andy," I said. "You want to start?"

"The first question, Danny," Andy said. "Why?"

"You mean what possesses a guy to write a couple of million dollars in bad money orders?" Danny looked towards Lana. "Can we get some water, please? This is going to be a long story."

Lana called the deputy, who soon returned with several bottles of water. She then re-started her tape recorder. "We took about a five-minute break to get some water brought in," she said. "Danny, are you still willing to speak with us?"

"I am," he answered. "Detective DeShong, could you re-ask your question?"

I thought it was kind of interesting how he put himself in the driver's seat. I got the impression he was enjoying this. It didn't matter. He was telling us what we wanted to know.

"Danny, why?"

Danny leaned closer to the tape machine. "That's a really easy answer? Back in eighty-five, I lost my job. The company I was working for went bankrupt. It turns out the CEO was skimming off the top and drove it broke. He was also skimming off our retirement fund. What we'd paid into it was gone when the news broke. He had booked a first-class ticket to anywhere except here long before anyone came looking for him and his little wife. Oh, so that you know, he's still out there. Last I heard he was living in some small island nation the U. S. doesn't have an extradition agreement with. Probably got a beautiful house, a yacht, and one heck of a tan. With luck, he'll die of skin cancer, or a shark will eat him.

"But I'm in the unemployment line. I've no job and no retirement. And I'm staring down the gun at sixty. I was counting on that retirement, you know.

"Now I went looking for other jobs, and I did find them. But none of them paid the bills and the ones that might have didn't seem to be interested in hiring an old man. So one day, I bought a couple of money orders from the 7-11 to pay some bills. It occurred to me I could alter these things real easy like."

"What made you realize that?" I asked.

"The typeface. We're talking plain old fashioned Pica type. It's all done on a dot matrix printer, but a typewriter is kinda close. I wasn't too concerned with the stuff at the bottom of the money order. I realized most people wouldn't even look at that. All I needed was a pencil eraser, a typewriter, and the rest was easy.

"Erasers I had, and the typewriter had been sitting in the closet for years. I just dusted it off and oiled it up. I was in business.

Danny hadn't said anything new. People had been doing this for ages. Indeed, the FBI had chased some guy who had created Pan-Am checks that were so realistic that Pan-Am honored them. It was all about a story and looking credible. This guy was smart enough and likable enough that looking credible wasn't a problem.

"So, what did you do," Lana asked. He was giving them a basic course in counterfeiting and me a refresher course.

Well, I purchased a couple more money orders. I got out the typewriter and went to work. I'd bought three money orders worth three dollars each. I made them worth three hundred each. Then I cashed them at mom, and pop's under an assumed name, of course."

"And . . ."

He paused; sadness came over his eyes. "My wife passed about two years later. She never knew what I was doing. I kept the roof over her head, the lights on, and the food and medical bills taken care of.

"I needed money for the funeral, and so I altered and cashed more. I gave my wife a first-rate funeral for a twenty-dollar investment." He sipped some water and then looked at the wall. "I'm not lying, it was a bit of thrill. I mean, it's the ultimate snow job. All I had had to do is be careful not to go to the same place twice. The ones I liked to pass them to were those check cashing places. I mean, it was a little revenge. The average guy goes in there and cashes the check he worked all week to get. They give him the money back but keep a huge chunk of it. That isn't right.

"I was avenging the little guy by playing their game, and screwing them with a piece of paper that was worthless."

I wondered if he realized that bypassing these bogus money orders, he wasn't helping anyone. All they did was increase their rates to cover their losses and then some.

The next several hours were an odyssey across several states as he told us about places he'd been and what he'd done. As expected, what we knew was the tip of the iceberg. There were thousands of money orders he'd cashed still out there. We kept a rough running tab, and Lana had been busy adding numbers. Taking into account what he told us, he'd written well over three and a half million dollars' worth of forged money orders.

"What happened to all the money," I asked.

"Well, some of it went into living. Cars need gas and tires, and I need food and lodging. I went all over America, living off the land and enjoying the retirement that was stolen from me. I did a lot of cool things," he said a smile on his face. "I rode the Mississippi on a paddlewheel steamer. I even took cruises to Jamaica and Alaska. And would you believe I flew the Concord once just to say I'd done it. I went to France and back. I even stayed there for a while. But most of it, I just gave away."

"Huh," Andy said.

"Panhandlers on the corner," he said. "Or maybe I'd toss a couple of thousand into some small churches collection basket. Maybe I'd find out about someone who had a bill they couldn't pay. Well, it got paid. Or some deserving soul would find a couple of hundred bucks just lying in their path.

"I tried to do as much good with it as I could."

I shook my head. "Mr. Kreps, I don't know if I should just arrest you, give you a civic award, or both."

"Just call me Robin Hood," he said with a grin.

Andy looked up from his writing pad, and said, "So you gave millions of dollars away? Can you prove any of that?"

He shook his head and said with a smile, "Sorry. Robin Hood never got receipts. Neither did I."

I knew he'd be convicted on and serve concurrent sentences on all counts. I was sure he had a fair chunk of money squirreled away someplace. It wouldn't be in a bank. More likely, a 50-gallon drum someplace.

He leaned back, smiled, and said, "In the meantime, I've three hots and a cot in the Iowa State penal system and free medical for a year or two."

I smiled at him and said, "I know, you got to love it when a plan comes together."

We shook his hand and left. Lana gave Andy the tape. "Gentlemen," she said with a sigh. "Who says crime doesn't pay."

Andy took the tape. "I agree. I'm sure he's got money to burn out there. That will make our retirement look puny."

"If we ever retire," Lana added.

"And his retirement is all tax-free," I pointed out.

We took Lana and the officers who helped with the takedown to lunch and then flew back to Alamosa.

Andy dropped me off, saying he'd get the tape transcribed.

Jewell picked me up, and I was home in time for supper.

I stamped "Case closed" on the 7-11 bandit the next day.

CHAPTER EIGHT

FALL

I was feeling pretty good about myself when I got into the office the next morning.

That lasted just long enough for me to pour my first cup of coffee and to read the briefing sheets from the day before. I almost threw up when I did.

Max had been arrested.

I looked up the patrol report and read through it. The charges were "Drunk and disorderly, 3rd Degree Assault, Domestic Violence, Resisting arrest.," What it all meant was that he'd grabbed, pushed, or struck Eva. There was a yelling match, he was intoxicated, and had put up a fight with the deputy when arrested. They were all misdemeanors, but still! Half of them would be thrown out, but the Domestic Violence charge was a big red flag. Judge Gordon was a stickler for that one, and rightfully so. Unless my deputies had seriously screwed up, that charge would stick.

Jonesy's warning seemed more a prophetic statement now than a heads-up.

And that put me right into an emotional and professional issue. I'd arrested friends before, even close relatives. When you work in a county where everyone knows or is related to everyone else, that is bound to happen. But none of them had ever watched my back like Max had. There was a tie there that, unless you've been in combat and relied on someone to help keep you alive, it is hard to explain to the average person, and that cannot be ignored.

I sighed. Today had just gone to hell in a handbasket.

And I hadn't even finished my first cup of coffee yet, I reflected.

There was a knock, and I looked up. The Sheriff stood at the door, the forever cup of coffee in his hand.

"Morning, Sheriff," I said, trying not to sound like I'd just blown out of Gunsmoke.

"How was your trip?"

"I closed that case out. It seems Iowa has a John Doe warrant chasing him around, too."

"Really? That's good news," he answered.

"Even better news. Iowa will be happy to extradite. We made a deal. He cops to all the charges here and serves time in Iowa. He'll be out in three years. Andy talked to a prosecutor in Iowa, and they're aboard."

"Do we know what he did with the money?"

"He said he spent some, gave some of it away. Of course, he can't prove that, and neither can we. My guess, he's got a bunch of it buried in a can someplace that he's not talking about."

"So when he gets out of prison . . ."

"He digs it up and retires," I finished. "I'd bet he's got at least a million two out there. You can retire on that, and unless he's dumb, he can live life well and not attract any attention. It fits in with his motivation."

"Good work. What else?" I knew he'd seen the jail report. He knew Max was my friend and had anticipated the problem it would cause me.

"Well, you know a friend of mine is out back," I said. I looked away from the Sheriff, and I realized that without meaning too, I'd clued him into knowing that his instincts were right.

"How do you feel about it?"

I leaned back in my chair, wondering when this old Marine had picked up a degree in Psychology. Of course, I thought, the School of Life University was still the best school around. By now, he'd probably earned triple Ph.D.'s from it.

"Well, part of me says he doesn't get any special treatment. The other part of me says we've spilled blood together, and that counts for something. That makes me want to help him."

He nodded, and I went on. "You were a rifleman in Korea. You were at Pusan. Those guys you were with . . ."

"I know," he said. "I killed for them, and they for me. If any of them were ever in trouble, I'd want to try to help them." He paused and then went on, "He wants to see you, you know."

I nodded. "I expected as much."

"And Will, you don't have to justify it to me," he said. "I understand perfectly."

"Thanks, Sheriff. I'll wait a bit. I need to think about what I'm going to say."

He understood that. On the one level, I couldn't let Max get away with beating his wife. That just wasn't something a man does. And you certainly don't go getting drunk and being a pain to the local cops. The NCO in me said that I needed to fix the problem. In the Army, we tried to salvage the soldier. If we couldn't repair him, we had to get rid of him.

Unfortunately, you can't discharge a civilian.

"We got a request for some assistance from APD," the Sheriff went on. "They'd like you to take a second look at a case they're working?"

"Oh?" We didn't get sheets from APD, and this must have been a pretty new case.

"B and E at the Railroad Jewelry Depot," he explained.

One good thing about all the training I'd been giving everyone was that it helped build interagency cooperation. The different departments were starting to play together to ask each other for help. The more they realized we were all in the same team, the better, I thought.

The Sheriff went on. "They say it doesn't feel right. It's meant to look like someone broke in and stole several thousand in jewelry. But the space they're supposed to have gone through is small, and then there's the problem of making a fifteen-foot drop down, and then back up. They're thinking an inside job, and they tried to make it look like a burglary."

"Let me guess," I said. "The owner has had a bad year and needs the insurance money to make ends meet."

We all knew the owner. David Wheaton was an outsider. He'd moved in from out of town, and among other things, opened a jewelry store specializing in 100% authentic Native American jewelry.

The problem was that anyone except Native Americans made the stuff he sold.

A guy in Taos had once seen the stuff and proclaimed loudly that "no self-respecting Native American would turn out such pathetic pieces of crap." David had tried to sue him. All that saved David's case was that one of his suppliers had just enough Navajo in her to qualify as a Native American. The judge threw the case out, and he could still make his claim. But people who knew better gave him zero business.

The guy also tended to have the most unbelievable luck when it came to high end losses. He'd lost a home full of priceless antiques to fire. The insurance check, or so I'd heard, was in the millions.

Lately, he'd suffered interesting injuries in various businesses around the Valley. Almost every attorney that specialized in those kinds of cases knew him. He'd made some good money that way, and had purchased several businesses and buildings throughout the area. The attorney's that had represented him in these cases had come to realize he was nothing more than a crook and wouldn't represent him anymore.

He had recently passed the bar. In addition to his interests, he represented some of the lower life forms in the valley.

The locals had crowned him the "Most despised man in the county." I was sure that some beautiful morning he'd wake up murdered, and the list of suspects would be as thick as a phone book.

"Tell them to bring it over. I'd love to look at it." I looked at my calendar. "I'm free this afternoon."

"What else?" he asked.

"I also want to start getting people trained up on entry tactics."

The Sheriff nodded, and I could see him getting ready to play Devil's advocate. "Everyone's going to say that's too big city for us."

"Maybe. But if no one's noticed, our population is going up. A lot of folks from the city are coming back, and they're bringing the problems with them. The way we used to do business is going to start endangering us.

"And of course, I'm going to preach even more Inter-agency cooperation. We're all small departments, and we need each other for backup and extra resources. We can't afford to think of individual fiefdoms anymore."

The Sheriff smiled. "The cops either already know that or are figuring it out. Your problem is going to be your city councils and the commissioners. You're going to have to get them to start thinking outside their little boxes."

"Oh, I already know the button to push on that one. What I want to do is an exercise. Say a school exercise where we have to go in. Like a student with a gun." I didn't know that was a scenario waiting to happen. Columbine and other such events were just a few years in the future.

I could see him thinking about it. "There's never been anything like that in Colorado."

"Not yet, but one day someone is going to bring a gun to school, and it's going to be all over the evening news. And we need the schools to start thinking about that as well."

"Mass casualties?"

I nodded. "It would give EMS some training."

"SWAT?" he asked.

"It's something we don't have. Don't know if we ever will, but we need to able to work together as one if needed."

The Sheriff was thinking about it, and he then said. "I don't envy your job, Will. That's one reason I brought you back aboard. So you could drag us kicking and screaming into the 21st century."

"I know," I answered.

"Now, if I were to put together a Christmas wish list for you to make this happen, what would you need?" he asked.

I'd been thinking a lot about it and had much of it already written down.

"I would love standardized weapons in every department. But that's not going to happen. At least not easily." In our department, we had several officers that carried 38s, others carried .357s or 9mms, and I carried a 45. Without the departments mandating a weapon to carry, and possibly even providing them, that just wasn't in the cards. "I would also like to see some AR-15s, but I don't see that happening. People will say it's to GI Joe for a small county. But we need some good rifles with scopes. Maybe even send some folks off to school to learn to snipe. I know, I know. Costs money! Money we don't have.

"What we do have is shotguns. That's in every department. Shotguns are the ultimate tactical weapon, and we need to know how to use them in tactical situations.

"We also need more shoot-no shoot training, and do it under realistic conditions."

"Like the Dodge City School you and a couple of others put together?" the sheriff asked.

"We put that together for almost nothing," I said, "and our people got some good training out of it. All we were out was gas and lunch."

"We can swing that," he said. "Go on."

"We need blueprints of all the schools and public buildings." And then I paused and thought about it. "We're getting a bunch of cast off from the military, aren't we."

The Sheriff nodded. "I've been racking my brain trying to figure out what we need. You have some ideas." He took out his notebook.

"I'd like a dozen Kevlar helmets if we can get them. If not, piss pots and liners will work. Flak jackets, LBEs, and gas masks would be nice. NVGs would be helpful. But I don't see Uncle Sam giving too many of those up.

"And while we're at it, see if you can pick us up an ambulance."

"Ambulance?"

"Yeah, like they used on MASH, only newer. We can turn it into a command/crime scene processing and team transport van. It will also be useful to help support Search and Rescue missions."

"People are going to comment."

"It's emergency equipment. And unless we need it, we don't use it. It stays in the trunks or the yard. "

The Sheriff wrote it down and said, "I'll see what I can do."

And in the meantime, I thought I'd better come up with a training plan. Let's start, I thought, by looking at what can be done for free or at a low cost. I could quickly imagine several places in the county where I could reopen Dodge City.

But, until then, there were morning reports that I had to finish. I went to my "IN" basket and started looking at what patrol had done while I was gone. A lot of it was open and closed. There'd been a fight at the pool hall in Romeo. Both suspects were taken into custody, charged with disturbing the peace, and bonded out. I read over the report and witness statements. Nothing significant there, I thought. Both offenders were frequent fliers. I'd probably see them in jail for a couple of weeks soon. There was a stolen vehicle out of Santa Fe, New Mexico, that had been recovered. Santa Fe PD had been notified that the car had impounded. Patrol, in their search, had found a receipt for gas purchased on a credit card. I wrote down where the gas was bought and made a note to check and see if maybe they had a security camera and to follow up on the credit card. The car was at one of the local tow yards, so I decided a follow-up with a search of the vehicle, and look for fingerprints. There were a couple of bad checks turned over to us for prosecution. I made a note to assign them to Joe in dispatch. While dispatch was his job, he wanted to move up, and getting experience in handling cases that were pretty much already solved was an excellent way to do that.

When I went back in for a coffee refill, I pretty much had a handle on what my day was going to be like. But I still didn't have a clue what to do with Max, and so when I went back to my desk, I called Jewell.

"This is your ten o'clock. I love you call," I said.

"How's your day going, Baby?"

I gave her a quick rundown on things and then said, "I need you to pray with me about something. Have you talked with Eva today?"

There was a pause, and I knew what she was thinking. "Max in jail?"

"Yep," I answered. "He wants to see me."

"What are you going to tell him?"

I shrugged as if she could see me over the phone. "I don't know yet. That's why I need to pray with you. I talked to the Sheriff about it. First offense and drinking were involved. I think I'm going to talk to the DA and the public defender and see if I can push to get his butt to the VA and probation."

"Think he'll go for it?"

I didn't know but said instead, "If he's smart, he will. Otherwise, the DA will push for jail time."

I could almost hear her thinking out loud over the phone, and then she asked, "How bad was Eva?"

"It wasn't as bad as the Germany incident Jonesy told me about. Eva got slapped around some. They took her to ER, got some pictures, and such. "

"I'll call her. See if I can visit and have a talk. And you?"

"I'm going to talk to Max. I think it's past time we gave them an invite to church."

"I'll extend it," she said. "I think we need to get that prayer going."

I agreed, and she took the lead. "Father, we come before you to ask for your guidance and wisdom. You know Max ended up in jail last night and that he and Eva have been having issues. Will is going to talk to Max, and I'm going to talk to Eva. Give us the words that we need and soften their hearts to receive them.

From human viewpoints, fixing this problem is a waste of time, but not from yours. It's all about them receiving what's said and to put it into practice. Whisper it in their ears that what they're doing is not the way to live, and only you can give them the peace they want. We pray that in your Holy Name. Amen"

"Amen," I said. I told her that I loved her and hung up. I then punched the intercom number for the jailor. "Can you bring Max Laurie to my office, please."

"I'll have him there in a minute," was the reply. I poured myself another cup of coffee and a paper cup for Max. A minute later, the Jailor escorted Max into my office. Since he wasn't a flight risk or dangerous, he wasn't shackled, but he was wearing jail orange.

"Thanks, John," I said. "Please close the door."

He nodded and closed it.

"Have a seat, Max," I said. I was feeling way too much like an NCO ready to chew out a soldier who had messed up.

He sat down, looked at me, and said, "We've gone suddenly somewhat formal here, haven't we Will. Are you going to preach to me again?"

I sat down, looked at him, and said, "If I'm going formal, then it's because you've put me in an awkward position. I don't know if I should be talking to you as a law enforcement officer or as your friend.

"And yes, I'll be preaching at you because you're wrong and you know it. And if that doesn't work, I might bash that thick skull of yours in for putting me in this corner."

He sighed and looked up into the corner of the room. "I could sure use a friend right now." He bowed his head and then looked at me, "Just like you needed a friend back in Saudi."

There it was. That's the trouble with friends. Someplace, somewhere, there's history. Among soldiers, that history is often rather intense. And some folks hold on to that history, turn it into debt, and try to collect on it.

"Max," I said. "I won't let you lay a guilt trip on me. The difference between you and me is I saw where I was headed and did something about it.

"And yes, it's true. I owe you more than you'll ever know. And because of that, we're here drinking some rather pathetic coffee." I took a sip of that rather pathetic coffee and marshaled my thought. "God damn it, Max. What the hell happened?"

He took a deep breath and launched into his explanation. "I ran into a couple of guys while they were doing some recon for their hunting. We stopped at the bar in Capulin and had a couple. And when I got home, Eva got all bent and got into my face about it."

"The report says you were intoxicated. The deputy said you were highly combative, swearing, and slurring your words. It sounds like a lot more than a couple of drinks to me."

I saw him backpedal and then say, "Honest, Will, I wasn't drunk."

"Then why the drunk and disorderly charge? Why the resisting arrest? And for God's sake, why the assault charge? I know my deputies. They don't lie. They're too damn lazy to lie!"

"You're not my father, damn it," he said, an edge in his voice. I realized his hands were balled up into fists. "You're not even my sarge anymore. I don't have to explain a thing to you. I'm a grown man. I know what I'm doing!"

I glared at him. "But I'm still your friend," I said quietly, getting control of the anger that threatened to boil up. "We've been through it together. I owe you a shot at redemption."

Slowly his face softened. He bowed his head. I'd played chess and cards enough with him to know what it meant. He was giving up.

"I don't know. We were sitting at the bar. OK, I had a lot more than a couple. Whiskey," he said as if that explained it all. "I left about ten, got home about fifteen minutes later. Eva was up, and she asked me why I was out. I tried to explain to her that it was business, and then she wanted to know what her name was."

"Excuse me?"

He paused and looked at the books on the shelves. "Eva thinks I was out there messing around on her again. She kept asking, and I kept telling her there wasn't anyone. And then she asked why I hadn't come home, and Will . . . I just lost it. She pushed me too much. Nagged, really." He gulped, and then remembered he had coffee in front of him. He took a deep drink of it. It was hot, and I wondered how he managed to keep it in his mouth and not spit it all over me. He swallowed, put the cup down, and kept talking. "Man, if she'd just backed off, I wouldn't have blown a fuse. She pushed me too much."

I let that one hang there for a moment, and then said, " Max, do you know what my standard for a man is these days?"

He shook his head but said, "Oh, boy. Here it comes. Yeah, I know your standard. It's Jesus."

"He is my standard," I said. "Maybe back when we were in BDUs and keeping the world safe from democracy, things were different. Maybe then it was all about drinking and chasing girls. No, I was wrong." He looked at me, his eyes strangely neutral, but I went on. "My life was in a tailspin, and worse, I knew it. You knew it. Everyone knew it. But no one was willing to broach an option that might change my life. I didn't think anything would or could stop the fall."

"I remember," he said, nodding his head slowly. "You were worse than a mess, Will."

"And that incident in Saudi? All that did was prove to me that I couldn't save myself. If you hadn't been there, I don't know what I'd have done."

"You would have killed Michaels," he said and smiled. "I wonder if he knows how close he came to taking one in the back?"

"I hope not," I answered, remembering that single most terrifying moment in my life. I pushed the memory aside. "Max, what I'm trying to tell you is that I'd painted myself into a corner by thinking I could run my own life. God was something I kept on the shelf and drug out on Sunday morning. I needed him to run my life for me, but I wasn't willing to let him. And no one was telling me that there was a better way. Maybe it's because they thought that real men don't need God, or that everyone would think they were Holy Rollers or something."

"That's what I don't get," he said. "You talk about letting God run your life. Well, what if he takes you someplace you don't want to go. Like the Amazon, or back to Iraq."

I laughed. "Are you happy being where you're at right now?" I asked. "God didn't do this to you. You did it. And you drug me into your mess."

"It's not your mess, Will."

"Just like putting your hand on top of mine when it was pulling a Colt from a holster wasn't dragging you into my mess?" I looked at him. I wasn't sure I was connecting. "Max, I'll be forever grateful for your intervention. You gave me my life back. All I'm trying to do is return the favor. It breaks my heart to see you in that orange monkey suit."

He nodded as if understanding. But his eyes were far from agreeing with me. "I must be an embarrassment to you as well as a huge disappointment."

I shook my head. "My friend," I said. "I've never been embarrassed or disappointed with you. Scared out of my mind? Now that's something completely different."

"Scared for me?"

"Every second of every day. I do that for people I call family."

"Is that why you preach at me? You're 'afraid for my mortal soul.' " He made quotation marks in the air with his fingers when he talked about his soul.

"What kind of Christian or friend would I be if I wasn't? I want to tell you there's a way to become the man Eva needs. A better way."

"But what about the woman I need her to be?" he asked.

"Let me tell you about a woman," I said. "Would it surprise you if I told you Jewell was praying for me well before we met?"

"She seems like the type that would. But praying for you? How?"

"She was working at a nursing home as an administrator. When we deployed to the Gulf, they gave out the names of the soldiers from the area that were going. Someone wrote the names on yellow ribbons and handed them out to the staff. You were supposed to pray for the safety of the soldier whose name you got. She got mine. "

"Really?" he asked.

"Really," I answered. "I think it was her prayers that kept me safe. It was her prayers that put you there to put your hand on top of mine. And it was her prayers that have made me who I am and what I'm becoming.

"That's the kind of woman you want. You've got one. But you need to be a man to her."

He looked at me like I was an alien from another world, and I was talking Klingon to him.

"My friend. Remember that riot we had up on the Hill? They were throwing rocks. I took one meant for you."

"And you spent several days in the hospital. I remember."

"And now here you are," he said, shaking his head. "It's like you've become some weird-ass fanatic."

"I prefer the term Jesus Freak," I answered with a smile. "It works very well for me."

"Well, good for you," he said, a mocking lilt in his voice.

I shook my head. "Max," I said. "Were you ever thankful for learning to use an M-16?"

The change in tactics stopped him. "I'm not following."

"I mean, if we got into a firefight, wouldn't you be thankful that you knew how to use it."

"Of course," he answered. "But what does that . . ."

"Everything," I said. "Now suppose you showed up for a gunfight with a knife. Or worse, completely naked!"

"Now, wouldn't that be a sight," he laughed.

"I'll top it. How about naked on a battlefield, only you don't know you're on a battlefield."

He didn't say anything, but I could see it on his face. Your lifespan would be very short, he was thinking.

"The Apostle Paul says we're on a battlefield every second of our lives, and unless we have God with us, we're not going to last long because we're up against an enemy that intends to destroy us. And sadly, he'd just as soon make sure we didn't even know there was a war going on."

He shook his head. "Will, you're talking religion. I've seen religious types. Talk about how good God is and how he can change your life. All you're doing is rubbing my nose in your," and made the quotation marks again, "righteousness."

"Max, I'm just telling you what I wish someone would have told me there's a better way and that it works."

"Again, good for you. I don't expect it to work for me."

"Here's a new one for my SMARTbook, I said. "Thou shall not have Daffy Duck in charge of my life. My standards were screwed up. I needed to replace those old standards with something new, and God did that for me. I'm learning that he's taken all the bad stuff that happened, and used them for good in my life." I pointed to a small plaque I had hanging on the wall above my desk. "Those words taught me that if I got out of the way, God could and would do awesome things for me."

He looked at the plaque. "I can't read it from here. What does it say?"

I looked up at it. I didn't have to read it. "It's from Jeremiah, chapter 29, verse 11. 'For I know the plans I have for you, declares the LORD, plans for welfare and not for evil, to give you a future and a hope.' "

"What does that mean?" he asked.

"It means get out of the way. Trust me; I know what I want for you." I had a thought. "Max, you've flown on airplanes, right?"

"You know I have."

"Do you remember flying to Germany from the States?"

"It was my first time on a 747."

"I remember flying to Germany also. I left St. Louis and landed in Frankfurt. Do you think I could have just walked into the cockpit demanded that the pilot let me fly and that I could get us safely from point A to point B?"

He shook his head. "No."

"Why not?"

"For openers, you're not a pilot. I've seen you crash paper planes, and a 747 is a pretty complex piece of hardware."

"Exactly. Add to that I'm going across an expanse where there aren't a lot of landmarks, and we'd have lived just long enough for us to die. That's how it was with me at the wheel of my life. I was lost because I didn't know the way. On a good day, I was going in circles, but mostly I was doing an excellent job of crashing my life

"I had to stand up, shut up, and let the pilot sit down."

"And what does that have to do with me?"

"Everything," I said. "You need to let the Pilot sit down in your life and do what he tells you to do. And the Bible tells us what he expects. It's about self-control about putting God first."

He shook his head. "I could never do that. My family is first."

"And how's that working for you?"

It was like I'd poked him with a stick. "What do you mean?"

"I mean, your family is your wife. You've slapped her around. You're sitting in my jail. How's that working for you?"

He shook his head and snorted, "I never thought I'd hear you in the Amen corner. God isn't the answer to my life, and I'll thank you never to bring Him up again."

He took a sip of coffee, and then asked, "Can you help me?"

I nodded slowly, but said, "Question becomes, do you want to help yourself?"

"I'm listening."

"OK. The good news is none of what you did is a felony. You're a first time offender, and since people still like soldiers, we've got some leverage. Here's what we're going to do. I'm going to get you a slot at a VA addiction center. I want you in counseling and away from booze. Keep out of the bars. And while you're in counseling, we're going to push for some anger management. I'll talk with the DA and the Public Defender, and we'll work out a plea arrangement. You go in for counseling, and we'll talk time served and probation."

He opened his mouth as if to say something, thought better of it, and then said, "If the DA and the Public Defender can hammer out the details, I'll go in for counseling like you suggested. But I've got bills to pay."

"Let me work on that. Did you ever talk with those ranchers I gave you names of?"

"No," he said. "I need to stay focused on my business."

"Again, Max. How's that working for you? I've no doubt it will work eventually. I'm just concerned you'll have starved in the meantime."

He shook his head. "No, I need to keep working on it. Besides, I've one or two sources of money."

He's not ready to get out of the way, I thought. "I'll see what I can do. Jewell will be talking with Eva and see what she's planning. Maybe she's looking for a job." I buzzed the jailor to come and get him.

"She's a nurse. It should be easy for her to find a job," Max said.

"One other thing. You and Eva are going to be going to church with us. Getting in the 'Amen" corner wouldn't hurt you any. We have an outstanding Pastor who cuts through the garbage. I want you talking to him before and after you go to the VA. Call it a favor for my helping you."

"Swear you won't bring this God B.S. up again, and I will."

"Then I'll just have to pray that the Father proves it isn't B.S. as you put it," I said. "And Max, I'll keep praying that you come around."

"Can't tell you what to do."

There was a knock on the door, and the jailor came in. Max stood so he could go back to his cell. He smiled thinly at me, and then said, "Will. Will. You think everyone is rational and will listen." He shook his head. "You're too good of a person."

" Max, maybe you better thank God for that."

CHAPTER NINE

THE MOST HATED MAN IN THE COUNTY

Sgt. Rob Gonzales of the Antonito Police Department arrived a little before two that afternoon. He had a folder full of reports, photographs, and documents.

He also brought along a couple of doughnuts from one of the diners in town. That made him my hero.

I met him at the door to my office. It was good to see him. I'd known Rob for years.

"Got one I want to consult with you on, Will," he said after I'd ushered him into my office and poured us some coffee. He handed me the case file, and I began leafing through it. There were several photographs taken with a Polaroid camera. Some of the pictures had a ruler or a tape measure in it. I looked at the photos taken inside the store, and the bar next door that shared a wall with the store. There was a ceiling panel askew in the picture from the bar. Right under the tile was a single pedestal table with a big black boot print on it.

"Looks like a hiking boot of some sort," I said.

"That's what I was thinking."

I pushed away from the desk, looked up, and then at him. "Let me see if I get this right. Sometime between about 12 AM and 7 AM last Sunday, person or person(s) unknown entered the building through a roof vent located on the northern side of the building. They then got into the bar section, where they obtained several books of matches and a couple of table candles which they used for illumination up in the attic. They removed two pieces of aspen tongue and groove by an unknown means, forming a hole about ten inches across, and 3 feet long. They then dropped to the floor and stole approximately one hundred and seventy thousand dollars' worth of turquoise jewelry. They then left, along with their loot through the hole in the ceiling, and exited out the roof vent. There is an alarm system on the door, and metal grating over the windows."

I looked at Rob. "Did I get that right?"

He nodded, and I went on, "And you find something wrong with this case."

"Several big somethings wrong."

"I do have a suspect for you."

He smiled, knowing I was about to put him on. "Who," he asked.

"Reed Richards from the Fantastic Four. He could easily do this. Too dang bad, he doesn't exist outside of the comic books."

Rob laughed then said, "You see the same things I do."

"There's a couple of problems I have with the way it's meant to look. First, how many people do you know could squeeze through a ten-inch hole? Then drop . . ." I looked at the picture taken inside the store. "What would you say that drop is, twelve feet?"

He turned to a page in the file and pointed. "From floor to the hole, it's fourteen feet, six inches."

"OK, drop fourteen and a half feet, rob the place, get the loot up through the hole, and then get back up the fourteen feet and a half feet to the hole. Also, they entered the bar, stole some matches and candles to light their way. And they left all the booze? Did they look in the register?"

Rob shook his head. "No, and there was about two hundred dollars in the till."

I couldn't imagine any crook passing up such an easy haul.

"And it looks like they dropped down from their entry point in the bar roof, and onto the table," I went on. "They got what they needed, table candles and matches, and then got back up, using the table as a step up."

"That about sums it up."

"Was the table knocked over?" Someone standing on that table, or landing on it would have knocked it over.

"No," he said.

"Why don't you think this happened the way we're meant to think it did?"

"It doesn't make sense. The table should have fallen over when they dropped from or tried to get up to the ceiling. And dropping the fourteen feet to the ceiling to floor and back? I won't even mention the hole."

"So what you're saying is there's a good chance that if it did happen the way it's supposed to look like it happened, then the perp hurt him or herself doing this?"

"Yeah. And in the bar. The chairs weren't pulled out. You'd pull out the chairs to step up on then onto the table."

"No blood on the floor or evidence of a fall?" I asked. "And did you check with the hospital regarding broken bones."

"No blood, and not yet on the hospital. I will check that out."

"Any threads, hair, or blood around the entry points into the bar or the shop?" I asked.

"No one's going through that hole without leaving something behind."

I continued leafing through the case in hopes that I might find something that would change my thinking. I didn't.

" This case stinks. That footprint looks like about a size twelve. Only one footprint, and on a pedestal table! Great sense of balance!" I scoffed. "Not to mention lighter than air. I'm not sure one of those tables would hold a man, and they wobble like crazy."

I looked at the picture of the ceiling construction. Logs, each about a foot thick formed the frame, with Tongue and Groove boards nailed to the top. I examined the picture of the boards that had been broken out. One of the pieces of wood that faced into the shop had an odd half-circle pattern about two inches across. The other had two near the end where it nailed into the log.

"Here's your biggest piece of evidence," I said. "No pry marks."

"The boards they broke out?" Rob asked. "I noticed that too."

"So, we're going to remove two pieces of t and g aspen. You can barely break one of those boards when it's by itself, lock them together, and it's going to take a lot of force. I'd need to get a pry bar of some sort in between the boards and then lift, right."

"Right," he said. "I can't figure out how they got those boards up otherwise."

Except for the two busted boards, the ceiling was pristine. "Those two marks," I said, thinking out loud. "Caused by something circular, maybe two inches across?"

"I thought they were hammer marks," Rob said.

"It does look like that, but look closer. All we're seeing is the external area of the strike. There's no center to them. Here's where I'm heading with this. We think that this was a hammer strike, maybe the result of a careless carpenter. But these are nailed from the top, not the bottom."

"Go on."

"Even assuming that some work got done under the boards, why should I see a hammer mark on the only two boards that got busted. I'd expect to see more."

"Coincidence?" he asked.

"Maybe, but that still leaves how the boards got busted. Now I only see one mark on one and two marks on the other. Two hits with a hammer aren't enough to knock up and break the board. And even if it could, then we're still dealing with it happening from the inside."

Rob knew I was close to figuring it out. "Then how did they pry the boards up and not leave a mark on the boards?"

I took a bite of the doughnut he'd brought for me. The doughnut was dry, and I preferred my doughnuts with chocolate and crushed nuts. But it would have been rude not to eat it. I swallowed and then said, "They didn't pry it. They pushed it."

"Excuse me?"

"Those marks, they'd be about the thickness of a two-inch metal water pipe. They put one end of a pipe up to the wood, and the other on a jack. I'd use a twenty-ton jack to do this. Very easy to use, they're common and portable. I'd begin pushing against the wood by jacking it up. You reach a certain point, it lifts the wood free of the nails and soon the wood breaks, just like we see in the pictures."

"And the second mark on the one?"

"The pipe slipped a little," I suggested. "You're right, Rob. There's just enough evidence to make you think someone came in through the roof. It didn't happen that way. This is an insurance scam."

"Why else do you think it?"

"Getting from the floor down and then back up," I said. "Takes an athletic individual to do that. A gymnast might be able to pull that off, assuming they had rocket assist on the takeoff. "

"Maybe they lowered a rope and helped him up," he suggested, playing devil's advocate.

"Maybe, but we're still dealing with a ten-inch hole."

"Zorro was a tunnel rat in 'Nam."

"How did Zorro come into this?"

Rob smiled. "David suggested him, saying he was in the store the day before."

"Can't be. Zorro's in jail in Alamosa. They scooped him up on a warrant." He's been there since Friday, and being in jail is a good alibi.

Zorro was one of the local bad boys. His real name was Diego Lopez. As a child, the TV Zorro was his hero. He'd ran around in a black cape then, had a toy sword, and the nickname stuck. He'd graduated from Antonito High School as the valedictorian. Then he was drafted and went to 'Nam. Too many explosions, and too much heroin later, he'd returned to a life of poverty and was an empty shell of a man. Because he was smart and unpredictable, people, of course, granted him superhuman status. Like the Devil, Zorro got blamed for a lot of things he had nothing to do with.

Zorro spent a fair chunk of time in jail. I was one of the few people he'd talk with. I always thought it was because I treated him as a man, a severely damaged man to be sure, but still a man. The job of a tunnel rat wasn't easy. It almost always went to the smallest, wiriest person in the platoon. Stripped to their skivvies, they'd crawl into the tunnel with nothing but a flashlight and a pistol. The tunnels were a haven for snakes, rats, and spiders. Occasionally, the VC would leave presents for the tunnel rat in the form of a grenade or punji sticks. Since the VC didn't dip their sticks in the same thing we did, even a scratch by one could be as devastating as the grenade going off.

Sometimes the tunnel rat ran into the VC, sometimes just cached supplies, more often nothing. It was enough for a human being to develop a case of PTSD a hundred miles wide. When we'd first met years before, I recognized the demon Zorro was fighting, and since he never asked for what had happened to him, I treated him with respect. From where I sat, he was following orders. Vietnam had killed Diego Lopez as efficiently as if the VC had put a bullet through his brain.

"He told me the thing he hated the most about the tunnels was the tight quarters. There were several occasions where I let him sleep on the couch because the cells were too small. A ten-inch hole might be utterly unbearable for him.

"And while we're on the subject, if they broke two boards, why not three, or four or five. It would make things faster for your entry man and easier on him. Might even allow him to get in," I said.

"Besides, once you get past the first board, the rest is easy," Rob finished saying. "I could have had that whole ceiling up in twenty minutes with a crowbar. It looks to me like they didn't want to do all that much damage because they'd have to pay to get it fixed."

"This is the work of more than one person, or so we're being led to believe. Look, they get in, and bring bags to carry the loot out. They have to bring a means to break the roof open. Then lower a person, not once, but twice down to the floor. . ."

"Why twice," Rob asked.

"They lowered him into the bar to steal candles," I said. "Oh, any scuff marks on the wall of the bar where he presumably went down and then up?"

Rob shook his head.

"If someone is helping pull you up, you help by digging in with your feet and propelling yourself along the wall. It's instinct. To deadlift someone at that point would be difficult at best. And if you jumped to help, you'd knock the table over."

"How about a child," he asked. He was exploring almost every thought a defense attorney might.

"Can't be too old, or you're still lifting a hundred-plus pounds," I objected. "That footprint is a size twelve. That wasn't a child."

"Maybe they didn't have a rope. Maybe they grabbed the person by the hands and helped him or her up that way."

"The bar entry, I'd buy that. It's against a wall. You can do that. The store? You're lifting straight up. I don't buy it."

"So assuming they have a rope to assist, get the bags out, and then get the person up . . ."

"Why the candles? I'm in an attic. I'd have expected to be doing this in the dark, and I forget to bring a flashlight?"

I could see that something was still troubling him.

"How do we prove this?" he asked.

"We don't," I answered. "When you write up your report, you state that the crime scene evidence doesn't support how the crime is meant to look. You say that entry appears to have been through a small hole, and give the dimensions, and all the particulars we talked about. Let the insurance company draw its conclusions. My bet is they won't pay off.

"Or we could get Wheaton in the interview room, read him his rights for fraud, and see what he has to say. That's your call since it's your jurisdiction."

"This is going to piss David Wheaton off," Rob said.

Now I understood why he came to me. Rob wanted an independent assessment to back him up. Rob knew he was going to step into a political shooting gallery.

"Terrific! You need to let your chief and police commissioner know what your report is going to say,' I said. "I'd still put a bolo out for anyone pawning a lot of Native American jewelry. I don't think you're going to get a lot of hits. After all, it's not like there's any serial numbers on them."

"And the Zorro angle?"

"That's the easiest of all. Just mention in the report that the person mentioned in Wheaton's statement as a possible suspect was in jail at that time. That he was mistaken."

He nodded and sat, thinking for a few seconds. "What do you think he's going to do?"

"He'll complain to your Police Commissioner. Probably call every town board member and the Mayor. And when they tell him to go to hell, he'll go to the press and say APD is incompetent and hasn't worked to solve this. If you're ready for that endgame, it won't go far. I'd expect him to try a lawsuit, possibly."

"Why that?"

"He needs the money. That's why this thing happened."

I could see the thought disturbed him. "If I know my mayor and council, they just might buckle."

"Tell you what," I said. "If it comes to that, then we put our cards on the table. I've always gotten along well with the press. I'll talk to them. In the meantime, we need to walk over to the commissioners office and photocopy this whole case file."

"What?"

"Trick I learned in the Army. Always protect your case file," I answered.

I took the copies home with me. Once I got comfortable, I took them from my briefcase and stashed them in my file cabinet at home that evening.

"You're playing Secret Squirrel with something," Jewell said when I came out of our home office.

"A case where I don't want things disappearing," I explained. I told her about my visit from Rob, and she nodded.

"Think he'd go so far as to have someone steal the case file?"

I shrugged. "David Wheaton is a low life scumbag. I think he'd prostitute out his mother for a buck."

"Guess I don't know him."

"You're not missing much. Now, how was your day?"

"Well. I spoke to Eva. It seems Max is out almost every night."

"He won't be out tonight," I said. "He's still in my jail."

She smiled and nodded. She knew I was just trying to be smart. "Eva told me that he's been hitting the sauce pretty heavy. She can't prove it, but she thinks he's been doing coke."

I rubbed my chin, knowing that a blood or urine test could determine that, but without an actual charge and a reason, I wouldn't be getting one. "Why does she say that?"

"Money mostly," she said. "Almost every dime they get in goes right out. He says it's for the business, but whenever he does anything for the business, he always has a receipt to back it up."

"Pushers don't give register receipts," I agreed. "What else."

"She's a stone throw away from tossing him out and going home," she answered. " I can't blame her. There's only one thing worse than being married to an addict, and that's being married to an addict that beats on you."

She had a point. The best thing for Eva might be to be on a plane back to Germany. But she had a claim to the property they'd gathered together. I wondered if it was enough to keep her here until there was a divorce settlement.

"I hate to see any marriage go bad, but being a punching bag is worse."

"I was in an abusive marriage, Baby," she said. "And I know a lot of pastors take a dim view of divorce. My ex was a pastor. He was beating me, snorting up our money, and sleeping around. I went and talked to an aunt and uncle who were pastors, and you know what they said?"

"No."

"They said to put on your make up, and wear sunglasses. You don't want to destroy his ministry."

"You're kidding." I almost refused to believe what I was hearing. But Jewell was one of those rare people that if she told you the sun didn't come up in the morning, then it was dark outside. Lying just wasn't in her.

I shook my head. "Sounds to me like he was doing a pretty good job on his own of ruining it. You don't do that stuff and expect to get away with it."

"I went around and around on that one. I prayed about it, and then one day, I found a scripture that cemented in my mind that it was OK to get away from him."

"What was that?" I asked.

"Malachi 2:16. 'The man who hates and divorces his wife,' says the Lord, the God of Israel, 'does violence to the one he should protect,' " She quoted. "I know some people would say I'm misquoting it, but he hated me since he was beating me."

"I know some folks would say the only biblical excuse for divorce would be immorality."

"I've heard that. Well, what can be more immoral than beating the one you're supposed to love?"

I couldn't argue with that one.

We had supper with the kids. Then we all sat down and played some cards before going to bed.

CHAPTER TEN

WHEATON

I got to the office early the next morning. I got my coffee and wandered into the dispatch office.

"Detective," Vicki, our day dispatcher, said. "There's a bunch of messages in your box for you."

Not good, I thought.

"They're all from the same person."

Even worse!

I pulled the dozen or so pink message forms out of my message box. Every one of them was from David Wheaton. He must have spoken with Rob and was royally ticked.

"How did things go at the MEPS station?" I asked.

"I got Military Police, with an assignment to Ft. Riley, and delayed entry till next year."

"Good, that will give you time to finish your POST training." Being a certified police officer and with some experience under her belt would translate into rank and good assignments when she got to permanent party.

I read through one of the messages. It was a rather forcefully worded message.

"He told me to write it down word for word," Vickie explained.

"Not a happy camper there," I said.

David Wheaton was none too happy with the investigation and my saying that there were problems with the scene. He'd requested that I call him back.

There was more to it than that. He called me every name except a white boy in it.

I sucked in my breath and went into my office. The problem with defending the truth is sometimes you have to put your mouth where the truth is. I dialed the number given to me. I didn't recognize it. It was a New Mexico number.

"Mr. Wheaton." I might as well be civil with him. It never hurt. "Detective Diaz returning your call."

"Diaz," he said. I noticed how he dropped my title. "I want to talk with you about your findings that you urged upon Antonito PD."

"My findings, Mr. Wheaton?"

"Yes, there are problems with the crime scene. That it doesn't support what is supposed to have happened."

"Mr. Wheaton. The evidence doesn't support what we're being led to believe happened."

"That's bullshit, Diaz. A blind man could see that someone broke through the roof, dropped down, robbed my store, and got out through the same hole."

I was ready to argue with him when I remembered the Biblical comment that you should never argue with a fool. I took a breath and said, "Mr. Wheaton, do you have a copy of the report in front of you?"

"Yes, I do."

"My analysis is based on the crime scene and the evidence. Any investigator in the world would come to the same conclusions I and Sgt. Gonzales came to."

"Well, I don't know where you earned your detective badge. A box of Cracker Jacks, maybe?"

I knew where this one was going, but said instead, "Mr. Wheaton, if you would like, I'll be happy to work with Antonito PD. We'll submit their investigation, photographs, and evidence to the CBI for further study. We can let them determine if we know what we're talking about."

He paused and then said, "Diaz, I've got a better idea. I think you're wrong. All you cops will look after each other anyway, so I'm not getting an impartial report. I think I'm just going to sue you and the Antonito Police Department for being incompetents. I'm going to have your job and that idiot Gonzales's as well."

Damn, not even an attempt to talk me into his point of view.

"Tell you what," I said. "Come in anytime tomorrow. My calendar is free. And we'll talk about this. But, bring your lawyer, oh, I forgot. You are a lawyer. I'll be advising you of your Miranda rights, and possibly charge you with making a false report and attempted fraud."

I figured if he were telling the truth, he'd show up. He didn't like the idea too much.

"I've got one better. You'll be hearing from my . . . Me!"

He was his own lawyer after all.

"Sounds like a plan to me, Mr. Wheaton," I said calmly. "And since there's a lawsuit pending, I have nothing more to say to you. Good day."

He growled something obscene and hung up.

I put the phone back on the cradle and looked up to see the Sheriff looking at me. He was leaning in the door with the forever grafted to his hand cup of coffee.

"I admire your restraint," he said.

I scowled and took a sip of my coffee. It had gotten cold, but I was too ticked to care. It was my turn to growl. "All I wanted to do was call him a liar. Worse than that, he's a God damn liar."

"Don't worry," the Sheriff said. "I already called him that for you. My name will be on that lawsuit as well."

I shook my head. "I'm sorry, Sheriff. You don't need this. Not during an election year."

He shrugged. "Will, if I had a nickel for every time someone told me they were going to have my job or threatened to sue me, I'd be the richest man in the state."

"That's what I just thought. Sheriff, that's the one thing I hate about being a civilian. Because you make a call, it entitles everyone to disagree with it."

"Of course he disagrees with it. I saw the same stuff you did. I came to the same conclusion. You don't have to be a NASA engineer to see the case has problems."

I shook my head. "He honestly thinks people would be stupid enough to believe it happened that way. I mean, we might be backwoods here, but that doesn't make us stupid."

The Sheriff nodded. "What's your degree in?"

"AstroPhysics."

"That makes you about the smartest person around."

"If I'm so damn smart, then how come I work for you?"

The Sheriff laughed. "So, the question becomes, what will he do next?"

I looked towards the wall. I was already thinking of the next move. "He'll go to the press. Try to put public pressure on the commissioners, so if he files his suit; they're more likely to cave and settle out of court. It's an election year for some of them also. They don't want the heat."

"And he keeps it out of the courts?'

"He keeps it out of the courts. He knows if it goes to trial, we stand a good chance of winning."

"That's reasonable. What are you thinking?"

"I'm going to get the reports together and ask CBI to take a look at it anyway. I want their input. That way, if he does try, we've got our ducks in a row."

"Anything else?"

I nodded and drummed my fingers for a bit. "My buddy from Routt County. Let's ask him if he'd be interested in some consulting work. Say a grand worth."

"Ouch," the Sheriff said. "See if he'll do it for five. And let's wait and see if we need to do that."

"And if Wheaton does go to the press, you let me handle it."

"You?"

"Hey, I'm the war hero here," I said, knowing that wasn't exactly true. I had a Bronze Star while the Sheriff had a Silver Star. But my war was a little more recent. "Might as well put that shiny medal Uncle Sam gave me to good use. If they call, I'll take a copy of the reports to them. Fight fire with fire. I don't like fighting things out in the press, but if he attacks, it deserves a good counter-attack."

When I called Jewell with her "10 AM, I love you call", we had a lot to pray about. "Don't worry, Baby. What's done in darkness will always be brought to light."

At 2 PM, the phone rang. It was Sylvia Fernandez, a reporter from the paper.

"Will," she said. "I'm following a story lead regarding a break-in in Antonito. The man who called said you and Antonito PD aren't taking it seriously."

Hmmm, I thought, all business. Sylvia was a nice person, but when she had a story, she was blunt and to the point.

"Hi, Sylvia. Long-time, no talk to. How you been?"

"Rushing for a deadline," she answered.

And so concludes the small talk portion of our conversation. "Your caller would be one David Wheaton. Correct?"

"Yes, it is," she said, a little amusement in her voice.

"Tell you what, beyond saying the man is full of it, how about you and I meet. I've got photographs, measurements, and all that. And then I'll tell you what I'm doing to meet his allegations. I'll let you draw your conclusions. Fair enough?"

Sylvia knew I knew how to fight back in the papers, and it almost always made good copy.

"Fair enough. How soon can you come up?"

"Let's see. It's two now. How about I meet you at your office at three. I know that's getting close to the deadline."

"Three it is." She said. She knew an allegation was always good press. A free for all in the papers was even better. I decided I was going to give her one. Probably wouldn't win her any Pulitzer, but sold a lot of newspapers.

I ducked into the Sheriff's office and told him what was going on. I then left to get to Alamosa and the newspaper office. I stopped at home and grabbed the copy I had of the investigation, and made it to the paper with five minutes to spare.

Wheaton had made one tiny mistake.

Sylvia and I went all the way back to college. She and I had taken several journalism courses together. We'd both worked at the college radio and TV stations. That's when I was trying to figure out what I wanted to be when I grew up, and so was sampling a little bit of everything.

I still don't know what I want to be when I grow up, but at least I ended up with a very well rounded education. I could talk with almost anyone from the janitor to astronauts on practically any subject. It had served me very well over the years.

Sylvia hadn't changed one bit. She was short, a little overweight, glasses, and a mind that could cut through the malarkey.

She was one of the few reporters I trusted.

"Will," she said as I came in the front door. "You haven't changed one bit since the last time we crossed paths."

"And you're still a total BSer, Girl. I'm older, got some wrinkles, and I'm getting gray."

"Well, I'm still short, fat, and I wear thicker glasses, but you don't hear me complaining!"

We both laughed.

She led me to a table that served as her desk. An Apple computer occupied one side, a riot of notepads, phone messages, and coffee cups filled the other. She offered me a cup of coffee and indicated a chair for me to sit down on that was next to her desk.

The coffee was surprisingly good.

"Will, you already know what he said."

"I got a pretty good idea. David Wheaton called me this morning, and called me an incompetent ass that got his detective badge out of a box of Cracker Jacks."

She had pulled out a legal pad and began writing. "Well, where did you get your training?"

"Well, let's start with the Colorado Law Enforcement Academy. Then a whole bunch of years of experience. I went into the Army, where I worked for two years undercover narcotics, a year and a half of plainclothes investigations, and then I went over to division MP companies and ran Garrison and Combat Military Police teams. I've been doing law enforcement now for a little shy of 15 years.

"Along the way, I went through the Military Police Investigations course, and over twenty-five courses in criminal investigation. Most of those were put on by the FBI, the Kansas Bureau of Investigation, or the German Polizei. I'm well up on evidence preservation, arson investigation, counter-terrorism, and believe it or not, Occult Crimes Investigation. I have a security clearance so high that it scares me. And here's one unrelated thing for the readers. I have a Bronze Star that's about worth a cup of coffee."

"I knew about that. Why do you rate it so low."

"Simple. I didn't deserve it."

"I found an article from Stars and Stripes on you. What's this 'Regulators' you're part of?"

I laughed. "It was a term hung on me and five others. It was meant to be derogatory, but we ended up wearing it as a badge of honor. A bunch of CID investigators thought we were just a bunch of yokels. We got working narcotics."

"This wasn't narcotics," she said, "but something that happened in the Gulf."

"I can tell you this much. Our suspect tried to toss it in our face, and the press got wind of it. That Colonel should be getting out of prison in about forty years.

"We were all cowboys, you see. We all went through basic and AIT together. We were all assigned narcotics and investigations, and we went through almost eight years in the same units. We all went to the Gulf War and were in the same platoon."

"That doesn't happen very often. The article I found was very flattering."

"They had to be flattering. It's not every day a bunch of cowboys stopped a massacre."

"Sounds like an interesting story."

"It is. I'm saving it for a novel," I explained. "Officially, it never happened."

"So, what do you say to his allegations that you and the Antonito PD aren't taking his case seriously?"

I opened the case file. "To the contrary. We're taking it very seriously. What we're not taking seriously is his interpretation of the scene." I then showed her the pictures of the crime scene explaining my reasoning behind each.

"So, overall, your interpretation of the crime scene is that it calls him a liar."

"'Liar' is a word I'd use. You might want to use something different.

"Let's say the evidence isn't jiving with what is supposed to have happened. The evidence is supposed to support a conclusion. In this case, it doesn't."

She wrote that down, and then said, "Why do you think he's insisting that someone broke in and robbed his place."

"This isn't for print, but you're a good investigative reporter. Here's something to chase. Pull everything from Conejos, Costilla, and Alamosa county civil courts on him. I think you'll find your answer. And then ask him how business was last year."

"What else have you done?"

"I'm sending copies to CBI. I want their people to give their opinion on it. And, if we have to, we'll be asking a separate office to give it a second look. The idea is to see if they draw the same conclusions we did.

"I've also extended an invite to David Wheaton to come down to the Sheriff's Office. I'd be happy to have him try to convince me. The problem there is I'd end up having to Mirandize him, and ask him some rather pointed questions. He's declined my invite."

She wrote that down. "Will, as always, you give a good story. I've got a feeling he'll be doing some serious back peddling when I call him back. I'm not a cop, and I came to the same conclusion you did."

"He's threatening a lawsuit. And I suspect the reason he came to you was to fire a couple of shots across the city and county fathers bow to get them to cave in so it wouldn't have to go to court."

"Election year?"

I nodded.

"Think he'd actually go through with it?"

"He might try, but you know me. I always try to find the good in people. But sometimes they make me pause and wonder.

"But if it comes to it, I love a good fight."

"Can I have copies of your investigation?" she asked.

I hesitated. "Only if you promise not to release any of the details or photographs. If it goes to court, it will be evidence."

"I can promise you that."

I let her make copies. Her word was good for me.

By the time I got home, Sylvia had called, asking that I call her back. I returned the call right away.

"Will, you were right. He backed down."

"Really."

"Yes, he blames it all on a misunderstanding. And I followed your tip. This guy likes suing people."

"That he does. And that's why I took him seriously. I figured he'd try to fight it in the papers. He knows if all that got introduced into court, he wouldn't be looking good."

"Well, it's too bad. It would have made a good story."

"I'll try to find you a good juicy one."

"I'll hold you to it."

I hung up and noticed that Jewell was smiling at me. "What?"

"Didn't I tell you he'd back down? That his lie would come out?"

"You sure did, Love of my Life."

"Surely he can't think people are so stupid that they'd just roll over and let him snowball them."

"I had this same discussion with the Sheriff. And stop calling me Shirley."

She laughed at the old joke, but said, "Why would he pull something like that?"

I shrugged but offered a guess anyway. "He had a bad year. He stages a phony break-in, collects insurance on stuff that may or may not have been there, and he's flush for a bit."

"And everyone's insurance goes up as a result."

"It's like I tried to explain to Max. Sin has a ripple effect. Somehow, someway, it impacts everyone. And while I feel for someone who has a bad year, this is a terrible way to try to stay afloat."

Jewell was smiling at me.

"What?"

"Did I ever tell you that you're a good man?" she asked.

"More than once. But I think you tell stories, Girl."

I gave her another hug, and while I was hugging her, something started nagging at me. I hadn't fully realized it, but she'd just opened a door on David Wheaton's psyche.

"He's not a native," I said.

"What do you mean?"

I was looking at the wall and just letting my brain run wide open. "Think about it. He's here for a reason. A largely unpopulated area. Poor, so we don't have the resources that larger departments might have. Why would he come here?"

Jewell came to the same conclusion I did at almost the same time. "Easy pickings," she said. "The man is a vulture."

I thought about it and then shook my head. "No, he's a coyote. He's smart like a coyote, and he takes advantage of an opportunity. And like a coyote, he likes the wide-open spaces. He has a larger plan. Something I don't see yet."

"Why?"

I hadn't added that piece in, and I wouldn't for a couple of years anyway.

"I don't know yet," I said. When I finally did get that piece of the puzzle, I'd kick myself because it was so obvious.

Despite his early defeat in this round, I hadn't seen the last of David Wheaton. His path and mine would continue to cross for some time.

About 9:30 the following morning, I was reviewing the plans I had for resurrecting Dodge City and getting our officers and deputies more tactical training when the phone in my office rang.

"Conejos County Sheriff's Office," I said, "Detective Diaz speaking."

"Diaz," I heard the voice on the other end say. I recognized it almost instantly.

"Mr. Wheaton. What can I do for you?"

"I underestimated you, Detective," he said. I noted he had used my title this time. Something had changed. "You play the game well."

So, that's what it was. To Wheaton, it was a game. But which one? Chess? Poker? Maybe a little of both?

"You don't win by letting folk walk all over you, Mr. Wheaton," I said.

"Opening gambit, Sir." Then he chuckled and said, "I look forward to the competition."

I smiled thinly, and it was a second before I realized my eyes had narrowed some. "As long as you understand how I play the game, Sir. I play for keeps."

"Well, so do I," he said.

I started to say something, but by that time, he'd hung up.

CHAPTER ELEVEN

DODGE CITY – ENTRY TACTICS

David Wheaton didn't vanish off my radar. And it's not because he'd left town or anything. It's just that dogs that aren't barking don't tend to attract a lot of attention. But like a moth around a flame, I knew he was flitting about. What I didn't realize was that he was slowly eating away and unraveling the fabric of the world I knew.

He was far from my mind, though, as I looked out at the small collection of police officers and sheriff's deputies gathered in the classroom. I was wondering what they were thinking.

When we first started up the Dodge City courses, they had attracted some attention. Most of the officers treated it as big-city tactics that had little to do with them. They continued to think that right up to the point they got zapped for the mistakes they made in the training exercises.

Then they started taking it seriously.

I'd gotten kids who were interested in acting from the local schools, and this gave them a platform beyond the school plays. They became my OpFor (Opposition Forces), a role they played with enthusiasm.

An example of the work they did was the very first course. We'd taught something every cop does every day, and that's vehicle stops. Most of them went like they usually would. And then we threw a twist into it.

A couple of young ladies from one of the local schools were cheerleaders. I had them show up in uniform, and I borrowed a red Mustang from a local dealer. They drove the car, the cop makes contact, and they sit there, flirting and batting their eyes at him. One hiked up her skirt just a little to show a bit more leg, and while he's distracted, they killed him.

In another scenario, a cop made another traffic stop only to have a bunch of guys come bailing out of it. Each person had a baseball bat and was yelling obscenities and approaching the car. That entire exercise was designed to answer one question. What do you do?

Some tried to get out and use their legal authority. When the exercise was over, everyone agreed that would end in either one or more the guys being shot or the officer seriously injured if not killed.

The correct answer to the exercise was to get the heck out of there and call for help. Then you engage them when numbers were on your side.

The idea was to teach them to stay focused (the girls weren't going to kill you with their eyes and thighs, but their hands) and to think tactically.

We covered traffic stops, arrest techniques, crime scene processing, and negotiation techniques. Jewell and I had asked God to bless it, and he did. Our monthly meetings had gone from just a few to a dozen or more officers per session.

Today's session had fourteen officers in it. Our host for today was Bob Mortenson, Town Marshall, for the Manassa PD.

Sgt. Jeff Sanchez of the La Jara PD was in attendance, and Pam Harmon represented Sanford Police. RJ Madril and Arnie Romero were from my department. Sgt. Rob Gonzales showed up for Antonito PD. There were also two deputies from neighboring Costilla County, Albert Montoya, and Timothy Gutierrez. Bill Thompson made it down from Mineral County and Sheriff Al Hendrix from Saguache County. The big surprise was a couple of officers from the Monte Vista Police Department and two from neighboring Rio Arriba County in New Mexico.

It was a shock to realize that this little assemblage constituted a good fraction of the total Law Enforcement contingent in several counties. I'd gotten accustomed to having law enforcement measured in company-sized elements in the Army. There was no way many of our smaller departments could approach the size of even an Army squad.

Our class was at the Headstart Building in Manassa, Colorado. It was a modern one-story building built entirely of cinder block. It had been painted canary yellow with brown trim, a color scheme I hated. This building had three classrooms, a lunchroom, office space, and a couple of bathrooms. It was perfect for today's training.

RJ, the Sheriff's son (his real name is Tony Madril, Jr. I've never asked where "RJ" came from), and I had gotten there early. We unloaded several boxes of gear. We laid out flak jackets, steel helmets, and liners, gas masks, and carriers. We'd used some blue spray paint to paint the helmets, and then using a stencil, the word "POLICE" on the back of the flak jackets.

"Perk," RJ said. "I never in my life thought I'd be wearing the badge again."

I could appreciate that. "Me neither, Mr. Ewings. I guess we should both be thankful we had somewhere to go."

I'd found the Sheriff's Office again after getting out of the Army. RJ had been a Spanish teacher at a school. Trouble is when schools get in financial trouble, anything that's not associated with the "three Rs" tends to be let go.

That includes Spanish teachers.

So RJ was back. Long ago, I'd hung the nickname of Mr. Ewings on him, A play on the name of the character Larry Hagman had played so well on the TVshow, Dallas.

He turned around and hung "Perkins" on me after one of the deputies on Dukes of Hazard.

The closest we had to a Daisy Duke, was Pam. I didn't expect the conservative Mormon girl from Sanford to run around in short shorts anytime soon.

The gear we had would be distributed to the officers within our county that attended today. They would form the backbone of our SWAT team. Each would sign for the equipment and promise to take care of it.

We'd purchased some plastic bins so they could store them adequately. In the weeks and months to come, they'd be using it, if not for actual tactical work, then for training.

There was a large whiteboard in the conference room. I had long ago learned the value of different colored dry erase markers and purchased a box at the local Walmart. We had a large pot of coffee going, and a couple of boxes of doughnuts from the SpudNut Doughnut Shop in Alamosa for today's event.

He was making the coffee when Pam Harmon showed up. I noticed them talking, and he introduced himself. When he came up to the front of the classroom, he asked quietly, "Who's Pam?"

"Sanford Town Marshall," I responded. "Ex-Marine Military Police."

"Hmmm," he said, which told me something. I wasn't aware that RJ liked blondes.

I smiled. Maybe it was about time he found a nice girl.

I had filed that away, and I got going with the class. "I want to thank everyone for coming today," I said. "And I want to thank Bob Mortenson of Manassa PD for hosting this month's training.

"Not too many months ago, several MPs and I had to clear a barracks in Germany. We had a soldier who raped a girl and ran into the barracks. The CQ and other NCOs managed to chase him into the basement area. He was down there armed with a Ninja sword. We were able to take him down successfully, and without anyone getting hurt by using the techniques, we're going to study this afternoon.

"We're going to cover Individual and team room clearing tactics. We'll finish before five o'clock. We will have an OpFor exercise so you can practice what you've learned. If you do it wrong, congratulations, you just got somebody killed. I hope you go back to your respective departments and show them the new tactics. Questions?"

Bob raised his hand, and when he asked, I knew he was merely playing Devil's Advocate. Bob was an old-time cop, but he knew times were changing. "Will, do you see us ever actually having to use these?"

"Bob, I hope and pray, we don't. But we have to admit that we're starting to deal with a different breed of criminals these days. It used to be these guys were friends and neighbors. Now, we have more people coming in from the cities. They're trying to get away from the problems there, but bringing those problems with them. That means we'll be dealing with those problems.

"So, yes. Someplace, somewhere, we will need them. And since we're always backing one another up, we all need to be on the same sheet of music and train from the same book. Good enough?"

He nodded and said, "Let's do it."

"OK," I said. "Here's the scenario. We get a call that there's been a disturbance at someone's home. People are panic-stricken. There's been some knife play involved. Someone has been cut up, and they're still inside. The perp is in there also. Everyone else got out.

"What do we do?"

I turned to the chalkboard and started drawing. "Here's our house." I drew a square, and then a line that indicated the front door and another marking the back. "Front door opens into a living room, " I continued drawing lines outlining the inside of the house, "and to the right is a hallway. Off the hall are two bedrooms and a bathroom, and in the back is the kitchen.

"Our objective is to clear the house, apprehend the suspect, and do so without becoming a casualty ourselves. We also need to make it safe for EMS to come in and get the wounded guy drawn in blue to the hospital.

"OK, what do we do?" I tapped the whiteboard with the marker.

We all knew that this is a real-world problem that could happen. Pam started the scenario. "Since I'm a one-man department, I'm covering the front, and then calling for backup." I nodded and drew a patrol car in front of the house.

"OK," I said. "We have a sheriff's deputy down the road. Where do you want him?"

"Covering the back," Pam said.

I drew another police car at the back of the house.

"Cool. Unless our perp slipped out, we have him sealed up. Now what?"

Rob from Antonito PD chimed in, "We could get on the loudspeaker, tell him to come out. "

"How about we call the house?" Jeff suggested.

I nodded and drew a speech balloon over the red stick man, and the words "Come an' get me, Copper!" in it.

"So far so good," I said. "We've got him contained. And we're trying to talk to him. Incidentally, the phone idea is good. We want communications with him. It also helps us narrow down where he's at, unless, of course, they have cordless phones. The loudspeaker can do the same and might bring him up to the front of the house. He might not think it through and try to shout out the windows at us. What else are you doing?"

"Calling for more help," Jeff said.

I nodded and drew a couple of more patrol cars in the front.

"Now here's where tactics come into play," I said. "Do I want every patrol car that shows up to park in front of the house?"

I could see I was making them think a little. "Why might I want all the cars in front?" I asked.

"Show of force. Intimidate him into giving up?"

I nodded and then said, "And why might I want them to stop a couple of houses down?"

"So he doesn't know our strength," another answered.

"Good, and who makes that call?"

"Well, if this is Sanford, then Pam makes that call," RJ said. "It's her town."

I nodded. The officers were thinking in terms of Incident Command, a course we'd covered a few months before.

"OK, so we have an officer outback. He shouldn't be in his car. He needs to be ready to tackle the guy, engage him, whatever needs to be done. So, Pam, you're Incident Commander. Bob and La Jara PD are upfront with you. The guy isn't coming out, and our knife victim is bleeding to death. Tell me, would you ever go in by yourself?"

Pam scratched her head and answered, "Only if I had to."

"And when would that be?"

"Only if life was seriously threatened. It depends on the circumstances."

"Good. The best answer I've got, and this is a tough call to make, is I wouldn't go in without backup. But suppose this is a schoolhouse, and we've got children . . ."

I let that thought hang out there in the air.

I could tell by their faces what their answer would be. To a man, they'd put themselves on the line. It was a tough call, and one that could quickly end up with more casualties than doing nothing would produce. But then a human has to do what a human has to do.

RJ chimed in, "Some folks would say that since we're training for it, someone might try it."

I nodded. "Some folks are right. But ignoring it doesn't mean it won't happen. What it does mean is we've thought about it, done some training, and drawn up a plan or two. But if I'm thinking about it, so's someone else."

I let them stew on that one for a couple of minutes and then went on. "Ok, so the perp is holed up in the house. Our victim is bleeding out, maybe dead already. What are we doing?"

Bob said, "We're going in."

I nodded. "Yep, we're going in. Now's there are four officers on the scene, with one watching the back. Pam, you're Incident Commander. What's your plan?"

She studied the diagram for a moment and then said, "I'd re-enforce the back with an extra officer, and then we hit both doors at the same time."

I nodded and drew a stick figure in black in the back. "Anyone see anything wrong with the plan?"

"Only if he jumps out a window."

"Could happen," I said. "When we hit the house, we want to bottle him up. So Pam, what would you say to have a couple of your reserve officers help guard against that?"

"Good idea," she said. She had several citizens who helped with parades, funerals, and the like. "That means we need to get them a bit more training."

"I agree. They want to play cop, let's start treating them like the real thing. So anyway, we've run her reservists through a cram course on arrest, and we've got four of them positioned at the corners of the house to keep an eye on things." I drew these guys as little green stick figures. My chalkboard was starting to get full.

"Before we do much more, what else do we need to do?"

A couple of ideas were tossed out.

"How about communications!"

"Layout of the house."

"Who the perp is?"

"Assault plan itself."

"Where is everyone located."

"How about guns? Are there any in the house."

I wrote it all down on the board:

- Communications plan.
- Target layout
- Personal information
- The plan
- Information
- Support

"How about a medical plan," RJ suggested. "Someone's likely to get hurt out of all this."

I drew an ambulance a few doors down.

"So, we've got the situation contained. Now we need to get resources and information. We're also planning, and we're filling in the blanks. A big blank is the layout of the house. We can make a lot of guesses, but eyes trump guesses any day of the week. So, where can I get a layout of the house?"

"County records!" someone suggested.

"Good, but it's after hours."

Bob raised his hand. "Assuming someone who lives there is standing outside, have them draw it out."

I nodded. "And while you're at it, find out where the victim is, where the perp was last seen, and about guns and other weapons. What other options do we have?"

"Looking," Jeff suggested. Sometimes the obvious is the best. "Binoculars are great for this kind of work, even if they turn the lights off. You can still see movement."

"OK, let's talk assaulting the house," I said. "Recon has put the suspect in a back bedroom.

"There's a couple of ways we can do the assault. Our incident Commander has already decided that we're going to hit the front and back door at the same time. Two points of attack will give our suspect something to think about. Now, what kind of assault will we do?

"The first option is what we call a Dynamic assault. We get in fast. We clear quickly, overwhelm the perp, and secure the scene. That means going into every room. In our scenario, we secure the front room and kitchen and hall, sweep down the hallway, and hitting each room till we're done. Since this guy may not have a gun and isn't holding the wounded guy hostage, it's a possibility.

"The good news here is we get this thing over and done. The bad news is there's a good chance someone might get hurt or killed.

"Another is what we call a Deliberate Assault. We know where the victim and the perp are. Our first objective might be to secure just the front room, the kitchen, and the hall and get the wounded person out. This kind of assault will mess with the mind of our perp. Up to this point, the house has been his fortress. Breach that, and his confidence is going to be shaken big time. It also changes the dynamics of the situation a bit. And how is that?"

"We're in control," Bob answered.

"Exactly. We've confined the perp to that bedroom. Once we gain control of these three areas, we've denied him access to water, food, and the bathroom. We try to talk him out. We could toss a tear gas grenade into the room or spray some mace under the door. That might make him come out. Or, we could hit the door when he's half blind and take him that way.

"And we've made him dependent on us for food and water. If it goes that far, we can always spike his lunch with something that will knock him out. The good news here is that there's a good chance this will probably end peacefully. The bad news is, we might be there a while.

"And who makes that call as to what kind of assault we do?"

Everyone looked at Pam. "Yep, it's her call. I'd probably say whatever your objective is might dictate, which we do. So Pam, given our circumstances, which do you want to do?"

"I'll go with the deliberate assault. Worst case scenario, we can always hit that backroom later if we have too."

"I think that's a good call. OK, so we've got a plan of sorts. Tell me about your communication plan?"

"Get off CSP, and go to Channel 4, Sheriff's channel."

"And how do you brief the guys in back?"

"I leave Rob watching the front, go around and do it personally. And I'll probably use the word 'Go' to begin the assault. I don't need to let everyone in ScannerLand know what we're doing or how we work."

"OK. So we know our perp is still in the back room. That means you don't have to be that stealthy in your approach. For weapons, what are you using?"

Pam already had that figured. "One shotgun per team, handguns for everyone else."

"Added wrinkle. When we approach the door, we discover they're locked. What do we do now?"

"Shotguns take out locks pretty well?" offered an officer.

"Yes, they do. But how about a fire ax or a sledgehammer, and just giving the door a good whack? Or asking if anyone has a key?"

That must have made sense because several people nodded in agreement.

"The problem with just kicking the door in like they do on television is that doors are made of some pretty stern stuff. The best-case scenario is you'll have to kick it several times before it opens. The worst-case scenario that doesn't work.

"Either way, you'll probably end up hurting your foot."

I noticed a few of the officers smiled at that. They must have tried it and spent the next few days limping about and wolfing down Motrin.

"Again, try to keep it quick and simple. Now in our scenario, we don't have a key, so we will have to whack that back door. If we're using a firefighter to bang in that door, well, they need to get out of the way once it's knocked open. The assault team will be rushing in, and he better be out of the way."

I pointed at the door. "We have a lot of names for doors. The book calls it the Fatal Funnel. Others call it the Area of Maximum Exposure. Others call it the Screwed Zone. There are other names I won't use because there's a lady present."

I'm sure that as a Marine, Pam had heard them before. Probably used them herself. But I was still going to respect the lady.

"Bottom line, it's a choke point, and if I intend to leave this Earth and want to take some company with me, this is where I'm going to do it. As the cops are coming in through the door, I'm shooting into it. For our scenario, this isn't a fatal area.

"But once we hit that door, we better get in fast. Here the guy with the shotgun comes in and covers left. The guy right behind him covers right. No one is there, so what's the first thing I need to do?"

"Let the other team know the area is secure," Jeff said.

"Communications is vital.We're going to be keyed up, and it's easy to end up shooting at each other. Communications are your first, best line of defense against that happening. If you go to clear the hall, make sure you announce you're going to clear the hall and make sure everyone acknowledges that."

I looked at Pam. "Okay, we've completed our first objectives. You're in the front room and the kitchen. What's next?"

"The hall is still wide open. We need to finish bottling him up."

"Good call. We have to pin him down a little more. Now, here's another place where people get themselves in trouble. Who's clearing that hall? Your assault plan should cover that because this is an easy place to turn into a shooting gallery."

"Give the job to team one," Pam said. "Team Two can support."

"So, Team One is responsible for securing the hall. What we don't know is if our perp has moved. Remember, this is happening quickly. Our perp has been alerted to doors being knocked down and strange voices. He might already be in the hall. Or he might have come out, dropped the knife, and be standing there with his hands up. How do you look down that hall and get it done quickly and safely."

"Just come around the corner with the shotgun," someone suggested?

"And if he's standing right there?" I asked. "He grabs the shotgun barrel. Our situation just went from bad to worse."

I could tell this a new thought for them.

"Remember, you've got to be quick about this."

"Can I show them how we did it in the Marines?" Pam asked.

"Go for it!" I urged.

She got up and approached the desk and then touched it. "Pretend that the table edges represent walls,' She said. "I want to clear that hall. When I begin my approach, I come parallel to the wall, and then I begin curving out, away from the wall. All the while, I'm keeping my weapon pointed down the hall until I'm looking all the way down."

She was pointing her finger like it was a pistol and demonstrated the maneuver.

"As I walk around, I clear my field of view and see more and more until I'm looking down the hall. Now, I'm going to end my curve on the opposite wall or stop in the middle. I'd rather have some cover so that I might end up on the opposite wall. At this point, he isn't coming out without my seeing him.

"I report hallway is secure. Team two can also look down the hall now, and they can position someone exactly opposite me, so we have it covered." She went to the board and drew in a couple of little stickmen to illustrate it.

"Notice where we're at, we're not in each other's field of fire. Questions?" There weren't any, then she looked at me, and a look of apology came over her face.

"Sorry, Will. I didn't mean to steal your thunder."

I shook my head. "No need to apologize. That's exactly what I was going to show them."

It was nice to have someone who knew something on the subject, and Albert from Costilla County nodded agreement. "That's exactly how we did it in First ID!"

"Cool, let's try it," I said."Okay, let's go out into the hall. Down at the back, there's a T intersection to practice this. Albert and Pam. You two know what you're doing. Demonstrate and then correct when people screw up. "

We went out, and Albert asked everyone to empty their pistols and then double-checked each to make sure they were empty. I sat back and watched, realizing what had just happened was a good thing.

By allowing them to go and run with it, I'd found my team leaders for the team I wanted to build. RJ was definitely in, but I didn't have a clue on team 2 and 3. Now I knew.

Albert had dropped his magazine and shown it to Pam and RJ, who confirmed the weapon was empty.

For half an hour, they practiced the sweep technique. I watched as Pam, Albert, and RJ demoed it, and then how they worked with everyone else and with each other.

My instincts told me I'd made the right choices for Team Leaders.

We took a break, and while we were drinking coffee and sharing war stories, there was a knock at the door.

"Detective," a voice said. A young girl waved to me. "We're here."

"Excuse me," I said, getting up from my coffee and cookie. I grabbed a paper bag and went out into the hall, where six teens waited.

'Hi guys," I said. "Thanks for coming down and helping me out."

"It's a gig," one said.

I figured if they ever made it big and got a gig on a cop show, this might help.

"Let's go in this classroom," I said, pointing.

Once in, I turned to them.

"OK," I said. "You've had a chance to look at the scenario? Good. Who are my kids?"

Two of the teens raised their hands.

"Now, you guys are the youngest, so your part is straightforward and the most boring. You're going to be kids and teachers both. The emergency plan is if stuff hits the fan, the teacher locks the door, and they wait for rescue. That's what you're going to do.

"The entry team will secure the hall, knock on the door, and you'll unlock it. Make sure they either show you a badge or ID themselves as police. If they don't, don't open the door. They'll direct you out the back. After that, sit down, eat cookies, and enjoy the show. Cool?'

They nodded.

"OK, one to each classroom." The two teens left.

I turned to the rest, two girls and a guy. "OK, Alexia," I told the girl who'd waved to me. "You're the director here. Monica, you're the secretary and Phil, you're our disgruntled dad.

"You and your wife have split up, and she's got custody of the kid. You got a little liquored up, and you've come to try to get him. Of course, they stopped you. Monica here, well, you shot her in the stomach. You've taken Aleia hostage, and you're demanding your son be released to you. You two will be in the office back there. Phil, threaten to blow her head off, and Alexia, be terrified out of your mind. They'll be calling in on the telephone to talk to you, so pick it up.

"I want you guys to sock it to them. Scream, threaten, whatever it takes. And if you get the chance, kill her or them. Make-believe, of course," I said with a smile. "Cool?"

I went to the bag I'd brought in and handed him an orange-colored plastic pistol, and Monica a t-shirt and a dispenser of fake blood. "You might want to change into this, and put this all over your stomach area. If you get it on your pants, it will wash out. I'll get you guys staged here in a bit."

Phil took the fake pistol, smiled, and said, "This is going to be fun."

"No matter what happens, we end the play at 4:30. I'm the referee, and some things will be simulated, so if I yell something, respond to it like you would if this were real. Just go with the flow."

They all smiled and nodded.

"OK, standby. I want to get all our cops outside before I stage you guys."

I went back into the room where we'd been and told the cops, "OK, its showtime. We're going to do an exercise and put to work what you've learned. Cleanup, and then I've got some presents for you."

Coffee cups and napkins went into the trash, and within a couple of minutes, the conference room was clean. I then motioned to the boxes of gear RJ, and I had brought in.

"Courtesy of Tio Sam," RJ said.

We went to a box and began handing out flak jackets. "These are flak jackets, not bulletproof vests, and sorry, they're only for cops from Conejos and Costilla County. Your sheriff or chief can get these, and if they don't know how, we'll be happy to tell them how.

"Be warned. These are flak jackets, and they're designed to protect you from things like splinters and glass shards that might be generated from a gunfight.

They might, and I do use the word 'might' lightly, stop a small caliber, low velocity round. I wouldn't want to bet my life on that. For this scenario, I want you guys to wear them."

We handed out helmets, gas masks, and carriers. "We'll be training with the masks next time. They need filters, and they haven't come in yet."

"Officers, take your stuff, get suited up, and wait outside."

Once they left, I went into the other classroom. Monica had changed into the t-shirt. She looked as if she'd just stepped out of a horror movie with fake red blood all over her stomach area.

"You two, back office," I said, pointing to Alexia and Phil. "Monica, I want you to lie down right here," and I indicated an area near the office door. She laid down, and I reached into my bag and placed a plastic puddle of fake blood next to her.

"OK, everyone, relax. It's showtime." I walked outside.

The officers were all suited up, looking somewhat clumsy in their flak jackets and helmets.

I opened a folder and handed out floor plans for the building.

"Bob, it's your town, so it's your problem. Here's the scenario. A divorced, drunk, and disgruntled dad has lost custody of his son. He's gone to the facility to pick up his child. He has a gun. The building is on lockdown, and we have kids in several of the classrooms. A mom who was in the back got out, and called it in. She says someone had been shot and is down in the hallway.

"We will pretend you called for help, and those assembled have shown up." I gave them a couple of small, commercial-grade radios donated by Radio Shack. "Use these for communications. We don't want to freak everyone in scanner land out. Questions?"

"What are my options as far as equipment?" Bob asked.

"Anything you've got in inventory, or another one of these departments might have is what you can bring to the party. So if you need a tank and haven't got one, you can't have it. Good?"

Everyone was. "Bob. You can ask me questions the caller might know, but as far as advice right now, I'm on vacation in Alaska." I looked around. "Everyone! The game starts now."

Bob started asking questions

"Lady," Bob said. "Do you know where they went?"

"Looked like he went into the front office," I said, slipping into my of the caller. "He was dragging the director in with him."

"And the person who you said had been shot?"

"The secretary? She was down by the door to the front office."

Bob called everyone over and began setting up the teams. "Team 1, you're Jeff and Pam. You're going in the front. Jeff, you take the shotgun.

"Team 2, that's Rob and RJ, you're going in the back door. Albert, you and your buddies from Costilla County are Team 3, and you'll go in right behind Team 2.

"Monte PD officers, you form Team 4, and you're out here with me.

"Any questions?"

There weren't any, so bob continued. "Here are our objectives.

"First, Team 3, you'll get all those kids out through the back door. Go in through the back, and move them out one classroom at a time. In the real world, we'd move them to the church over there. That would get them to safety.

"Team 2, you provide security for them.

"Once done, we concentrate on getting the shot girl out. If we have to, we drag her out of the field of fire towards the back, and EMS takes her from there.

"Team 2, once they get the kids out, that job falls to you. Team 1 will provide cover. Once they get her out, take a position covering the hall with Team 1."

That made sense to everyone.

"Here's how we're going to play this. I'm going to be on the phone (Bob held up a bag phone. I didn't realize he had one, but according to the rules of play, he could use it), and I'll be talking to the perp inside. I want to keep him busy in that back office while we get you guys in. Team 1, the entrance is a little offset to the office. You should be able to get into the lobby. Stay there, real quiet-like, and be ready to move to support Team 2 if things go south for them.

He looked at the teams. "Quiet is the operative word here. Questions?"

"Then what?"

"I'm still talking to him. That's where Team Four comes in. There's a small window in that back office, about seven feet up. You'll simulate breaking that window and toss in two tear gas grenades. I'll radio out "Gas," and that's your cue. Everyone mask, and we go in."

"Here's a radio for each team," he said, handing each team one of the small Radio Shack radios "Channel Seven. Wait for my signal to move in."

I walked back to the Headstart building. I'd forgotten that Bob had ran an infantry platoon in 'Nam. He knew his business.

I walked into the office just in time to hear the phone ring. Alexia picked it up, and when Bob identified himself, she went into acting mode. "Jesus. He's got a gun and . . ."

"Shut up! Shut up!" Phil yelled, playing his part now. He put the mock gun to her head and said, "Give me that." A tear rolled down her face as she handed him the receiver. She might make a good actress someday, I thought.

"Who is this!" he demanded, putting it on speakerphone.

"This is Marshal Bob Mortenson. Who am I talking with?"

"What's it to you, Marshal!" Phil snapped.

I could hear Bob fall back and mentally regroup. Bob was perfect for the Incident Commander. He was older, been around a bit, and not much ruffled him.

One of my concerns with Bob was he was older than most of us. Heck, his daughter and I had gone to school together, which would put Bob over fifty. Hanging with the pups might be harder for him, but maybe running the strike center or maybe there was some other job for him.

"Sir, I'm trying to be polite here, and calling someone by 'hey you' is not good manners. So, I introduced myself, who are you?"

"My name is Phil Jack," he snarled, staying in character.

"You're not in the front office, are you, Phil. Are you in the Director's office?"

"Why are you asking?"

"Because I can't see you through the window. So that must be where you are."

"Yeah, we are."

"So, Phil, what's going on here?" Bob asked after a pause.

"She's the problem!" Phil screamed towards the phone and gestured angrily with the pistol towards Alexia. "She won't let me see my kid."

"And why's that, Phil?"

"My wife and I. We split up! She's got custody, and the court says I can't see him!"

"Is the director, OK?" .

"For the time being. Marshal, I want to see my kid."

"Listen, Phil, you hurt her, and you'll never see your kid again. You'll be sitting in a prison cell, and you'll never see him. I promise you that."

Bob changed tactics. "They said someone had been shot?"

Phil, still in character, deflated a little. "Yeah, I think she's the receptionist. She jumped at me, and the gun just went off. I didn't mean to . . ."

Bob paused. He had a handle on the man now. "Well, that's an accident. It's not like you meant to, right?"

"Right."

Outside, I heard a door shut a little louder than it should have. Team 2 and 3 were in the building. I'm sure they were kicking themselves for being a little too noisy.

"Someone's in the building," Phil said.

"A mom going in to get her kids. An EMT stopped her from going in." Rob was a good liar.

"EMTs?" Phil said.

"We've got a woman out there who's hurt. We need to help her, Phil. You understand that. That's why the EMTs."

Bob let him digest it for a second and then said, "Will you let us help her?"

"And if I do, can I see my kid!"

"Look, Phil. I can't decide that for you.   can contact a judge. I can ask him to permit you. . ."

"I've got all the 'permit' I need right here with this gun, Marshal!"

"Phil. You didn't mean to shoot that woman," Rob said over the phone. I knew he wanted to shout, but was playing it cool. "That was an accident. You said so yourself. But if she dies, and it's because you wouldn't let us help her, then that isn't an accident. That's murder. And we both know that's against the laws of God and Man."

Bob let it sit there for a second and then said, "And you're not a murderer. You told me that."

Phil paused. The character he'd immersed himself in was thinking it through. "I'm not a murderer, Marshal. But I don't want any funny business. Have your medics come in and get her. I'll be watching."

I walked out of the office and watched as Team 2 came down the hall. A couple of the actors who had been teachers and students had been pressed into service to act as paramedic players. Phil went to the door, still holding Amy in front of him.

He was looking out. One of Team 2's members made himself visible, his face hidden inside the gas mask, his weapon held at ease in a non-threatening manner. The two EMT players helped the girl up and chuckling; they went away.

I watched it thinking that a good sniper with a good scope could have ended this right then and there. A headshot and it's goodnight world. I seemed to recall something

Phil smiled, and we went into the office. He'd noticed the gas mask. He closed the door. "She's out of here, Marshal. Why was your man wearing a gas mask?"

"Because, Phil, I just chucked two tear gas grenades through the window into the office you're in."

Phil looked at me for stage direction.

"Gas. Gas. Gas," Bob shouted over the radio.

"This room just became a gas chamber," I said. "You can't see, and you can't breathe. What would you do in real life?"

"Ah!" he said, and then went right back into character. "Jesus Christ," he screamed and started coughing. He clawed his way to the door, Alexia right behind him.

I had to give them credit for acting. While there was nothing there, they sure acted like there was and were putting on a convincing performance. The door opened, Phil fell out, and a shotgun was pointed at his head by a gas-masked individual.

"Game over," I shouted. "Unmask, and let's go back into the classroom for critique." Then over the radio, I called, "Team 1, 2, 3 and 4. Games over!"

A few minutes later, we were all in the classroom, students included. "OK. Critique."

"We've got to find a way to keep doors from slamming shut," RJ said.

"Actually what you'd do is one of you would hold the door, and then close it, make sure it didn't bang shut. We'll have to train on that." I looked around. "How were communications?"

"Good," Jeff said. "Something we might want to try to get is headsets. In a real situation, we need to hear the radio traffic better."

"What would you think of using these radio shack radios instead of police channels for tactical situations?" I asked, taking the small radio Bob had. "They can go on the belt, and we can get headsets for hands-free communication."

"It would work. I'd prefer something encrypted, but that costs money," Albert said.

"Noted," I said, writing down to look into headphones and encryption. "Was the assault plan solid?"

"Very. We could have used more people, especially on Team 2," Albert said. "In the real world, we might not have had Team 3. Team 2 would have been doing double duty. And the Incident Commander might have been doing the job of Team 4. More people would have been perfect."

I nodded. "Well, Christmas is only a few months away. Maybe Santa will bring us some."

Everyone chuckled, but we all knew that more officers were a luxury our cities and counties couldn't afford.

"One thing I liked was Bob and his bag phone. It made it possible to be in two places at once. It freed him up to command the incident and allowed him to negotiate at the same time. Anything else?"

No one had anything.

"Next month, I should have real filters for the mask. We'll practice masking in a hurry. We'll learn how to take care of them, and then we'll do some real gas. Anything else?"

One officer raised his hand and asked, "Do you think we'll ever actually need this?"

Another officer answered it by saying what we all knew. "Let's hope and pray, we don't."

CHAPTER TWELVE

CHRUCH

Max was good to his word. I promised to help him, and he came to church.

He went to rehab as the DA deal requested. He returned, looking rested. He'd put on a few pounds, and looked like he was in as good a shape as when he left the Army. The rehab center had a gym, and they encouraged people to use it.

But his eyes weren't showing what I'd hoped to see. She seemed calmer, but at the same time, restless. It was like he didn't know what to do with himself.

Eva seemed happy having him back, and I hoped and prayed that they were getting along. With God's help, the bad times were left behind, and tomorrow would be a brand new day in their relationship.

While Max was at the VA, getting anger management and alcohol counseling, Eva had been going through counseling as well. Jewell had been working with her, and it seemed to be doing her a lot of good.

Jewell never told me what they discussed.

But one thing Jewell did was to start helping Eva find work.

Jewell had cultivated a lot of contacts when she worked as an Administrator for a local nursing home; She had maintained those contacts out in the medical industry, and she was able to put Eva in touch with the right folks. Eva had a nursing degree and had gotten work at the Hospice center. She joined us for lunch once.

We were all at the kitchen table. The kids were clustered about, talking among themselves and letting us adults chat. Jewell had put a big slow cooker full of her famous red chili on the table. When she took the lid off, the spicy garlic and hot peppers filled the room with the smell of the south-west.

Quickly, she filled the soup bowls and set them while The Brat placed two baskets of cornbread and a crock of butter on the table.

Everything was ready, and we sat down.

"Let me say a quick prayer," I said. As is the custom in our family, we all held hands to pray.

"Thank you, Father, for this food and bless the hands of the one who prepared it. I thank you for the guest at our table and that you bless our time together. And Father, I ask you to meet the needs of those who go hungry this day. In Jesus's name," I said.

We all said "Amen," and the hands that had held each other a second before were now reaching for the cornbread and spoons.

"So, Eva. How's it going?" I asked.

She swallowed the chili she'd been eating. I was surprised that a girl from Germany, a place that is not exactly known for spicy foods, had developed the asbestos tongue and stomach required to enjoy the meals we take for granted in the American South West.

"I miss Max, Will," she said. I saw her eyes sadden a little. "It's strange not having him around."

"Does he call?" Jewell asked.

She nodded. "Every night if he can. He said to tell you guys, 'Hello.' "

"Tell him I said 'hi' too, and that I'm praying for him." I stirred the chili to mix the onions and shredded cheese a little.

"I appreciate that, and yes, I'll tell him."

"Does he say if it's helping him any?" Jewell asked.

She shook her head. "He doesn't talk about it much. He did say he's starting to understand why he's so angry all the time."

"Oh," I said.

"They gave him a diagnosis of Post Traumatic Stress Disorder. He got it in the war."

That didn't surprise me. Almost everyone had come back with at least some issues. For months we'd walked on eggshells, waiting for Saddam to drive his tanks into Saudi Arabia. We were isolated in a lot of ways, the constant go-go-go, and then days of combat. While we saw mostly the aftermath of the carnage, it was still enough to overwhelm most and leave them changed forever.

"What can they do about it?" Jewell asked.

Eva sipped some of the soup. A small smile curled her lips. She was enjoying her meal, and that was a good thing.

"They're putting him on some medications. More counseling," she said. "He still has a long way to go."

She looked at me, and her head cocked slightly. "You went through more than he did, Will. And you were a policeman before you went into the army. Don't you have PTSD?"

"I do," I said, swallowing some food. "What's different between me and everyone else is I have PTSD. It doesn't have me!"

Jewell nodded at me. "God healed him."

A confused look came over Eva's face. "I'm not sure I understand."

"Healing," Jewell said. "God healed him."

"I'm afraid I still don't understand," she said.

"In the Bible," Jewell explained. "We read where Jesus healed people. Everything from being lame right up to raising them from the dead. Will asked God to heal him."

"That simple?" she asked.

"Not entirely," I answered. The Bible also tells us we need to confess our sins. I hate that choice of words because it sounds like we did something wrong. What I needed to confess and work through was all the years of hurts and pains caused by police work and combat. Part of it is getting it out there, looking at it, and then letting it go.

"If you need to forgive, you forgive. If you need to let go, you let go. You make a choice not to live there anymore. Then God can help you. Until you let him, it isn't going to happen."

"But isn't God all-powerful. Couldn't he just make it go away."

"Sure he could," Jewell answered. "But people miss the point. It's our dependence on God that makes us better when it comes to things like this." She paused.

"You're familiar with the story of how Israel wandered in the desert for forty years after their deliverance from Egypt, aren't you?"

"I've seen the movie," she answered, with a smile. "They don't exactly encourage many of us to read the Bible in Germany anymore."

"Really?"

"Really,' Eva said.

Jewell looked at me with a shocked look, and I nodded. She just went on with the story, "God led Israel through the desert to their promised land. They sent a team of spies in to go and to scout out this promised land they'd bed led to.

"But they came back with stories of powerful armies and walled cities that were fortresses.

"They told Moses that the men were so big that they looked puny compared to them."

"Were they?" Eva asked.

"Physically?" Jewell shrugged. "I rather doubt it. A lot of theologians try to say they were giants, but as a counselor, I say they weren't. I'm sure there were some pretty good sized people there. They called them giants, but they probably weren't much bigger than the spies who went in were.

"The spies came back saying to everyone that they'd be squashed like bugs by these people.

"But there was only one group of spies that gave a different report. They said, yeah, they got armies, and there are walled cities, but as for giants? No, we sure didn't see any of those.

"But, so what. Even if there are giants and we missed them somehow, we've God on our side.

"We can take them."

"I remember that," Eva said. "So why did they end up wandering the wilderness for all those years?"

"Well, the spies who gave the negative report were partially right. They were bugs in the sight of the people that lived there. As I said, they weren't any larger than the Israelites were.

"It was the Israelites that were small in their own sight. They were still thinking like slaves. They couldn't get past that, and as long as they kept seeing themselves as slaves and as nothing, that's all they were ever going to be.

"So, they ended up wandering the desert for years, kicking butt and taking names. And when forty years had passed, this was a whole different breed of people. Now they were the giants, and they were tired of wandering. So there's the point.

"They had to grow past that slave mentality. You've got to get tired of wandering, and you've got to change the way you look at yourself. God doesn't see you as a battered wife. He sees you as tall, beautiful, and courageous."

I remember I saw a tear in her eye that day.

Now, as I stood at the door of the church, Max and Eva pulled up in his Ford pickup. He went around and opened the door for her as a man should.

"Just like the old days," I told Jewell.

Max wore jeans, a red plaid shirt, and his cowboy hat. Eva also wore jeans and a plaid shirt. They weren't at all out of place with the cowboys, farmers, shopkeepers, and everyday families who attended.

My biggest concern was wondering how they were going to handle this church.

The small Cowboy Church wasn't the quiet, "sit on your hands, sing a couple of hymns and tune out everything else" kind of church.

Not this one.

This church had its roots in the old Pentecostal movement, and some of the high energy voltage from ages past still coursed through the congregation. These folks were the raise your hands, throw your head back and shout "Amen," fall on their face before the altar types. A lot of folks called these kinds of folks, "Holy Rollers."

I wouldn't argue the "Holy" part, but I had yet to see anyone roll around. I'd come to learn that this old-time religion wasn't everyone's cup of tea. A lot of people liked their God not so nailed to a cross and not their spine. They wanted Him kept trapped between the covers of a book on the coffee table, and visited on Easter and Christmas. Most people acted like they were afraid if they prayed out loud, God just might hear them.

Be that as it may. If plugging into the very thing that can change your life scares you off, then you deserve your lot in life.

And I kept having the nagging feeling this was Max's last chance. I hoped I was wrong. I smiled as they came through the door.

That smile got broader as I glanced at my wife.

Jewell was dressed in her Sunday best and looked radiant. Being the daughter of a preacher, she wouldn't have looked any other way. The kids were all dressed neatly, as well.

If there were anyone in this church not so neat, it would have been me. I looked like I was ready to go to work. Jeans, boots, a white long sleeve shirt, and the black vest that I wore almost every day. But Sundays were a bit different. I buttoned the top button on the shirt. The tie was a clip-on. I'd never learned to tie a Windsor knot, and besides, a tie was the first thing a bad guy grabbed for. My crossed pistols tie tac completed the ensemble.

I looked more like a cowboy than a detective. The only thing that would have clued someone in otherwise was the Walther PPK tucked into a belt holster and my badge in my wallet.

You just never knew who might show up for church and for reasons other than to hear the Word of God.

While I hadn't exactly signed on the dotted line, so to speak, God and I had gone from casual strangers to good friends. I realized that He was providing the structure I needed to overcome the pains and hurts in my life.

I was sure that a little dose of it wouldn't hurt Max or Eva one bit.

"It's good to see you guys," I said, giving Eva and Max each a hug.

"A deal is a deal," he said.

I hoped he wasn't just trying to amuse me and that he might get something out of today. The problem was that if you had no interest in becoming a Christian before age fifteen, then the chances went down drastically when you became an adult. That made me a rarity. Maybe it was because I'd always been interested in the things of God. Perhaps all I needed was a nudge.

I hoped the same was true of Max.

But I noticed he watched two daughters of local ranchers, walk past. It was much more than a glance, but a definite undressing of them with his eyes. They felt his eyes, glanced at him, and smiled.

He returned it.

Max, I thought. Your wife is right here. Somehow, I got the feeling that even if I'd shaken him to get his attention and explained that to him, it wouldn't have made a difference. He'd have checked the girls out anyway. I turned my attention back to the conversation.

"How's it going?" Jewell asked Eva quietly.

"He's staying sober," she answered. "And thank you both for that recommendation with the Hospice Center. I got the roving nurse's job."

That was good to hear. It meant traveling and more money. Before she was doing just office work. Now it was hands-on nursing. I didn't envy her job. Making it comfortable for the dying was much more than a job. It was a calling from God.

"Lunch after services?" I asked.

"Where?" Max asked.

"I was thinking of Campus Café. Best cinnamon rolls in town."

Max nodded and then looked at Eva. "I could use a good cinnamon roll."

"Our pastor and his wife will be tagging along," I said. I looked where Pastor Morgan was standing and chuckled. I noted his jeans were fitting a little snug. "He likes a good cinnamon roll too."

"He's the guy you've been talking too?" Max asked.

"He's the one. Been there, done that got the t-shirt. He was a SEAL team medic. The Morgans are good people."

I noticed that Eva was looking at the stage at the electric piano, guitars, and drum set. It seemed less like the churches, I was sure was she accustomed to, and more like what might be in a Cowboy Bar. She looked at Jewell and asked, "What kind of music do you have here?"

Jewell smiled. She couldn't resist the opening. "We've got both kinds. Praise and Worship."

Eva got the joke and chuckled. Max stood there with a blank look on his face and said, "I think I missed something."

Several folks came by, and I introduced them around. Community is what a good church is supposed to be about, and you get that by building relationships. The Smith's, long-time members, knew Eva. She was the nurse working with their elderly grandmother. I knew the old woman was in the final days of her life, and it would be terrible to see her go. But she was strong in the Lord. When she closed her eyes here, she'd open them there.

The praise and worship group went up on stage and began turning on the piano, and guitars. A few trial chords and Tony, the leader of the group, came up to the microphone and with the electricity of a prizefight announcer called out, "Good morning and welcome to our service! Let's all stand and give God a big old shout of praise and thanks for our just being alive today!" And every living, breathing soul stood up, and a roar went up from dozens of throats and hands went right up into the air.

I glanced over at Max and could tell this had taken him a little aback. I smiled at him. He hadn't run for the door, and that was 95% of the battle.

A projector beamed the words of the song onto the screen, and we all broke into a hymn quickly followed by another. The first several hymns rolled with the twang of the guitars and the beat of the drums like something you'd almost expect to hear at a concert. And between numbers and with the music still playing, Tony said, "Thank you Lord for your sacrifice, that means my past is no more. Thank you for the goodness you've shown me in my life. Thank you for answered prayers and thank you for not giving me everything I've asked for. Thank you for being real in my life. For taking a kid from the streets and making him into a better person . . ." And the music changed, slowed, became majestic, and eyes closed, hands raised, everyone just let God and his goodness wash over them like a tide.

Our singing went on for several minutes, and then Pastor Morgan stood up, got behind the pulpit, and thanked the group. He turned to the congregation and said, "Thank you all for coming, and may God bless you. May he also open our hearts and minds to hear and receive his word today. Amen!"

And the congregation roared out a loud "Amen" in response.

Pastor Morgan looked out over the congregation. "Do we have any newcomers today?"

Eva raised her hand, and I smiled at Max's reaction. The look on his face showed he'd just wanted to blend into the background, but now that couldn't happen. One of the older women came over and gave them both a small basket. It had pens, a pad, a card with the church contact information, a card to fill out and drop in the offering basket, and a couple of freshly baked scones and a small jar of jelly.

"And while we're welcoming new faces, greet one another," Pastor said. For a minute or two, the placed dissolved into neighbors shaking hands, women hugging each other, and chatting.

Soon, everyone went back to their seats, and Pastor Morgan launched into his message. "Michael Jackson. How many of you like Michael?" A few of the younger folks raised their hands. "Michael Jackson has a song called 'The Man in the Mirror!' Maybe you've heard it." He sang a little bit of it, and then went on. "Most of the cowboys and farmers in here cringed a little, and I'm sure you guys thought, 'Hey if it ain't Waylon Jennings or Johnny Cash, I'm changing the station!'"

That got a laugh.

"Anyway, this is not the Gospel according to Michael Jackson. But it is about who that person is looking back at us in the mirror every morning. I know a lot of us get up, we go to the mirror, and we see that person. I'm sure that most of our thoughts are anything but reflective.

"I know when I get up, I see the sunlight through the windows. I hear birds chirping outside. And then I get to the mirror, look in, and you know what I do next?"

He paused for effect and then smiled. "I look in the mirror and go, "Eck!"

Everyone laughed.

"For the rest of you, you look at the reflection and go, 'Good Lord, I need to cover up that gray' or 'how the heck did I get that old?' You young people probably look in and go, 'Oh no! A zit! My life is over!' "

I glanced around. Everyone was chuckling, and I could see he had the congregation hooked. In high school, Robert Morgan had been an excellent public speaker. Being a preacher had only improved him.

"But the mirror shows only the outside. When you look in the mirror, you also see your eyes, and it's who's behind those eyes the mirror can't show. Let's talk about the piece the mirror doesn't see. Turn with me in your Bibles to Luke 18," he said, flipping through the Bible on the podium. The sound of his page-turning blended in with the dry leaf rustling of dozens of other listeners sorting through their Bibles. "If you need help finding it, you'll find it someplace between Genesis and Revelation."

There were chuckles at the well-worn joke, and a lot more turning of pages, some old and worn, others crisp and new.

"Let's take a look at verse 9. This is the parable that Jesus told about the Pharisee and the Tax Collector. Most of you know the story, but let me read it to you.

"'To some who were confident of their own righteousness and looked down on everyone else, Jesus told this parable: 'Two men went up to the temple to pray, one a Pharisee and the other a tax collector. The Pharisee stood by himself and prayed: 'God, I thank you that I am not like other people—robbers, evildoers, adulterers—or even like this tax collector. I fast twice a week and give a tenth of all I get.'

"'But the tax collector stood at a distance. He would not even look up to heaven, but beat his breast and said, 'God, have mercy on me, a sinner.'

"'I tell you that this man, rather than the other, went home justified before God. For all those who exalt themselves will be humbled, and those who humble themselves will be exalted.'"

He paused and looked around. "The Pharisees prided themselves on being the best of the best. They had a bunch of laws that governed everything they did. You did this before eating. You did that with your shoes. The whole thing was they took a few basic things God had told them to do and blew them out of proportion. Before too long, what they did had become more important than God. They looked in the mirror, and if they were meeting the letter of the law, then they were good to go. Don't believe me? Look at the text. He's saying, I do this, and I do that. If you were to ask him, he'd give you this big list of what he's done. I'm sure he had a checklist someplace that he marked off against just to make sure he was good to go. Tithes? Sure, I give tithes! Pray every day too. I do it when I'm supposed to, at the exact time, and for the exact amount of time. I come to the temple, I get down on my knees, and I pray to God. Fasting. Hey, I've lost weight fasting, don't I look good? I'm so cool, he thought!"

Pastor went on. "He was pretty cool." He paused for a second, letting folks digest the picture of this man. "Or at least he thought so," he went on. "Everything this guy did was external. Nothing he mentioned had anything to do with who he was. Want an example? Let's be honest about it guys, a good looking girl walks by in skin-tight jeans, and what's the first thought that goes through our minds." He paused, smiled, and in a mocking lilt said, 'Oh, yeah, baby ... .'"

There were a few nervous giggles. Everyone knew where he was going. It was clear that more than a few of these cowboys had checked out the cowgirls. I managed a glance over at Max. He looked like he had been hit with a board.

"So what did Jesus have to say on the subject of looking at a woman with lust? He said, and I'm paraphrasing it here, 'Hey, you look at a woman with lust in your heart? Well, you might not have done anything physically with her, but your desires prove you might as well have. It's still adultery, guys!' Don't believe me? Check out Matthew 5, verse 28.

"Now, did the Pharisee do that? I don't know, but he's a man and subject to at least the temptation. I'm sure his checklist included 'Did I sleep with a woman, not my wife?' As long as he could check 'No' right next to it, he was OK.

"I'm sure his checklist said nothing about, 'Oh, yeah, baby!'"

There were a few chuckles.

"How about gossip? Did he talk trash about someone? He sure did. He was running down the tax collector right there in front of God. What does the Bible say about that? Try this on for size. 'They were filled with all manner of unrighteousness, evil, covetousness, malice. They are full of envy, murder, strife, deceit, maliciousness. They are gossips.'

"You'll find that in Romans 1, verse 29." He paused. "That's a rather scathing comment, don't you think.

"So what we have here is a guy who is standing before God on an ego trip. Gee, God, check me out, he said. Ain't I cool? Aren't you lucky to have me on your team? I'm so cool and such a sweet guy that if you gave me hot tea, I'd give it back to you sweetened and in a frosty mug."

Pastor laughed. "This guy is in love with himself and can't see beyond the end of his nose that he's just as bad as everyone else. He was justified in his own eyes. I do this. I do that. I'm playing the game. I'm sure not like that loser across the aisle there."

He paused, looked up, and said, "Let's talk about that loser. The Bible tells us he was a tax collector. In the Jewish world, there was almost no one lower than a tax collector. Lepers were a lot higher in the social registry than they were. Just like the folks who work for the IRS today, this man worked for the government. Today, someone says, 'Oh, I work for the IRS' and folks cringe a little. Back then, it was worse because he worked for a government they didn't want. He also worked for himself.

"It might have been a bit different if Israel had been its own country, but it wasn't. It was a conquered land. A foreign power had come in and imposed their will upon them. They'd given them a king that they didn't want. They'd put a Roman governor over them, and Roman soldiers patrolled the streets. And anyone who complained was quickly jailed or killed.

"And here's this guy. This loser has a commission from the Roman Empire to rob people. He takes money from their pockets and gives it to a government they didn't want and hated.

"Now, if that's not bad enough, then there's a little bonus. The tax collector only had to give a certain percentage of whatever he collected to the government. The rest was his to keep. And there didn't seem to be any real guidelines on how much they could collect, all he was required was he give 'x' amount of it to the empire. The Bible, the great historian Josephus, and other related sources tell us that some of these tax collectors were wealthy men.

"Most viewed the Tax Collector as a traitor and a thief. So, the Pharisee was right. He wasn't like this man."

He paused before going on. "He was worse. When the Pharisee looked into the mirror, he saw a pretty cool guy. The Tax Collector saw something different.

"The Bible says it was the Tax Collector who went away justified before God.

"Why? Maybe it's because he wasn't wasting God's time. Someplace, somewhere, he'd taken a good look at himself. Perhaps it happened when he'd gotten up, washed, and looked in his eyes and wondered who that was looking back. He had to ask the question, 'Who am I really?' He took God's yardstick and asked, 'How do I measure up to the only yardstick that matters.'

"He found out he couldn't."

"This man didn't even dare look up to God. He knew his sins were so bad he didn't even know where to start to list them. If there was a commandment out there, it was a bet he'd broken it. He'd stolen from people. He'd robbed the Empire as well. He'd condemned whole families to poverty.

"Who knew what they'd done in the holy name of survival. Had children starved to death or been pushed into servitude because of his actions? Had his actions forced women to resort to prostitution to have food for their children? Had men taken their own lives because they'd lost everything? Was the crushing weight of the poverty he inflicted more than people could stand?"

He looked around and then said, almost quietly, "What we do has an impact on others."

I wondered what that was about.

"Someplace, he saw what he'd done. He knew one thing, he had sinned. He was anything but perfect. It scared him so badly, he didn't even dare raise his head. The Bible says all he could do was beat his chest and beg for mercy and repeat over and over, "I'm a sinner.'

"And the Bible says he went away 'justified' before God."

I looked over at Max. His eyes were wide, and I was astonished to see a tear roll down his face. Somehow, this simple country preacher had whacked him right between the eyes and was connecting.

"What does that word 'Justified' mean? It means God found him righteous. God is a forgiving God, and all we have to do is stop being a phony with him. The Tax Collector ended the charade.

"And maybe . . . Just maybe, we're running a con game against God. Is it time we stop the charade?"

He looked at the congregation. You could have heard a pin drop in the place. "Are you tired of being a phony with God? Are you're tired of trying to be something you can't be and know it? Maybe it's time you came clean and admitted it. If so, come up. Or if you want to come up here and spend some time with God, the altars are open."

Carol, the Pastor's wife, had stepped up behind the piano and was quietly playing as he concluded.

"Come on down, folks," he invited.

And then I heard Max say, "I'm going down there. I need to get it right."

Max, followed closely by Eva, went down to the altar and prayed. Jewell and I stood behind them and prayed with them. And I remember thinking that maybe they were going to be OK.

Events would prove that I didn't have much of a future as a prophet.

CHAPTER THIRTEEN

THE BULLET

Max and Eva came to church for a month straight. Once when services were over, we all spilled out of the church. Pastor Morgan and his wife were standing at the door, chatting with everyone.

I usually tried to give them space, but this time we stood on the walkway, talking with Max, Eva, and The Smiths.

It seemed the old woman had had a dream. That she was wading ashore onto a beach, and a man was standing there waiting for her. The dream had brought her a lot of comfort. In it, she wasn't an old woman anymore, but young and healthy again.

I think we all knew what the dream meant.

After several minutes, the congregation melted away to their pickups, jeeps, and homes. Pastor Morgan and Carol came over.

"Want to grab some lunch?" Pastor asked us.

"Sounds like a plan. Where?"

"Campus Café. Where else?" he said. "I invited your buddy Max and his wife along, but he turned me down."

I could use a good cinnamon roll, I thought.

But I wasn't sure about why he'd invited Max beyond his just being a friend. Maybe he thought if he lowered the wall between them, Max might come in and speak with him.

I was a little disappointed with Max. He came to church, but other than that, he kept a low profile. I'd invited him to coffee, lunch, and aside from the one time he met me at the Romeo Lunch, he'd either turned me down or been a no show.

I'd even placed my Bible on the table, and all he could talk about was the old days, and how his business was going to make him rich.

I was seriously wondering if his "conversion" had all been show.

"You folks ready to go?" Carol asked.

"We are," Jewell said.

Pastor Morgan was already thinking about getting there. "We'll drive."

That sounded like a good idea.

We all walked out and loaded up. We stepped out of the church just in time for me to see Max's pickup turn down the road.

I couldn't help but think I was failing with him.

Carol drove, and soon we turned down the Waverly Road towards 285.

"So, Will," Pastor said. "What happened?"

"What do you mean?"

"What I read in the papers. That someone took a shot at you."

I realized Pastor Morgan was eyeing me. "That's one reason I wanted to talk to you. What's going on?. It sounds as if it's been rough out there."

"Being shot at tends to make it a rough," I answered.

"Any suspects?" Carol asked.

"Got a ton of suspects, just no proof to nail it to them. There are a few people around who wouldn't mind seeing me dead. But I don't think that's what they were trying to do."

Pastor Morgan nodded. "How you taking this Jewell?"

"Oh, I'm upbeat, quoting scripture, acting like nothing ever happened."

"In other words, terrified," Carol said.

"That I am,' she said.

"I hope you don't mind that I'm bringing a friend to church with me these days, Pastor." I meant the PPK tucked in my belt.

"What are you packing?" he asked?"

"Walthers PPK. I figure if it's good enough for James Bond, its good enough for me."

"So, what happened?" he asked. I noticed Carol leaned back a bit to hear the story. Jewell had already heard it a few times.

I stopped and thought it through, and then started talking. "We'd been running Dodge City for a while now. We've covered all kinds of interesting things like traffic stops. I drug in some of the stuff we did at Ft. Riley with our MPs, and applied it here."

"Where do you guys do the training?" Pastor Morgan asked.

"It floats around," I said.

"So, what have you done so far?"

"Well, traffic stops, as I mentioned. We've done domestic disturbance training, Incident command, more crime scene processing, and analysis. We spent a couple of months on that one. Then we did hostage negotiations, and more recently, we've trained on entry techniques and gas masks."

"Think you'll ever need it?" he asked.

"I sure hope not," was the best answer I could give. "But sooner or later, we might."

"What else do you have planned?"

"Well, in light of recent developments, evasive driving just popped up on the radar."

"I would think it would." Pastor said. "How did it help you get through your most recent problem?"

I smiled. "You have an amazing ability to get one to talk, Pastor." He knew I was dancing around the issue, so he forced me into it. "The tricks I know might have saved my life."

"Tell me about it."

No sense in putting it off, I thought. "Well, some of it you already know from the papers. So, let's talk about the rest of it."

I let my mind drift off, remembering that day in late October.

October is one of my favorite times of the year. Winter is just a few short months away, but by the same token, the hard work of summer is over. As a boy, summer was all about working hard. I drove cattle, fixed fence, hauled bails, and chopped wood.

Summer was all about work.

And then September comes. We went back to school, and at last, I had a chance to rest. Someplace around the middle or end of September, we brought the cows down from the mountains.

Bringing the cows down always signaled a major shift in the typical day to day work. Yes, bitter cold was on its way. Yes, the cows would be calving in that cold. We'd have to keep water holes open and feed the cows. But the hard work of summer was over. There would be ample opportunity to sit down, warm ourselves by the fire, and maybe even watch television.

As a cop, it also signaled a slowdown. Most people stayed indoors during the winter. Of course, they got on each other's nerves, and there's almost always a spike in domestics.

One thing I loved about the fall was the change in leaves. Driving up Conejos Canyon was always a treat. The aspens turned shades of red, orange, gold, and yellow that just never seemed to exist before. The canyon and the mountains would be veined with the yellows and reds intermixed with the evergreens.

I always enjoyed the ride up, even if I was headed up to a crime scene.

This call was routine. The caller had reported he'd come in to go hunting and found his cabin broke into near Platoro. The patrol deputy was tied up in the north end of the county.

I was at the Sheriff's office, working on cases when I heard the call come through.

"What's up?" I asked the dispatcher.

"B and E up towards Platoro. Cabin break-in. Caller is John Coward of Dallas."

 1

111111

erer William R. Ablan

I nodded. I knew John. I wondered what he was doing up here so late in the year. He was an old cavalryman from when the Army still rode horses. I always enjoyed talking to him, and he was a good storyteller.

"I'll head up," I said. It had been a quiet afternoon, and a chance to go up and do some leaf-peeping was welcome. Let the patrol deputy know I'd handle it. I'd end up going to process the site for prints anyway.

I got my notebook and walked out to Trigger. October had been beautiful with temperatures in the 60s, and no snow in the high country.

"Conejos SO, Conejos 4. 10-8, 10-76 Platoro," I called once I had the cruiser started and was pulling out of the driveway.

"Conejos 4, Conejos SO. Copy your 10-76 Platoro. Time 1134 hrs."

It had been a quiet and lazy day. I ran into only a few cars during my drive, and it looked like everyone in the county was settling in for their long winter naps. The little towns of Las Mesitas and Mogote were quiet. The most activity I saw was a farmer on a tractor out in a field. I rounded the corner and drove through Foxcreek,

This time of year, it was just one of the many sleepy hamlets this time of year. A lot of folks came up and lived there in the summertime, but would head out after hunting season was over.

Locals called them "Snow Birds" because they didn't care for the snow.

About a mile outside Foxcreek, I entered what I thought of as the start of the real forest. It was like someone drew a line, and the junipers suddenly began

237

to give way to pines on the other side of it. Some were somewhat scraggly to be sure, but in my mind, this is where the forest started.

I was admiring the distant aspens when the right side of my windshield shattered. Trigger seemed to buck from the loud thud and impact.

As fragments of glass sprayed out and over me from the windshield, the car seemed to scream like a mortally wounded animal. Smoke was billowing up around me, and it took me a second to realize the scream, and the smoke was coming from the car.

I'd slammed down hard on the brakes. As I was trying to register that something had just happened, another hole, this time a little larger than the last blew out right under it.

While the intelligent part of me tried to catch up on what was happening, another part already knew and was reacting.

My reflexes and training had taken over.

"Someone has just taken a couple of shots at you," a voice screamed in my brain.

As it seemed to happen so many times, the calm, cool, logical part of me stepped aside, and something deep and powerful took over.

It was like I was watching myself do things automatically without thinking about it. The conscious part of me was now a mere spectator while another part slammed into automatic.

Part of that automatic response was to freeze a picture of the area into my memory. I saw what appeared to be a puff of smoke, just off to my one o'clock, and up the hill behind a fallen tree. That same part filed that image away like one would save a file into a computer.

"What do you do when someone is shooting at your patrol car?" I remembered asking that question of my MPs in a Dodge City course.

Many were all for stopping, taking cover, and returning fire. While that might seem like the manly thing to do, it's also the most dangerous.

The correct answer is, "you run like hell."

The car was shuddering to a stop, every bolt in it groaning from the sudden stop. Trigger had barely stopped and, I'd thrown it into reverse and floored it. The big 440 Magnum howled as the four-barrel carb flashed open and fuel dumped into the waiting engine. The car shuddered in protest as the motor delivered every bit of horsepower it could into the drive chain. The tires screamed on the road as they dug into the pavement for traction. I'd put one arm over the seat and was steering backward at almost 50 miles an hour. Thank God the road was empty. Otherwise, this maneuver would have been dangerous in the extreme.

Like I'd done dozens of times before in training, I let up off the gas, and cranked the wheel down counterclockwise from the 12 to the 6. Almost instantly, the nose of the car swung around in a 180.

The maneuver I was doing is called a "J turn." It's also called a "Rockford Turn" because James Garner did it all the time on the TV show, The Rockford Files.

When Rockford did it, he was always so calm and collected and ended the maneuver with a grin on his face and not a hair out of place.

What they never showed on Rockford is what really happens.

As the car began to whip around, plain old fashioned centrifugal force rears its ugly head. The G-forces climbed from the sudden stop to accelerating backward and then whipping around, and everything loose in the car seems to explode. Every piece of dirt under the seat, every coin ever lost, every pen dropped, comes exploding out in a tidal wave of debris. I watched this flood of debris come sliding out from under the seat, joining my briefcase and clipboard on the opposite side of the car.

My body was trying to follow the centrifugal force induced flood. Only the seat belt and my own iron grip on the wheel kept me from falling that way. The straps of the seatbelt cut into my waist and shoulder. It seemed that every muscle in my body had tripled in weight.

Like I was trained, I kept watching the area where I wanted to come out of the spin.

A wave of dizziness swept over me from the sudden increase in G-forces, but my body was still on automatic.

I was halfway through the spin. Trigger leaned over hard, and as I shifted it from reverse to drive, I had a terrifying feeling that the car was going to roll right over and keep on rolling.

But the G-forces subsided, the tidal wave of debris stopped, and the car was coming up on having made a half-circle.

Instantly I cranked the wheel right back from the 6 to the 12 and punched the accelerator. The car seemed to skip as it gathered momentum, and then the tires grabbed, and I was accelerating out of the kill zone.

The engine was screaming like a banshee as I punched free of the cloud of tire smoke. Within seconds I was hundreds of yards away from the area from where the shot had originated. I kept going until I was two miles away, slammed on the breaks, and skidded to a stop.

Only then did I grab the radio.

"Conejos SO, Conejos 4," I called, My voice sounded weak and shaky. It wasn't the only thing shaking. So was my hand.

"Conejos 4, go ahead," came the reply.

"Joe," I said. "Get hold of Conejos 1, and start rolling me some back up this way. I'm one east of the KOA on Hiway 17.

"Someone just put a couple of rounds into my car."

I took a deep breath, and Pastor Morgan said. "So, what happened next?"

"We got a roadblock set up, and they started running every car that was coming down the canyon. Rio Arriba did the same on their end, but there are plenty of places a suspect might have gone," I said. "Once I got a few more cops in the area, I took a squad-sized element up to the area where I thought the shot had come from. Whoever had fired the shots was long gone, but we found two empty casings placed next to each other, and a Mosin-Nagant rifle next to them."

"Any prints?" Carol asked.

"Nothing. The weapon was clean, and so were the spent casings." I said. "And there's no record of the weapon ever coming into the United States."

There should have been a paper trail someplace on a Russian rifle. In this case, there was a big fat nothing. What's worse is there were only about a billion Mosin's made, and they've been farmed out all over the world. It could have come from anywhere.

"Why a Russian rifle?" Julie asked. The way she said made it clear to me she was thinking two or three steps ahead/

"Well, the Mosin is one of the best bolt action rifles ever made," Pastor Morgan explained. "And it's got some great range."

"I'm glad they were lousy shots," Jewell said.

"That's where I have a little trouble," I said. I don't think the shooter intended to hit me."

Pastor Morgan frowned. "I'm not following you."

I thought about it for a second and then said, "I think it was a warning."

"Warning against what?"

I shrugged. "I don't know yet. I think someone was trying to scare me off."

I didn't have the data to figure that one out yet.

If someone sends you a warning shot, they usually tell you what it's all about.

What I didn't know was that this was the first shot in what would prove to be a very long and protracted war that wouldn't end for a couple of years.

"And what are you doing to protect Jewell and the kids?" Pastor asked.

I hadn't thought much about it. The thought that my family might be in danger was something I needed to think about right then and there. Maybe my mind hadn't wanted to go there. Or perhaps I felt that the imaginary line drawn between the two counties was some barrier that nothing would cross.

Pastor's simple question made me pause and think. If they were trying to scare me off, pulling something on my family might be next.

"As much as I hate to admit," I said, "very little."

"Maybe that's where you need to start. I've got a spare 38 if you need it."

"I might take you up on that," I said as we pulled up and parked in the parking lot of the Campus Café. I got out, rushed over, and helped Jewell out.

"Smells good," she said. She wasn't lying about that. I could smell the sweet smell of the warm syrup they served with pancakes and waffles from outside.

"Have you eaten here, Baby?" I asked.

"I used to work in Alamosa, remember. Campus Café has always been a good place to eat."

We were approaching the door when it opened. A man and a woman were coming out.

My good mood vanished as I went to Red Alert. I grabbed the door and held it open for him. I nodded slightly at him, not once taking my eyes off him.

"Good morning, Mr. Wheaton," I said.

I looked at the woman, wondering who she was. She was young, blonde, rather pretty, and about half his age. The way she carried herself said she wasn't from around her.

She's Ruskie, a voice in the back of my head said. She did look like the girls from the St. Petersburg area, I thought.

David Wheaton nodded in return.

"Good morning, Detective," he answered, glancing over at Jewell, the Morgan's, and the Laurie's. I realized Wheaton was doing the same thing I was. He was remembering faces and details and filing them away into a database he kept in his brain.

I'd done the same with the woman already. I had remembered a lot about her and filed her in the "Potential Threat – More info needed" category. I'm sure Wheaton had done the same with the members of my little group.

The girl moved up on the threat list when I noticed she appeared to be cataloging us as well. I wondered why a Russian girl would be interested in us? And why she would behave in such a fashion.

Americans and Russians tend to be very much alike, in they ignore a lot of people. If you're not a friend or relative, they will ignore anyone they don't know.

She wasn't doing that. We all seemed to be of intense fascination to her.

We went in, and Jewell asked quietly, "Who's that?"

"David Wheaton. The man who complained to the newspaper about me," I answered.

"And the girl with him?"

"Heck if I know. I think she's Russian."

"Hmmm," she said. "Russian girl. Russian gun."

I had to admit, it was an interesting coincidence.

As restaurants go, the place was pretty simple. It had a mom and pop feel to it, with plenty of booths and open tables. It took a couple of minutes while the waitresses wrestled two small tables together to accommodate us, but within a few minutes, we sat down.

"That somebody, you know?" Pastor Morgan asked.

I nodded.

"I don't think he likes you much," he said.

"He doesn't," I confirmed.

Pastor Morgan was doing a pretty good job of reading my mind. "Hey, just because you're paranoid doesn't mean they aren't out to get you."

I recognized the quote from Catch-22 and nodded. I put the thoughts behind me and enjoyed my breakfast with friends, trying to forget that someone was out to get me.

CHAPTER FOURTEEN

"TWAS THE NIGHT BEFORE CHRISTMAS . . ."

Christmas has always been a magical time of year for me. There's snow and gaily lit Christmas trees, and Midnight Mass is said while the organ plays softly in the background. All the churches are decked out with lights and Christmas trees and candles glitter behind stained glass windows.

Then there was the holiday get-togethers, the opening of presents, and seeing relatives you haven't seen in months or years. It's a time of magic and miracles when almost anything can happen, and the whole world seems to stand still with hushed anticipation.

But since becoming a police officer, Christmas has been one of the days that makes me cringe a little. The top of the list was the fact that working holidays were a given. You're away from the kids, spouse, family, friends, church, trees, and presents. And while you wait with hushed anticipation, it isn't for a miracle.

The whole world feels like a powder keg, and you're waiting for it to explode. The bars are full of people who don't always get along. Music that has zero to do with the Christ child's birth or even Santa Claus comes out of amplifiers at a volume that threatens to shatter glass.

Then there are drunk drivers going to and fro, every roll of their tires threatening to turn "Oh Holy Night" into "oh Terrible Night."'

As I walked down the street, watching the revelers, I couldn't help but wonder how many of them I'd be taking a professional interest in before the Sun came up.

It was a rare night for me. I was in uniform. I had a badge pinned on, a Sam Browne around my waist, my pistol at my side.

Tonight was about making extra money. Holidays are rough on small PDs, and Antonito PD was always shorthanded. Tonight, I'd earn an additional $260.00. That would pay a lot of bills.

I hadn't worn a police uniform since before joining the Army. Not that I felt unsure of myself. Being an MP had just made me a better cop.

It's just that a detective doesn't wear a uniform much.

RJ and I were working together tonight. The town was full of cars dragging main, the bars were Standing Room Only, and it was way more than the two APD officers could handle safely. So the town contracted the

Sheriff's Office to help out. Those of us that were able signed on to make some extra money.

Jewell and her band, The Boys plus One, were playing at one of the local bars. She could make $600.00 for a weekend gig. Holidays always commanded more. Between us, we'd make nearly $1300.00 for this weekend's work. That was a month's wages for me and then some.

If it weren't for what the band brought in and the occasional side job, we'd have gone under long ago.

We had already done a couple of walkthroughs of the Mother Lode Bar where they were playing, and I'd had at least talked to her.

It was a rowdy crowd, but I wasn't too concerned about her safety. Her bandmates wouldn't allow anything to happen to her, and being seen with me was usually enough to dissuade anyone from pulling anything. Everyone knew you could do anything you wanted to me. Toss so much as a dirty look at my wife, and I'd ruin your evening.

At least when this night was over, we'd be able to drive home, catch a couple of hours of sleep, and enjoy a Christmas Breakfast of tamales and eggs. We'd wait till morning to open presents with the kids.

"I miss the kind of Christmas we had when I was a kid," I said while watching flakes of snow filter down out of the sky. They glistened like slow falling meteors in the Christmas lights. As they twisted and turned, they caught the different colored lights. The entire effect was like multi-colored confetti drifting from the sky.

RJ nodded. Walking cold streets and working was the last thing he wanted to do tonight.

We watched some girls walk past. They were loud, laughing, and going from one dance to another. They smelled of expensive perfume and cheap whiskey. It was clear they'd had one too many already.

What an evening, I thought. A great evening to get drunk, throw up, pass out, beat up, raped, maybe even killed, all on the same night, and all in the holy name of having a good time.

Man, I thought, I'm getting old thinking that way.

"Do you remember the movie house in La Jara?" RJ asked. He pronounced "La Jara" the way the locals did, by rolling the "R" in the name

We started walking, making sure everyone saw us Cops walking the beat keeps trouble down, and I wanted to keep trouble down. I didn't want to have to work to earn my pay.

My breath came out in puffs, as I answered. "I remember that. Thomas Washeck owned the building. The movie house was closed since before I was born, I think?"

"Yeah, but he'd open it up for Christmas," RJ said. "It was a big deal, and the fire department would bring Santa Claus in."

I smiled, remembering, and RJ went on. "Yeah, kids from all over the county showed up. The fire truck would come up from the fire department, the lights and siren going, and the cops would escort it. And riding in the back of it, old Saint Nick." RJ chuckled. "And he'd be tossing penny candy, and just laughing and waving and having a good time.

"The truck would pull up right in front of the old movie house. He'd get down, wave, and unlock the doors. nd then with a shout, he'd invite us all in, and tell us that an early Christmas treat awaited us."

I watched a blue Pontiac roll past us and down the street. The windows on the car were rolled up against the cold. But the stereo was turned up loud. I could hear the music. Some rap thing full of foul-mouthed words and curses, a great song to be played on Christmas Eve.

"I remember that," I said. "And we'd set there for hours watching Bugs Bunny and Road Runner cartoons, or Mickey's Christmas Carol."

"The first time I ever saw an old Tarzan movie was part of that Christmas movie fest," RJ said. "It was in black and white, I remember."

We walked into the Mother Lode Bar once again. I shook hands with a couple of the locals standing by the door and wished them a Merry Christmas. I could smell the sweet odor of marijuana about them, and they had a drink in their hands. They were always good for a bar fight or two, but they were in a good mood and not itching for any trouble.

The Mother Lode Bar seemed to be wall to wall people. Many were sitting on their favorite barstools. Others were at the tables or booths. Extra tables and chairs had been shoehorned in, leaving almost nowhere to walk. The waitresses grabbed drink orders from the bar that they somehow managed to deliver to the table without spilling them on anyone.

I wondered what the capacity was to the building, and what the Fire Marshall might say, and if he even cared.

The noise level was deafening.

The Boys plus One were belting out Garth Brooks, "I've got friends in low places." The guitars were cranked up loud so the folks on the dance floor could hear it dance to.

Of course, anyone sitting and trying to talk was, in reality, sitting and screaming to be heard over the music, and everyone else was screaming to turn the music up because they couldn't hear it and dance.

We'd made our way up to the bandstand and paused there.

"We're going to take five, so don't go anywhere," Joey, the lead singer, said.

Jewell came out from behind the keyboards and came up to me. She gave me a big hug. "How's it going, Baby?"

"Cold," I said. We hadn't had a White Christmas in years, and I was wondering how much of a zoo the ride home would be. "You guys sound amazing tonight."

"Thanks. It's a good crowd," Jewell said.

"Seen any potential problems?" I asked.

"Not yet," she answered.

I studied the crowd. It seemed good-natured, and I was hoping we'd get away without doing too much work tonight. We chatted with Jewell and the band for a few minutes before looking at my watch. I didn't want to pin us down to one place.

"Baby Love, we've got to get on our rounds," I said.

"Keep checking on us," she said.

"We will," RJ promised, in that tone of voice that told me he was teasing me.

RJ and I plowed like icebreakers through the crowd as we made out way to the door. We nodded at people, smiling, but always making sure a hand was covering our weapons. You never know what people might try.

We watched for a few minutes as people drank, making sure our presence was something people saw and felt. It was a show of force that promised if you did anything stupid, we'd make it a Christmas to remember.

We made our way out and continued walking the streets. We kept an eye on the cars. here hadn't been any car break-ins recently, and thieves hate the cold. But you just never knew when one would strike.

All we saw were people sitting in the vehicles smoking. Most were no doubt hitting the bottle a little, something illegal under city ordinances. But stopping to enforce that meant tying us up, and we wouldn't be available for the inevitable bar fights.

"Getting colder," RJ observed. The light snow that had been falling was getting heavier. It had been warm during the day, and the roads had soaked up the heat from the Sun. Now, the snow was melting as soon as it had hit the pavement, making it wet. As the temperature continued to fall, the wet roads would freeze, and snow would build up over it. The result would be a layer of ice under the snow. It would be just one more challenge for drivers whose driving ability would already be questionable.

We stopped and talked to a few guys who were standing outside, and then continued on our way. We'd walked up by City Hall, cut behind it, and were walking down the alley.

You almost always caught people in the alleys on a Saturday night. Holiday nights just multiplied that by a factor of three. Some were out there smoking dope.

Occasionally, you caught folks having sex. Most of the time, they were merely trying to get the noise out of their ears and talking, and you had to ask them to take the beer back inside.

We were just about to cross the street when we heard it.

Out of reflex, I stepped back into the shadows and cover of the building.

"What the . . ." I started to say, and my hand went to the butt of my gun. I was looking for the source of the muffled crack as I drew the Colt out of its holster.

"That was a gunshot," RJ said a hint of alarm in his voice. He, too, was trying to locate the source of the gunshot.

And the radio began confirming that we had heard a gunshot and advising us that our night had just gone from quiet to terror.

"Antonito 2, Conejos 4, we have a report of shots fired at the Mother Lode Bar! Believed to be one individual with a gun."

"Shit!" RJ exclaimed.

I keyed my lapel mike and responded. "Conejos 4. Roger that. Antonito, we'll cover the back door."

"Already pulling into the front," Antonito 2 responded.

With weapons drawn, we ran across the street. The people on the side street and in the alley had heard the gunshot as well. And when two deputies come charging across the street, guns drawn, people tend to get the hell out of the way.

There were a couple of shouts of "What's going on?"

But we crossed quickly, focused on covering that back door.

I thought that if our shooter was smart, he'd stay in the bar. That would force us to go in after him. There were several hundred people in the bar, and that made for a lot of potential hostages. I was counting on him not being smart, and that he'd try to run. Having to go in after him in a crowded bar was about as dangerous a situation as I could imagine.

We were about twenty yards from the back door of the bar when I saw a man come rushing out. The lighting in the alley was already terrible, so all I saw was the shape of a man. But there was enough light for me to see he held something glittering in his hand.

"Gun!" I shouted as my pistol came up.

"Police, drop your weapon!" RJ shouted. RJ was coming up with his weapon.

I couldn't help but remember the last time I'd pointed a weapon at another human being. For an instant, I found myself back in the rain of Iraq instead of a Christmas snow. For a second, I saw the Iraqi soldier standing in front of me.

No, a piece of me shouted. That happened a long time ago.

"Focus!" I said to myself.

I shoved that memory down. I had a man with what appeared to be a gun almost directly in front of me. Remembering Iraq was the last thing I needed to do.

The man spun towards us before I had a good sight picture, and I saw a flash and heard a crack as the pistol fired.

We'd both seen the gun coming up and were diving for cover before he ever fired. I dove one way, RJ, the other.

The bullet buzzed past us like an angry bee.

I rolled, came up on one knee, pistol extended.

The man was already fleeing down the alley.

I jumped to my feet and continued running after him. RJ was right behind me.

Small caliber weapon, I thought, to judge from the sound of the report. It was either a .22 or a .25 caliber pistol, and a rather small pistol.

That meant he'd be down to three, maybe four bullets now. That is unless he had a spare magazine in his pocket, then that changed everything.

"We're taking fire in the alley behind the Mother Lode. Male suspect running north along the alley on foot," I heard RJ yell over his radio.

"Stop, Police," I shouted uselessly. "Drop your weapon."

He ran past someone. I heard them cry out in terror as they saw the gun, and a second later, I was passing them. A guy and a girl, both wide-eyed pointing in the direction the guy was running as I ran past.

Then a car turned down the alley.

For an instant, the man stood silhouetted in the car headlights. He was a perfect target, and less than 20 yards away. Instinctively my gun came up, but my brain stopped the shot. He was still moving. There was a chance I'd get him if I fired.

There was an equal chance I'd miss, and the heavy .45 ACP bullet would slam into the car. I didn't know if it would penetrate the body or window of a car, and now wasn't the time to find out.

Our suspect wasn't constrained by my rules of engagement, however. I saw him stop and extend his hand towards the car.

He fired a single shot at it. The small-caliber bullet ricocheted off the car and went whining into the darkness.

He was panic-stricken, and what he'd done changed the dynamics of the situation considerably. The guy intended to go on shooting till he was out of bullets, which by my count would be very soon.

But he still had a few rounds. He could still kill.

My pistol came up, and my sight pattern was perfect for a shot into his mid-back. But before I could squeeze off the round, he turned and headed in behind the Castle Hotel. As I rounded the building corner in pursuit, I could hear him pounding up the old wooden staircase, and throw his body against the back door.

I came running around the corner, and I was shouting at him to surrender. My weapon was up and aimed at him. He threw himself against the old door one more time. The door splintered, and swung open, dumping him inside.

There was a light on in the small landing, and for an instant, I was able to see him. He was just in a shirt, no doubt having left his coat behind. Dark headed, a light beard, and I could see the fear in his eyes. He knew what he'd done and knew he wasn't getting out of it.

In that instant, I had a brief window of opportunity to fire at him. I got the sight picture.

Fired.

Missed! I saw the wall plaster explode in a puff of white as the bullet impacted behind him.

"Antonito 2," RJ was reporting. "He ran upstairs into the Castle Hotel. Second floor!"

"We're right out front," another Antonito cop reported.

RJ and I stopped at the bottom of the stairs, taking cover behind the building corner. The pursuit had just gone from full speed ahead to stop and think this one through.

I'd never been upstairs in the Castle Hotel, just the first floor, and knew nothing of the layout upstairs. The lobby proclaimed that once it had been the Queen Bee of places to stay in Antonito. Decorated in a style that went out at the turn of the 20th century, it had old dusty overstuffed chairs and equally dusty carpet with faded floral patterns. There was a massive wooden desk where the check-in clerk had worked.

Behind the Desk were mail slots that had once held messages and telegrams. Now they contained dust. When the railroads had boomed through here, it had been the grandest hotel in the city. Now it was home to a few old folks on pensions and people struggling to make ends meet.

"RJ. Didn't your uncle rent space on the first floor for his barbershop?"

He nodded. "Yes, and I know how things are laid out upstairs."

"What does it look like?"

RJ thought for a second and then said, "This staircase opens up onto the second-floor landing. About ten feet to the left is the grand stairwell which descends into the lobby. The second floor is one long hall, and there are four or five rooms down that way on each side."

As he was talking, I heard a door open up there, and a room about halfway down that had a light on in it went out.

I pointed it out to RJ. "I think he's in there."

We reported that to Antonito PD.

"Will," Antonito 2 said. "We're getting this crime scene secured."

"Understood, got anybody reporting in yet?"

"Chief is coming in, and Pete is running home to get his weapon. A couple of volunteer firemen are offering their help."

He was talking about Pete Sanchez, a former Marshal about a million years before in this very town before he became a county commissioner. He was solid and knew what to do.

"OK, Let's go to Sheriff's channel and get this op set up," I said. "Be with you in a minute there." I keyed the microphone, thinking about who was out tonight. "Manassa 1, you there, Bob?" I asked.

"Manassa 1, I've been following. Want me on Sheriff's channel?"

"Please, and Bob, can you start heading this way. And can you round Pam up? I'd appreciate it."

"Will do. I'll go to Sheriff's channel as soon as I get hold of her."

I switched over to Channel 4, the Sheriff's Channel. "Antonito 2, Conejos 4."

"Go ahead."

"Here's what I want to do. We need to block off 285 for traffic for a block around the hotel. No cars, no foot traffic. If we can get fire at both ends of the street, we can send cars down and around. And please have them light up the streets best they can.

"And if they can get another truck in the back and light up the back, I'd appreciate it. And when Pete gets here, send him around the back. In the meantime, I'm going to get EMS and some more Sheriffs' resources in here. Can you get someone to watch the front?"

"Affirmative. Beano (nickname for the Antonito Police Commissioner, I never asked where it came from) is here along with a few others. They're all armed. They've got the front covered. If you need anything, have Beano do it. His call sign is Antonito 5."

"Copy that. Antonito 5, Conejos 4," I called.

"Go ahead, Conejos 4," Beano answered a second later.

"Did you copy my discussion with Antonito 2?"

"Affirm. We're setting that up now."

"Roger. Tell everyone to stay behind cover. We don't have this guy fully contained yet, and I'm not sure what he'll do next."

I called the Sheriff's office and told dispatch to let me talk to the jail deputy.

"Patrick," I said. "Call Linda. Get her in to relieve you. Then drive the Hulk down here. We need our equipment. Get it down here fast!"

"Consider it done," he answered.

A moment later, one of the fire trucks pulled into the alley, and I directed the driver where to stop, and turn on his floods.

"Shine them up onto that window," I said, pointing it out. We were somewhat exposed if we had to approach the stairs, but the bright floods would destroy his night vision. All he'd see is the light, and we'd be almost invisible in the shadows.

"Stay behind the truck," I said. "I think he's down to his last few bullets, but I don't want you catching one of them."

Antonito 2 reported that Antonito 1 had made it in and that they were at the crime scene.

"Send along any information they can give me concerning this suspect," I said.

Antonito 2 gave me a "roger that."

"Now what?" RJ asked.

"There's no other way out of there, is there?" I asked. "No back stairwells, anything like that?"

RJ stopped, thought for a moment, and then said, "Just the two. This one and the grand stairwell."

"What a fire trap," I said. But that was working to our advantage right then and there. "Let's get him pinned down to the second floor. Stay here and watch the back till Pete gets here. He can still jump out the second story!"

I keyed the radio. "Antonito 5, I'm going to get up to the second-floor landing. Any activity upfront?"

"None," he reported. "And the front door is locked." I didn't want to know how they found that out. Probably actually tried it. While that technique worked, it was also an excellent way to catch a bullet.

"OK, starting up now."

RJ moved so he could shoot up the stairwell. I left my cover behind the wall. My pistol was up and pointed straight up the stairs. The Fire Department had their floods shining straight into the window, and hopefully blinding him.

I moved slowly, trying not to make too much noise. I might be almost invisible in the shadows, but the old wooden stairs made plenty of noise, and I didn't want to alert our shooter I was coming. For all, I knew he was waiting around the corner of the landing for me.

Climbing stairs without making noise is as much an art form as a science. It takes lots of practice, and it still doesn't always work. You point your toes down as you lift your leg straight up. Doing it that way helps minimize the possibility you'll snag your toe on a rung, trip, and fall. You place the outside of your foot down first, and then slowly begin rolling from the outside in. Finally, your heel comes down, and you gradually shift your weight to that foot. Then you repeat the process.

It sounds easy. It is easy. The problem is if you don't practice it often, you have to think about what you're doing. Holding a pistol and maintaining a sight picture just complicates things.

It took me almost a full minute to get up to the second-floor landing. I stepped through the door, careful not to step on the debris from the door. Keeping the pistol pointed out ahead of me, I made the semi-circle sweep like I'd done dozens of times before. The hallway was empty.

"Hallway is clear," I said quietly over the radio. We'd just pinned him down a little bit more. "RJ, is Pete there?"

"Yes. He has his son and daughter with him. One's armed with a shotgun, the other with a thirty-odd six. The back is secure."

"Good. Whoever has the rifle, have them watch the window. If our suspect starts shooting out of it, tell them to take him down. Then, come on up."

A minute later, RJ was crouching right behind me. "What's next, Will?" he whispered.

"You watch this area, I'm going to move to the grand stairwell, and sweep the lobby."

"I think you should wait for backup for that."

I nodded. "I think you're right."

I needed to be careful. I was getting a little bit of buck fever. Time was on our side.

"We'll wait for Bob and Pam."

We watched the hall. I could hear the floor creaking from the rooms scattered down the hallway. People were up and moving around.

That complicated things. Gunplay was something we were going to have to try to avoid, and with an armed suspect, that was unlikely. That meant getting the non-combatants out.

And if I couldn't get them out, then I had to get creative.

"Conejos 4, Manassa 1," my radio squawked quietly.

"Go, Bob," I said.

"Sanford 1 and I are here. Your deputy is here with the gear."

That was good news.

"Roger, you guys get suited up. We'll need two shotguns for this. Grab your masks and a couple of gas grenades."

"Give us a few minutes."

A few minutes later, I heard them come slowly up the stairs. They were both suited up. We'd managed to pump a few dollars into our gear during the interim. We'd dyed the flak jackets black. The word "Police" was still stenciled across the back using white spray paint. I figured it made a great target. We'd also had fabric badges sewn onto the front where an officer would wear a badge and name tags.

"What do we have?" Bob asked as he and Pam joined us.

I pointed down the hall to the left.

"Third door down," I said. "That's the room we think he's in. The suspect is a Hispanic male, about thirty years of age. Dark headed, light beard.

"Keep an eye down the hall. We've got civilians in the other rooms. Any of them come out, motion them over. Be very careful of anyone coming out."

"Are we talking to him yet?" Bob asked.

I shook my head. "No. We've been sitting on him till we got some more muscle. I don't even know who he is yet."

I looked at RJ. "Let's get suited up and grab the Rammer."

"We've got it covered," Pam said as she quietly pumped a round into the shotgun.

RJ and I went as quietly as possible down the back stairwell and to the Hulk.

The Sheriff had managed to fill another of my requests and had obtained an old MASH style ambulance. Because we didn't have much money, we'd spray-painted over the red medical cross on the side with Olive Drab paint. And because the ambulance was big and green, we had hung the name of the "Hulk" on it.

An inmate with an artistic flair had drawn Marvel's Hulk on the side. He was wearing a ripped to shreds Conejos country uniform and a hat eight sizes too small.

Patrick was waiting for us.

"Your party clothes, Gentlemen," he said. He'd already laid out our flak jackets, helmets, and masks.

Quickly we began suiting up. I pulled on my flak jacket, zipped it up, adjusted the steel helmet that was painted black with the word "Police" stenciled on the back. A badge had also been stenciled onto the front in white. Quickly, I cinched the gas mask carrier around my waist.

RJ grabbed the Rammer, a large steel pipe with a flat end. Made for us by a local welder, it weighed almost fifty pounds, and in tests, we'd managed to knock in steel doors with heavy-duty locks.

This would be the first time we'd use it for real.

We rejoined Pam and Rob a few minutes later. I crouched down between them. RJ crouched next to me.

"Here's what I want to do," I said. "Pam, let me have the shotgun. You and I are going to move to the grand stairwell. I'll take point. I'll clear it, and then we'll both go down quickly.

"Let's get that first-floor lobby cleared. We need to check that the office right behind the desk is secure."

Pam handed the shotgun to me. "I've got double 00 buck in the chamber."

I nodded, and let Antonito 5 know we were coming down the stairs to clear the lobby and back office. They acknowledged it. I glanced at my watch and nodded. Officially it was Christmas day. What a way to spend it!

I pulled out my flashlight, turned it on, and nodded. "OK, here we go!"

"We got you six," RJ said.

We moved quickly to the stairwell.

Pam paused, her gun pointed down the hall as I stepped out and around into my semicircle, clearing the staircase. I nodded and began moving down. Pam pulled the muzzle of her weapon up as I went past and then quickly fell in behind me.

The Grand Stairwell was a fancy name for a carpeted staircase. Once upon a time, it might have been nice. But the oak had been painted over, and the paint was flaking. The carpet was dirty and showing it's age.

Behind us was a wall, and it opened into the lobby. As we passed between the floors, I held the flashlight down and low, so it would attract the shooter's attention first and maybe give him that to shoot at first rather than us.

Soon, I could look into the lobby. All I saw were the dusty, threadbare old chairs with equally dusty magazines lying on the faded carpet next to them.

Nothing moved, and we walked quickly down and through, checking behind the desk.

The office door was padlocked, as was a closet. The barbershop was secured, and the front door had a chain and padlock through the bars.

"First floor is secure," I said quietly over the radio. I got a couple of acknowledgments. We were partway up the stairs when Antonito 2 called, but I waited until Pam and I had gotten back with Bob and RJ to acknowledge.

"Antonito 2, this is Conejos 4. Go ahead."

"Will," I heard him say. "Your suspect is a Jose Montero. He's up here on a visa from Mexico working for Ernest Mortenson as a sheepherder."

"Speaks English?" I asked.

"Very poorly" was the response. "And so you know, the victim was his wife. Shot her in the head. She was dead when we got here."

I looked at RJ. A degree in the Spanish language made him our designated interpreter.

He smiled, already having figured that piece out.

"Do we know what happened?" I asked.

"Just that they were at the table and drinking. our wife saw the whole thing. She said it looked like they were arguing, and then he stood up, pulled a gun, and shot her. They live there in the Castle, room eight."

At least we'd guessed right on the room, I thought. But, he's probably had a chance to reload if he had a box of bullets with him.

"Your wife says to be careful, and she's praying for you guys," he finished.

"Tell her 'thank you,' and we will be," I responded. "Conejos 4, out."

"Objectives, Will?" Bob asked.

"You're the Spanish speaker. We'll try to talk him out first," I said. "Here's what I want to do. I want you about five feet from his door. Rob, you on the other. Pam and I will knock on doors once you start talking, and try to get folks out."

I let Antonito know what we were going to do. "We'll be sending them down the back stairwell. Make sure Pete and his kids know that."

They acknowledged, and then we moved quickly.

I nodded and RJ called out, "Jose Montano. Esta es la policía. Ponga abajo la pistola y Salir con las Manos en la Cabeza. No queremos hacerte daño, y no se si salen pacíficamente. "

Roughly translated, RJ had told him we were the police, put down his gun, and if he came out peacefully, he wouldn't be harmed.

I knocked quietly on a door, but no one seemed to be home there. Pam got an older man to come to the door she knocked on. He knew something odd was going on, and it only deepened when he opened the door to see a girl with a helmet and wearing a flak jacket.

She put her finger to her lips. I took him and motioned him to follow me, and when we got to the back door, I motioned for him to go down. Pete's daughter, was waiting at the bottom with one of the firemen. I was surprised to see they had some blankets. I hadn't thought of that and was glad someone had. They put a blanket around the old timer's shoulders and moved him quickly to safety.

"Sending another down," I said quietly over the radio, as Pam got an old woman out. As she cleared the rooms, Pam would mark the door with a red "X" drawn with a magic marker.

It seemed that was all that was home that night. Now to get our suspect out.

I considered my options.

He had a gun, and kicking the door in might get several of us injured or killed as we rushed the door. He'd already be thinking in terms of the Fatal Funnel, and I quickly put that idea aside.

While we'd have to go in that way, I needed to tip the scale a bit more in our favor.

We could kick in the door, empty a shotgun around the room and then go in. The idea had its merits but was messy in the extreme. While we'd knocked on doors, we had no guarantee that we'd gotten everyone out. All it took was someone who was a very sound sleeper or too scared to come to the door, and if they got hit by some buckshot, that could prove fatal.

I didn't know if buckshot would penetrate the slat and plaster construction of the walls. I was pretty sure it would. If it did, and it got someone, then we'd be liable for that.

That left tear gas. It would certainly tip the scale in our favor, and delivering it would be straightforward. We would hit the door with the Rammer, busting it open. One of us would toss in the grenade. It would go off within a second, and then we'd give it a five-count. The gas would quickly fill the room.

One of three things would happen, and I would work that into my plan.

"OK," I said to the team."Here's the plan."

I'd lead the assault. In most operations, I'd be in a van someplace, directing the takedown over the radio. We were too small for that. I'd need RJ's upper body strength to break the door. Being in his fifties, Bob wasn't as agile as he'd once been, and that counted against him. But he could still toss a grenade.

That left Pam to sweep in behind me. A talent taught and highly valued in the Marines is the ability to shoot and scoot. I'd need that talent if this was going to work out.

"RJ, you hit the door with the Rammer and break it open and get out of the way. Bob, you toss a gas grenade in. We give it a five-count, and then Pam and I go in.

"By the time we rush the room, it should be filled with tear gas.

"One of three things will happen.

"He'll come out on his own, possibly with a gun, possibly surrendering.

"Or he'll try to go out the window and right into Pete's arms.

"Or we go in and get him.

"Either way, expect him to be firing. What do you think?"

"I think it's the best move we got," Bob said.

I looked at RJ and Pam. They both nodded.

I let the cops outside know we were about to go in. Gas grenades get hot when they discharge and can cause a fire, so I asked that they have fire ready with a couple of extinguishers. I warned them to be wearing bunker gear and air masks.

I wanted EMS standing ready. They all acknowledged.

"One more time, RJ. Ask him to come out."

RJ nodded, and called out, "Señor, esto es la policía. Dejar su pistola y sale con las manos hacia arriba." Again, loosely translated, RJ had once again identified us as the police, told him to drop his weapon, and to come out with his hands up.

We didn't get an answer. I didn't know what our suspect was thinking. One thing he'd be sure of was that our just leaving him wasn't going to happen. Perhaps the realization of what he'd done had finally hit him, and dying was an option.

I'd already decided we wouldn't give him that way out.

"Let's give him about two minutes," I said.

He'd expect us to do something, and if we did it right after the demand to come out, it would increase the chances he'd be ready. If we let a little time pass, he might relax a bit, and that would tip the odds more in our favor.

"Two minutes," I said over the radio.

I kept an eye on my watch and made a quick prayer. I prayed quietly for our safety, the safety of everyone involved, and that we'd be able to take him alive.

The seconds crept by, I finished my prayer and then said quietly, "It's ShowTime. RJ?"

He'd stood up and made a couple of practice swings with the Rammer. He nodded. He was ready.

"Bob?"

He unfastened the strap that held a grenade. He nodded.

"Pam?" I got a nod. She was ready.

"Hnd signals from here on," I whispered. "Mask."

We pulled out our gas masks and donned them

I've never liked wearing a gas mask. Tactically speaking, they cut down on your field of vision, and make communications difficult. As I pulled the mask over my head and onto my face, I blew out like I'd been taught in Basic Training and felt the mask seal against my face.

While we'd trained to fight in them, they were such a bear to breathe in I'd always thought actual combat would be difficult at best. Now I was about to find out if that was true.

I stood, checked to make sure the shotgun wasn't on safe, and then held up my hand. Holding it out and away was "Attention."

My next move was my hand went up and then down. "Move out." Quickly but above all quietly, we moved to our designated areas. RJ was watching me. Pam and I were in position, and Bob knelt by the door half turned away from it so that he could see us and the door at the same time.

We were ready,

I held up my hand and spread it out.

RJ nodded.

I began counting it down. On two, RJ brought the Rammer up, took a deep breath, and twisted his body to get as much power as he could out of the swing.

I hit zero and then pumped my arm back and forth. RJ swung the Rammer down as hard as he could on the door handle.

The door exploded open from the force of the blow, ripping the old lockbox right off the wall. RJ was already jumping out of the way as Bob rolled the grenade through the door. The door swung open as far as it could, and then bounced closed only to bounce open again.

I heard a cry of fear from within, and a shot went off. The bullet screamed through where the door had been an instant before, and impacted the wall, causing a soft explosion of powdered cement.

. Then with a pop and an evil hiss, the grenade went off. Within a few seconds, a cloud of white-gray smoke rolled out through the door into the hallway. I held up one hand and then swept it down.

Pam and I exploded into the room, our flashlights piercing the rapidly spreading gas fog, our voices muffled by the protective masks as we shouted, "Police. Drop your weapon."

The guy was right in front of me, standing on the other side of the bed, bathed in the light of my flashlight and the floodlights shining through the window. He was choking on the gas, his eyes watering and blinded. But the pistol was still in his hand. He was turning it towards me as I ran into the room.

I stepped up on the bed and vaulted towards him. I was holding the shotgun between us like a bar, and he caught it full force in the chest. As he crumpled, momentum from the leap kept me going into him. And with a loud bang that deafened us, the shotgun went off. My finger had still been on the trigger, and my flying tackle had caused me to pull it. I heard glass shatter. I'd just blown out the window. A part of me was already analyzing the mistake. Instead of shooting out the window, I could just have easily shot Pam.

I landed on top of him in a heap, the flying tackle knocking the breath from me.

"Get up," a part of me screamed. "Get up and get moving!"

I sucked in air, the mask collapsing tight against my skin. Painfully I pulled myself up. Bob was already there to help me up. Pam holstered her weapon. I'd knocked the guy out cold. We still rolled him over and quickly cuffed him. We carried him out into the hall and away from the tear gas.

"Suspect is in custody," I called out over the radio. "I need fire up here now. Smother that grenade, and ventilate this place."

RJ had gone into the room, did a quick check, and noted that the grenade had stopped discharging. There was no real reason to open the window. I'd shot it out. He'd found and brought out the weapon.

It was a chrome-plated 25 caliber Raven, just as I had suspected. He'd note in the evidence custody log that before he cleared it, there were three rounds in the magazine and one in the chamber when he recovered it.

Our suspect had reloaded. A box of bullets was on the nightstand.

We went outside, carrying the suspect. As we went down the stairs, we each pulled our protective masks off. The sweat on my face chilled me as it hit the cold December air.

EMS was waiting at the end of the alley. On a signal from one of the firemen, they brought the ambulance up to park right behind the fire truck.

"Might want to let him air out a bit," I said.

They quickly got his clothing off, and we secure that for evidence once we'd let it air out. I'd noticed some blood splatter on his shirt, and we'd certainly want that. They covered him with a couple of blankets and wiped the residue gas from his face. Then they loaded him, still handcuffed into the ambulance. Antonito 5 jumped in with them for the ride to the hospital.

The Fire Chief came out and gave me the thumbs up. They'd opened most of the windows on the 2nd floor to ventilate the gas, and had taken a fan up to help blow it out. I could smell the gas as it settled out into the winter night. It wasn't enough to stop a person, just enough to cause a twinge in the nose and a tear in the eye.

We all walked up to the end of the street. We stood for several minutes with arms raised, letting the slight breeze wash the gas from our uniforms.

And that's when it hit.

I noticed that everyone was shaking a little. At first, I thought it was just because it was cold. But it wasn't that. We'd been keyed up for the assault, it happened, and now it was over. The tension had to go someplace, and our bodies were letting it out.

"Assault team," I said. "Let's get this scene processed, and then to the Sheriff's office for the debrief."

As we walked back up to the fire engine, I saw Jewell.

The fire department had set up a perimeter using yellow caution tape and had kept everyone behind it. She ducked under and came up, hugging me tightly.

"William Diaz," she said, running her hand over my face. "You sure know how to make me worry."

"Are you OK?" I asked.

"I saw the whole thing happen," she said, trying to find her words. "I was standing there, singing and playing. I saw him stand up, pull out a pistol, and shoot her. Right there in the head. I saw blood spurt out, and all I could do was keep playing and singing and thought, this isn't real. Did I really see what just happened? Then Joey pulled me down behind my amp."

Then she backed up quickly, and I saw a tear in her eye, and her nose started running.

"Tear gas?" she asked.

I nodded. It wasn't entirely out of my clothes yet.

"Just stand upwind of us, and face into the breeze, it will blow it away," RJ told her.

"Remind me to thank Joey," I said. "Did you give Antonito a statement?"

She nodded. "What are you doing?" she asked.

"We've got to process this scene. And then debrief. I figure we've got about two or three hours work ahead of us."

"Going to the Sheriff's Office for that?"

I nodded.

"I'll head over there," she said. "We already got our instruments and are out. Anything you want me to do there?"

"Coffee," I said. "Some sandwiches would be nice. And I might be referring some of these folks your way for mental health purposes. If you can put some thoughts together for PTSD, I'd appreciate it."

"I'll see you there."

She disappeared quickly into the crowd that was still standing and watching in the cold.

We were busy for the rest of the morning. We took dozens of pictures of the assault scene, drew the scene out with careful measurements, and then went to the SO.

Jewell had coffee and sandwiches waiting for us. We ate and drank our coffee while we got our gear ready for the next mission. Then we all sat down and wrote quick statements regarding tonight's events.

We were dog tired, and while the coffee helped, we had to get the debrief done while the incident was still fresh in our minds.

I asked Jewell to set in on it in her counselor's capacity. She had already thought about her quick talk about PTSD, and she was watching everyone.

I flipped the big chalkboard in my office over, wiped it clean. Then with a piece of chalk, I wrote, "After Action – Debrief – 25 Dec."

"What could we have done better?"

RJ raised his hand. "We've still got to get better communications. We need hands-free, and a frequency meant just for us to use.

"And while we're at it, we've got to figure out a better way to hold the flashlights."

"It felt really clumsy," Pam said, agreeing with him. "The flashlight hold might work for clearing a building, but the combat end was different."

I'd held my flashlight alongside the slide on the shotgun. If I'd had to crank in an extra round, I might have dropped it.

I wrote that down.

"I don't think CSP can accommodate us on another freq. Could we use the radios we used for training? And, except for duct taping the flashlights to the weapon, I don't know how to fix that."

"Might not be a bad idea on the radios," RJ answered. "If we can get a hands free headset, that would be perfect.

"How about holders for the flashlights?" Bob asked.

"holders?" I asked. I didn't know what Bob was talking about.

"Yes. Did you ever see Escape from New York?"

"Kurt Russell?" Jewell asked.

"The same. I was reading in one of my gun magazines. How to make a holder for a rifle barrel so you could clamp them on so you can have a flashlight on your weapon like they used."

That sounded interesting.

"Probably wouldn't cost much to have someone make a couple," he said.

Now, if we just had some money.

"We might be able to get some and fit them onto our shotguns. Not sure what to do about the pistols."

"Look into it, Bob. It might be something we can use."

"Not much we can do about this," Pam said, "but I felt we were a little slow in getting going."

I wrote it down.

I think most of that was waiting for our gear. Maybe, centralize things a little bit."

"This is the first time we had to do this," RJ said. "I think the tempo will pick up with training and experience."

"I thought having everything in the Hulk worked well," Bob said.

"There's a place we might be able to improve response speed," Pam said. "Maybe we need to deputize a firefighter to bring it in. After all, we had to wait for someone to get in and relieve the jailor so he could bring it in."

I wrote that down.

"Still not enough people," RJ said.

"I think we were good to go, but everything else got stretched thin," I said. "Antonito was tied up on the crime scene, and we had to have fire and EMS do crowd and traffic control."

"That's what I meant," RJ said.

"Sorry," I said. "Maybe more training for them?"

Everyone thought that would be a good idea.

"Or bolster our own reserves."

"We have to practice more with the masks on," Bob said. "They cut down on what you can see."

I wrote it down, wondering if I could get my hands on a different of a mask, ones that offered better visibility.

While we were talking, Antonito PD brought the suspect into the jail. He was quickly booked in on a charge of 1st-degree murder. There would be others, such as firing upon law enforcement officers and resisting arrest. That would all be leverage for a deal.

He was going away for a very long time.

I introduced Jewell. "Jewell," I said, "I think we all want to go home. Can you give them a quick brief on PTSD symptoms?"

She took the floor and explained, "As a counselor, I often see people suffering from issues caused by events similar to what you went through tonight. Here are some things to look for. If you start experiencing them, we need to get you some help. There's a whole host of others, but these are common and could indicate an issue.

"Often, you'll start having issues sleeping or loss of appetite. Those are biggies. If you find you're easily startled or even having problems concentrating or you're staying focused on what happened tonight, then, get help.

"Starting to smoke or drink more than you usually do also can be an indicator of problems. So keep an eye on yourselves."

She handed out her card, and said, "I'm a Christian counselor, and if you have problems talking to me, I can get you hooked up with the SLV Mental Health. PTSD is something that with work can be brought under control."

She looked at the strike team and then said. "I will be doing some follow-up to make sure everything's good with you. If you start to experience any of what I just described, please don't hide it. PTSD can do a pretty good job of ruining your life."

I nodded and then looked at the team.

Every one of them looked like death warmed under. "People, let's go home, and Merry Christmas."

There was a chorus of Merry Christmas's and good nights, and everyone was heading for the door.

As the sun was coming up, Jewell and I left the sheriff's office for the drive home. I'd called home, and the kids met me with my robe and slippers on the porch. Once home, I stood in the cold, stripped to my underwear, and bagged my clothes into a black plastic bag. They would be washed in a commercial laundry.

I slipped on my robe and showered.

It was good to have made it through the night.

CHAPTER FIFTEEN

CHRISTMAS DAY

"Will," Pastor Morgan said, greeting us at the door of the church. "You look like heck." Then he looked at Jewell and added, "You don't look much better."

"Thanks, and Merry Christmas to you, too," I said, shaking his hand.

I noticed that Carol was frowning, and then she said, "Were you in that mess they had in Antonito last night? I heard about it on the radio this morning."

I nodded. "Both of us, right up to our eyeballs," I said and made a motion with my hand that ended at eye level.

"What happened?" she asked.

I looked at our eldest daughter.

"Chica," I said, using my nickname for her. "Why don't you take everyone and grab our seat."

"Sure, Dad," she said. She herded the Bratt and Gerry into the church. With the kids out of the way, we could talk.

"I was a witness," Jewell said. "I saw it all happen."

"Really," Pastor Morgan said. "You saw the whole thing?"

That someone would witness a murder and that it would happen in front of them seemed incredible to him.

Carol's eyes went wide. "Jewell!"

"I'm OK," Jewell said. "I just couldn't believe I saw what had happened. I'm singing, playing piano, and I see this guy stand up, pull out a gun, and shoot this woman. I just kept singing and playing. I couldn't believe what I'd just seen, and then Joey is pulling me down behind the amp."

"And you, Will?" Pastor Morgan asked.

"I led the team that did the takedown," I answered.

"No one got hurt?"

I shook my head. "Not on my team. The guy got some bruising, and they had him checked out to make sure nothing got broke when I tackled him."

I saw the looks on their faces, and explained, "The guy was armed. We ended up using tear gas and tackling him. He did take a few shots at us while we were chasing him."

"He shot at you?" he asked.

I thought I'd just said that, and then nodded. "The shot was wild. But yes, he shot at us, and then at a car that had turned down that alley at the wrong moment."

"What was he using?" Pastor Morgan asked.

"Little Raven 25," I answered. "The gun's hot (meaning it had been reported stolen) and we're trying to sort out how he got it. He isn't talking."

"You both look dead tired," Carol said. "Are you guys OK for Christmas dinner?"

"Not yet," I answered.

"We got extra," Carol said. "We'll bring it over this evening."

"You don't have to do that," Jewell said.

"Oh, yes, we do," she said. "Goes with the territory. Besides, we're inviting ourselves."

And I thought a cop's job was never-ending. Being a pastor and his wife is almost as bad. Maybe even worse.

"We've guests coming over," Jewell said.

"Don't you worry about that," Carol said. "We've enough to feed an army."

"I appreciate it," Jewell said, meaning it.

We'd been seriously considering Chinese food for Christmas. Peking duck, extra crispy, I thought.

Not this year!

Pastor Morgan was looking at me, and Carol picked up on some unspoken verbal cue. She took Jewell by the arm and led her into the church.

"You really OK," he asked once the women were out of earshot.

"I'm OK. Almost had a flashback, but I fought it off."

"That's good to hear. It means that you're in control. And I'm glad you guys are OK," he said.

"We're OK," I answered. "Scared us all to death. We've been training for this, but this was our first real outing. We found out there's a lot of things we need."

Several of the local families came in, and we spent a couple of minutes shaking hands and hugging these tough old cowboys. The women went in, leaving us men talking at the back.

"Will Diaz!" George, one of the old-time cowboys, said. "You made the newspapers!"

I'd been introduced months before to George, and knew he was a local rancher. He also ran several saloons with another old cowboy, Everett.

But I knew almost nothing else about him.

He'd brought a newspaper in, and handed it to me.

Frontpage, I thought. Frontpage news is either good or bad. I looked it over. The large picture that dominated the front page showed RJ, Bob, Pam, and me carrying our murder suspect out.

Odd, I thought. I didn't remember there being a camera there.

Our faces were clearly visible in the newspaper pictures, and the headline read "THERE'S A NEW KIND OF SHERIFF IN TOWN . . .". I read the byline and shook my head.

"Sylvia!" I groaned. "Girl, what are you trying to do to me?"

I skimmed the story. She'd interviewed the Sheriff and Sgt Robert Gallegos from Antonito PD. They talked about the murder in the crowded bar and mentioned how several people had seen it happened. Then they told about how local law enforcement had been putting a team together and had managed to get some surplus equipment to help outfit it.They were also careful to point out that this was our first actual mission.

"Is the story true?" George asked.

"Yes," I answered.

"You really jumped over a bed and knocked the guy down?"

"Yeah, I did."

George laughed. "You got big ones, boy. Big brass ones!"

I took it as the compliment it was meant to be.

"I'd have shot him!"

"Thought about it," I said. "Our perp was half-blinded with tear gas. I figured I could take him alive."

"Looks to me like you're using old gear," George said. "Are those flak jackets even bulletproof?"

I shook my head. "We tested them. They stopped some rounds, but not others. We found that they'd sometimes, and I mean sometimes, stop a round from a 32, and 38. Anything else, forget it. Bullets went right through. What surprised us is a 22 penetrated.

"They're better than nothing, but we all know that nothing just might be what we're wearing."

"And you're using military-style gas masks."

I looked at him, cocking my head slightly. "George, are you going someplace with this, or just grazing?"

He chuckled. "I'm going someplace with this. You and Pastor Morgan come over and see me today. Bring our wives. Rhonda would appreciate the company. "

I looked at Pastor Morgan. "When?"

"How about right after services," he said. "We can have some pie."

I was hoping to catch a nap but didn't say anything. "I can do that."

Pastor Morgan nodded consent, and George hurried off to catch up with his wife, a slight smile on his face.

"I wonder what that's about," I said, watching him go.

Pastor Morgan shrugged. "Haven't a clue. But George doesn't do anything without a good reason."

"I should go to my seat."

I walked into the old church. It had been decked out by the Youth Group in the top-flight holiday style Christmas is known for.

Some of the older kids had gone to the Forest Service and gotten permits to get the Christmas trees. They'd taken their four-wheel-drive trucks up into the mountains, and found the trees that had been scouted and tagged earlier in the year. They'd cut them down, trucked them in, and put them up at the front of the church. The kid's church then decorated the trees with lights, bows, and ornaments, some of which dated back to the late 1800s.

Interspaced here and there were small homemade ornaments that had pictures of young men and women in uniform. They were photographs of men and women who had attended the church throughout the years the church had existed. All were military pictures.

The pictures included some who had paid for the freedoms we take for granted with their lives.

My picture was up there someplace, a rather new addition.

As long as this church existed, the pictures would be on the tree, and we would always be remembered.

The smell of pine hit me the moment I walked in. I smiled, remembering riding through open country in the mountains and how clean the air smelled because of the trees. I always enjoyed the memory.

I sat down next to Jewell and told her, "George McCaffrey invited us and the Morgan's over after services."

"Aren't you tired?" she asked.

"He was quite insistent. I think it has something to do with what happened last night."

"They seem like such a nice couple."

"Good," I said. It was settled. Jewell was game for some pie as well.

The praise and worship singers were getting ready. Cowboys tend to dress rather casually, but today was Christmas day. A few suit jackets and bolo ties were in evidence, and the boots had an extra coat of polish on them.

It appeared the drums and guitars wouldn't be used today. We would have more traditional music today. When services started, I saw I was correct. They started with "Away in a Manger" and ended with "O Holy Night."

Pastor Morgan stepped behind the pulpit, and after we'd welcomed each other, he launched into something I hadn't heard in years. It was a speaking piece that I remembered Johnny Cash doing years before called, "Here was a man."

"Here was a man," he said when he finished reciting it. He looked up at the congregation and said, "Today, some people want to silence that man. They say what he has to say is offensive to them. John 3:16 tells us this, 'That God so loved the world that he gave his only begotten Son so we could have eternal life.' But two sentences later, it tells us something that should chill us all right to the bone. Here, let me read it to you.

He paused for a second, finding it in his open Bible, "'This is the verdict: Light has come into the world, but people loved darkness instead of light because their deeds were evil.' "

He paused. "So, what does that last piece have to do with Christmas? Jesus came into this world to be a perfect sacrifice for sin. Before Jesus, there was only one way to atone for sin, and that's by a blood sacrifice.

"The problem was, it wasn't even a temporary fix. It was at best an acknowledgment of guilt because the sacrifice, no matter how perfect, was of this world. It took something else to pay the price for our sins, and that meant the price had to be one hundred percent perfect. The only thing that could make that sacrifice was God himself.

"So God took on flesh and became that sacrifice for us. His name is Jesus, and thirty-three years after his birth, he'd pay the price for us.

"Now a lot of preachers will say Salvation is free. Well, it is, you know.

"But there is a price to pay. It's the price Jesus paid. If he hadn't been born and died for our sins, there isn't any way we would be saved.

"But there is a price you have to pay, also. The price is you walk away from what you used to be. Matthew 13, verse 44 tells us, and let me read that to you, 'The kingdom of heaven is like treasure hidden in a field. When a man found it, he hid it again, and then in his joy went and sold all he had and bought that field.'

He looked around. "There was a price the man paid for the treasure. He walked away from everything he had just to own the piece of land the treasure was on.

And that's what we do. We walk away from the bars, the affairs, and the person we used to be to find something better. Something that gives us life, not death.

"And that's why a lot of folks don't accept Jesus as our Savior. They look at what he offers them and then look at what they have and would rather have what they've got. They can't see walking away from the familiar.

"Maybe it's out of fear of what people might think. Maybe it's fear of stepping away from the comfortable into something new. Maybe it's because they say they'll do it tomorrow completely missing that tomorrow isn't a given."

He looked up and pursed his lips. "I look out across this church. I know who some of you were. I've men and women here who were drug addicts, alcoholics, and some of you dabbled in adultery. At least one of you an almost murderer.

"The difference is your choice. You wanted life, and you were more than willing to walk away from that darkness and into the light.

"And that's why we look at that little child, and that's why we celebrate that fantastic Man's birth. He gave us not a candle in the darkness, but a blazing sun. The Sun brings life and warmth. Just as the Son brings us life and hope.

"And I do believe that's the greatest gift of all. A life we can call our own."

We sang some more hymns, and then service ended for that Christmas day. As we walked out, George said: "Follow us over?"

"Will do," I answered.

We followed them to their house, which was about a mile from the church.

The McCaffrey's Ranch consisted of the main house, corrals, and several large horse barns. The house was a two-story brick structure with a large porch. It was partially hidden by trees and had a sturdy fence around it. Several fields led up to it. In a pasture, I could see an artesian well from which water flowed into a cattle trough. This old-time cowboy had a dollar or two.

I'd driven by it several times and had never thought about who owned it. I figured it was just a very nicely laid out ranch.

The Morgan's pulled in behind us.

"Come on in," Rhonda, George's wife, said, motioning us in.

We all followed with Jewell directing the kids to make sure they didn't track snow into the house. The house looked old on the inside, with 5-inch plank flooring, and high-end paneling on the walls. I could smell apples and cinnamon. Rhonda must have been baking, and my mouth watered.

"Come in," George said, pointing to a side room. "There's a Nintendo and pool table in the rec room there for you kids. And you'll find soda and candy bars in the fridge."

Rhonda motioned the ladies into the kitchen, and George led Pastor Morgan and me into a large room. Once upon a time, it had been a bedroom. Now it was a library and office. One whole wall was filled with books. There was everything from textbooks on animal husbandry and accounting to Time-Life books on the Old West to Zane Grey novels. I was surprised to see that most of the latter were in a hardback edition. I wasn't sure if I'd ever seen a Zane Grey in hardback.

"Make yourselves at home," he said, gesturing for us to sit in two comfortable looking wingback chairs that occupied the center of the room. "Coffee or eggnog?"

"Black coffee," I said. I was tired and needed caffeine.

"You look like you could use some. Pastor?"

"Make it two," Pastor Morgan said, and George quickly left to get us our drinks.

I looked around the room, and several frames caught my eye on the wall. I went and looked at them. In a small shadow box was a medal with a slightly faded red, white, and blue ribbon on it.

I looked at Pastor Morgan and said, "That's a Silver Star."

He nodded, and I looked at a picture of a soldier receiving the medal.

"That's General Patton in that picture," I said.

I'd learned more about cowboy George McCaffrey in the last 20 seconds than I'd known from all the previous encounters with him.

George came back in with the coffee and noticed me looking at his medal.

"I understand you have a Bronze Star," he said, noticing my looking at it.

I nodded. "I told the Army to shove it. I didn't even know I'd gotten it anyway, till I left the service and saw it in my DD214."

"Why would you turn down a Bronze Star," he asked.

"Because I got into a gunfight with a man who had an empty gun," I said. Besides, they were giving them to people just for showing up.

I changed the subject. "Isn't that General Patton in the picture?"

George sat back in his old office chair, his coffee in his hand. "The General came out and gave me my medal. He acted like I'd done something great. It was nonsense," he said with a snort.

"Oh?" I glanced at Pastor Morgan. Obviously, he'd heard the story a few times but still enjoyed hearing it. This was one of those stories told only among warriors.

"The commendation reads that I single-handedly attacked and captured a German machine gun and crew by using fire and maneuver. What happened is a little different."

"It always is," I said, sitting down and taking a cup of coffee from the tray. I had to hear this story.

"We were moving up to Bastogne during the Battle of the Bulge. We'd walked for days, and we went right into combat. Anyway, before we'd started the walk, I'd gotten word that my mother had passed away. I put in for leave, but they wouldn't let me go home. So here we are, walking, getting more and more tired. It's cold, and I'm just completely pissed about everything.

"We're going through this one small town. The Germans had built a machine gun nest to defend it, and they started shooting at us. We took cover, tried to shoot back, and then I looked at it and said, 'screw it, I'm going home.'

"So I stand up, left cover, and I start walking towards the machine gun. There's no running. There's no taking cover. This is a casual stroll up to the machine gun nest.

"All the time, they're shooting at me with one of those Hitler's Zippers, and I can see tracers coming close to me, but not hitting me. So I kept walking.

"I walked right up to the rim of the foxhole. The Germans are looking up at me like they can't believe it, and I'm looking at them and figure, 'well, while I'm here, I guess I should do something about this.' I pointed my rifle at them, and they all surrendered."

I laughed. The story sounded impossible, but it wasn't the first time I'd heard stories like that, especially from the battlefield.

"So, they gave you a medal for wanting to go home."

He laughed. "Yep. The worst thing that happened to me was my boot laces that were sticking out of my boots were shot off."

I sipped some coffee. It tasted like freshly ground from beans coffee.

George turned to his desk and picked up the newspaper he'd shown me that morning. "Will," he said. "Sounds to me like you're trying to do something important here."

"What do you mean?" I still wasn't sure what he wanted.

"I mean, it looks like you're trying to pull your county out of the dark ages of law enforcement and into the future a bit."

"It's kind of hard when you've still got a 1970s budget. We know things are changing, and we need to be ready."

"Changing how?" Pastor asked.

"I mean, it's not the place I left almost ten years ago. The criminals have gotten a little crafter. And there are threats we didn't have before."

George rubbed his chin. "You went away, you learned a whole bunch of new tricks, and your eyes got opened. The problems were there all along. But back then, you couldn't do anything about them. Now you at least have the training to see them and try."

I looked at the picture behind him.

George Patton was still pinning a medal on a young man, but now I saw what he was saying. That young man in the picture being decorated by one of history's most famous generals wasn't the same young man who had left the ranch maybe months before. He was a different animal when he came back.

The same was true of me.

I'd complained to Pastor Morgan that I often felt like who I had been was now a ghost wandering the Middle Eastern deserts. Now George was telling me that wasn't exactly a bad thing.

"As the song goes, 'home ain't home anymore.' "

"Everyone else stayed behind. The same problems and the same solutions," Pastor said.

George cocked his head and said, "You're trained in the hard sciences, aren't you?"

George had been studying me.

"Yes, I took my degree in Astro-Physics."

"Then you're familiar with this. If you toss a frog into boiling water, it will jump right out . . ."

"But if you put it in the water, and bring it to a boil, it will happily die there," I finished. "What are you saying, George?"

"I'm saying that your problem is you don't have the money, and you're making do with second-hand gear."

"Go on."

"If we were to go shopping, and you had a blank check, what would you buy?"

"That's easy," I said. "Hands-free communications gear. Radio Shack has the stuff, and it doesn't cost that much. We're not transmitting over miles, just a few hundred yards tops. I'd buy Level 3 bulletproof vest. And I'd get some protective masks that have better vision.

"And I would love to have a few more non-lethal options besides just gas. Rubber bullets and the like.

"There's also training we can use."

"Such as?"

"Well, we need someone who's trained in sexual assault investigations."

"You'd be talking a woman?"

"Considering most of the victims are women, yes."

"And what else."

"Investigative tools. An Identi-Kit for starters."

George stayed leaning forward. "How about some shotguns that are easier to handle, and maybe even some proper carbine type weapons for working close."

"Hadn't thought about that," I admitted. "Haven't shopped much for that because that would cost money I don't have. I've scrapped stuff together from a dozen sources what we do have."

"Detective Diaz," he said, using my title. "I'm prepared to write you a check so you can buy the gear you need."

I put the coffee down and leaned back in the chair. "Excuse me?"

"Get a shopping list together. We'll buy what you need."

The confusion on my face was obvious, and he chuckled.

"You're not the only one who wants to leave the world a better place than we found it. And sometimes, that means drawing a line in the sand and fighting to hold it. You've drawn the line. I want to make sure you've got the tools you need to hold it."

He smiled at my confusion and then leaned back in his chair. "Do you know what an angel is?"

"If you're not talking about an entity in the Bible, then you're talking about someone who funds something out of their pocket without a promise of return."

"Well, Rhonda and I are your angels. We're prepared to fund your program with a thirty-five thousand dollar grant, right here, right now."

I shook my head. "Wow," I said. I didn't even have to think about it. I leaned forward and shook his hand. "Thank you. It will make our job easier and safer."

"That's the idea. Anything else you can think of you need?"

"I need someone to get blueprints and such together for public buildings. Take pictures and make plans," I said. "Then they put them into a book, so we've got them for response purposes. I've made a start, but there's a lot of work there."

"What are you thinking?" he asked.

I rubbed my chin, putting int words what had been a vague hope ten minutes earlier

"The book with the plans will be broken down by town and buildings. Each will have certain pieces of information to include phone numbers, some preliminary plans, and resources we'd need. It would be nice to send someone around with a camera to take pictures and map out staging areas and those areas best for cover and concealment, and such."

"Here's what you need to do," he said, "and its one reason I asked Pastor Morgan in. I want a witness to this. You'll need to talk to your sheriff and county commissioners, maybe give them five or ten percent for administrative purposes. From that, you can buy your gear and hire someone to do the work you just detailed to me."

"Wow," I said, shaking my head. Talk about Santa Claus coming to town!

"We'll see how well this goes," he said, "and if it goes well, we'll talk a yearly grant to keep it all going."

A sudden thought occurred to me, and I said, "Mr. McCaffrey, why are you doing this?"

He paused for a second and then said, "Years ago, my brother was a deputy sheriff in New Mexico. He was killed because he didn't have the tools he needed to protect himself. So, I'm doing this in his memory."

That I could understand.

"I'm sorry to hear about that."

"I've waited a long time for this to happen," George said. He looked at his watch and then said, "Come on. I'm sure Rhonda has some apple pie for us all right about now."

And with that simple pronouncement, the meeting was over. We went into the kitchen and sat down. Sure enough, there was a more than adequate piece of homemade apple pie for me.

We left shortly afterward, and I told Jewell that my little team had actually gotten money for equipment.

"Do you have a shopping list?"

"That I do," I assured her. "I've got the list from last night, and that's a good starter."

That evening, Pastor Morgan and Carol brought over a Christmas dinner of baked ham, mashed potatoes, green bean casserole, and freshly baked bread.

The table had been set days earlier by Jewell. It never ceased to amaze people how she could do something like what she did on such a small budget. A candle was in a crystal base that, in turn, had a small wreath with some ornaments on it. A red bow finished it.

She had gotten out her best silverware for the table also. Through an odd coincidence, her ex-husband and I had the same starting letter in our last name, so it worked.

The Morgan's had already said they were inviting themselves. After all, they had brought this perfectly awesome Christmas dinner over, so that was only right. While Jewell and Carol warmed the meal and made gravy, Pastor Morgan and I sat in the living room, talking, and sipping coffee.

Our living room was decorated to the hilt. A large, real tree went from floor to ceiling. It was buried under white lights and ornaments. he majority of the ornaments were red though the color gold was well represented.

There was also a smattering of Hallmark ornaments. This being our first Christmas together, Jewell and I had taken the kids down to the Hallmark gift shop and purchased an ornament for each of us. I found a Star Ship Enterprise ornament that had been overlooked for the last dozen Christmases, and that became mine. Jewell purchased a couple of plastic roses and had them interspaced throughout the tree. It just made it even more magical.

I had a fire going in the stove. We kept a teapot on top of the stove, and a wisp of steam was coming up from it. The tea pot's purpose wasn't for making tea, but to put a little humidity into the dry winter air. That helped keep the winter colds down. A couple of cinnamon sticks in it made the room smell all warm and welcoming.

Outside, the sun had set, and the small hint of blue in the sky was rapidly fading to purple. Soon it would fade to black.

I heard a truck roar up into the driveway, got up, and looked out.

" Max and Eva are here," I said. "Just in time, too."

I stood by the door, waiting to let them in. As I waited, the first winter stars starting to appear in the rapidly darkening sky. Then the sky was erased away as the timer hit 5:30 PM, and the exterior Christmas lights blazed on.

I watched as Max and Eva got out of the truck and approached the house, their breaths small puffs of vapor in the cold. As they got to the door, I opened it for them.

"I smell tear gas," Max said, the minute he and Eva hit the door. He was carrying an armload of presents, while Eva carried a plate of baklava.

"And a Merry Christmas to you," I replied with a dismissive wave. "Don't stand out there, Come in."

Nighttime had settled in full force outside, and a slight breeze kicked some of the snow off the roof. In the white Christmas lights, it filtered down like diamond dust. Guess we had a White Christmas after all, I thought.

Still, it was hard to reconcile the Norman Rockwell moment with what had gone down the night before. Somehow, the two realities just didn't mesh.

"Come in," Jewell said. She ushered Eva in, and I quickly took her and Max's coat. Jewell and Eva went off chatting, joining Carol in the kitchen.

Pastor Morgan stood up and shook Max's hand. "It's good to see you again," he said.

"Likewise," Max answered. I gestured for Max to sit down and asked, "How's it going."

He sat down and shrugged. "I closed the books on last year. Took a loss."

"It is your first year," I said. "You've made some big purchases this year. We'll pray for a better next year."

"Fortunately, Eva is getting plenty of hours," he said. "It helps keep the lights on."

"Well, I may have something coming down that might help."

"Law Enforcement?"

I shook my head. "Sorry, no. The Sheriff doesn't like hiring folks who have been in his jail. More a consulting gig."

"Let me know." He looked towards the kitchen and then said, "You look like Hell. Pastor, what you been doing to this guy?"

"That's a look you should know. It's called chasing bad guys."

"I'm running on zero sleep," I answered. "Jewell isn't doing any better,"

"Yeah," he said slowly. "You look like you did that one night in Iraq. What happened last night?"

I told him, and he nodded in understanding. "I sure miss that stuff."

"I thought you didn't like Law Enforcement."

He shrugged. "It gets in your blood."

"Well, another ten years, and I can retire," I said. "I won't miss working holidays. Where are my manners? Can I offer you some coffee?"

"Sure. Put some Irish whiskey in it," he said with a chuckle.

"Coffee I can do. The rest, you wish for. Be right back."

I walked into the kitchen where Jewell, Eva, and Carol were talking. I tried not to eavesdrop. After all, it was girl talk.

As I came in, I looked at Eva. There was something about her that bothered me a little, though I couldn't put my finger on it.

Max walked in right behind me, looked at his wife, and said, "How are you doing, Baby?"

I caught a hesitation in her voice. Something is going on here, I thought. Things aren't good anymore between them.

And what had been an animated conversation between the women suddenly quieted down, and Max said, "I got a brand new 308 for Christmas."

"Really," I said. I had never priced a 308 rifle, but I was sure they weren't cheap.

"Bolt action, nice scope. Be perfect for hunting big game. And 60 rounds of ammo to boot. She's one sweet gun."

"And what did you get?" I asked Eva.

"Pots and pans. And a vacuum cleaner," she answered.

She looked at Max, and he looked at the floor.

"The house has been a little messy," he said. "And we've been eating late almost every day."

We went back into the living room and sat down, and I looked at Max.

"Max," I said. "At the risk of pissing you off, maybe you can pick up some of those duties?"

He already knew where I was going, and if it was physically possible to watch a person put shields up, I saw it happen.

Easy, I told myself.

"I take care of the horses, and research ways to drum up business," he said, sitting down. Pastor Morgan looked up, and I was sure he was wondering what had just gone down.

"How long does that take?" I asked. "Max, she's doing a forty plus hour work week watching people die. That isn't fun. You need to be helping her out."

"It's not her job that's going to put us on easy street," he said. There was an edge in his voice now.

"Give her a break. Making a meal is easy, and if you don't know how I've some cookbooks, I'll loan you."

He was about to say something, and I had the feeling he was going to say that cooking was her job, but he shut his mouth. "I don't do things that way," he finally said.

"And cleaning? It doesn't take much to take out the trash, sweep the floor, and square away the bathroom. And I know you were taught to make a bed in the Army."

He took in a breath. I was wondering if I'd pushed a button I shouldn't have, and finally, he said, "You're right. You're right."

"Are you appeasing me, or have I shown you the error of your ways?" I asked.

"What do you think, Sarge," he answered.

If George Patton had been standing there, he'd have slapped Max into next Tuesday. I know I thought about it. If I'd known what was about to happen, I would have.

"Max, you want a good marriage? Let her know you've got it covered. She's your wife, not a slave."

He looked at me with narrowed eyes and said, "What about the scripture that says, 'Wives submit to your husbands'?"

I glared at him and then realized that my eyes had narrowed also. Max had pushed a button or two, and I'd missed it. He knew I was dog tired, my shields were down, and he was using it against me. For the first time in our relationship, I wondered how good a friend he really was.

Pastor Morgan must have seen the look and said, "Try reading the entire chapter, Max. Later you'll see Paul wrote that 'husbands love your wives like Christ loves the church.' Christ died for each of us, he washed feet, and he certainly waited tables. What makes you any better?"

Max leaned back into the sofa. He knew he'd lost that one.

He nodded, but I felt like all I'd managed to do was to annoy him. Finally, he looked up and asked, "What did you get for Christmas?"

I took a breath and remembered, I can't change a soul. Only God can!

"A telescope," I answered. "You know I have a degree in Astronomy." He nodded. I was sure I'd only told him that a half a million times. "Jewell thought it strange that I was an astronomer without a telescope, so she fixed that."

"And what did you get, Jewell?"

The girls came in about the time he finished asking the question, and I tried not to look at Eva because she got pots and pans and a vacuum cleaner.

I felt sorry for her when Jewell answered, "A Christmas ring."

"The one they had at Wal-Mart?" Eva asked.

I was surprised she was familiar with it.

While the ring was nowhere as spectacular as something from Tiffany's. It was also a lot cheaper. But it still cost a small fortune as far as a $1200.00 a month detective might be concerned.

"We'll be ready to eat in about five minutes," Jewell said.

"Outstanding," Pastor Morgan said. "I'm starved."

There were a few seconds of silence, and then I told Pastor Morgan and Max, "Come on, guys, I'll show you my telescope."

I took him into the small room that served as an office. We had a desk in it, a file cabinet that had been in the shed when Jewell bought the place, and bookshelves. An old manual typewriter sat in one corner of the desk.

My telescope sat in one corner. As telescopes go, it wasn't anything to brag about. It certainly couldn't be mentioned in the same breath as a say a Meade refractor. It was a simple Tasco refractor on an Alt-Azimuth Mount. It had a small finder scope that I'd zero later and a handful of eyepieces. It was very much like the first telescope I'd ever owned, and I'd pushed that one to its limits and looked at every star, nebula, planet, comet, an asteroid I could find.

Two of the most breathtaking things I'd ever seen had been through that small telescope. The first time I looked at Saturn, the rings were tilted towards me against a background of stars. I remembered standing in the early spring night, looking across the gulf of space that separated me from it and peering through the eyepiece.

The view was so stunning that I'd forgotten to breathe for several minutes. Saturn looked unreal, and I remembered thinking that if God made Christmas ornaments, that distant world would certainly hang well on the cosmic tree. It looked like some tiny glass blown object, beautiful and serene against a field of stars.

Off to one side was a small, reddish star, which I learned from an almanac was one of Saturn's moons, Titan. The Pioneer, Voyager, and Cassini missions were still years in the future, and that tiny red dot would fire my imagination. In years to come, I'd read every scrap I could regarding it.

Then there was Comet Kohoutek. The comet was found far from the sun but very bright for the distance. Everyone was sure that it would be the comet of the century. And right up to perihelion (that point at which the comet was closest to the Sun), it seemed that it would live up to that promise.

But it never became this incredible sight in the sky everyone hoped for. It passed very near to the Sun, and something happened to it there. It came out dimmer than when it went in and never brightened as they expected.

But it was still a very good comet. I remembered we'd had several days of bad weather and clouds had covered the sky. This was my first chance to do some stargazing since Christmas. I stepped out into the January cold and set up my telescope. I'd shoveled an area clear of snow where I could set up without standing in the snow. Orion was high in the sky, and taking a look at the nebula was always a treat.

But above the western horizon was a fuzzy bright green ball, with a faint tail that streamed out behind it like a fan.

It was Kohoutek. I remember people saying that it was invisible. They were wrong. I stood for several minutes, admiring it as it glittered in the night sky and marveled at how stars were still visible through the tail.

Then I turned the telescope towards the nucleus, and when I peered through it, I could see where gases were evaporating away from it, and the Solar Wind swept them into the broad tail. I studied the tail and how it curtained around and where some areas were heavier than others.

I then went in and asked my parents if they wanted to come out and see it.

"You can't see it," they told me. "The news says it's invisible to the naked eye."

"Well, it's up there, and it gorgeous."

"No, you don't know what you're looking at."

My parents had always considered me stupid.

What I didn't realize until much later was that the comet was a watershed moment in my life and that the further it drifted away from the Sun, the further I'd drift from my parents.

"Neat," Max said. "I've never looked through a telescope at anything in the sky."

"Well, we just might take it out then. There's the Orion Nebula. Always good for a look."

Jewell called us for dinner. The kids came rushing down from their rooms. ur daughters were dressed well, and their hair was combed perfectly. Gerry was dressed in a plaid shirt, and his hair looked like it and a comb were strangers.

We all sat down at the table, me at the head, Jewell directly opposite me. The Morgan's on the left and Max and Eva were at the right. The kids were all clustered around the rickety card table that every family seems to own. That's the kid's table, and the only way you move to the main table is if someone around it dies.

On the table, between us was the meal that the Morgan's had brought over. It smelled like heaven.

We all bowed our heads, and I said grace. Then the food began to be passed around. As I took the ham from Max, I got a good look at Eva's face, and I realized what it was I'd noticed earlier but hadn't put my finger on. Her cheek was swollen, and there seemed to be bruise hidden under concealer.

"What happened to your cheek, Eva?" I asked while putting a slab of ham on my plate. I already knew the answer, but I wanted to hear it from her. I thought if I didn't act like it was a big deal, I might get an honest answer.

She seemed to stop for a moment, and she got that deer caught in the headlights of a car look. The secret was found out, and she knew it. Then she glanced at Max and back to me.

"Oh," she said, and the way she said it made me sure it was a lie. "One of my Alzheimer's patients. He punched me the other day."

"Those old-timers with dementia can sure ring your bell," I said, as Pastor Morgan and I traded a look.

I knew she was lying.

What I didn't expect was for her to own up to it.

She knew we knew.

Eva put down her fork, and tears welled up in her eyes. She was quiet for a moment and then said quietly. "I'm sorry to ruin your Christmas."

I looked at Max. I saw his eyes go wide, and his lips quivered just a little. I already knew what Eva was going to say.

She dabbed at her mouth with the napkin. She took a breath, summoned up all her courage, and then said flatly, "Max has been hitting me again."

I don't know why she said it right then and there. Maybe because we were all there and she knew we'd watch out for her. Maybe she felt safe, or maybe she was just sick and tired of being sick and tired.

"Max!" I said sharply as if I were scolding a child. It was a mistake.

Max stood up so suddenly, his chair tipped over backward and landed with a loud bang on the wooden floor.

"Why you lying . . ." he said. His face went red with rage, and his fist came up. I was already jumping up, but he'd swung, proving she was telling the truth.

For a tenth of a second, I couldn't believe it was all happening. A major bombshell had just been dropped right in front of my family and guests, and a violent response was playing out right behind it.

And a whole lot of things happened almost instantly. Except for Eva, every adult at the table was on their feet. I'd grabbed Max and yanked him away from Eva. His fist passed through open-air instead of into her face. Pastor Morgan had moved and put himself between Eva and Max.

Max was thrashing about. He was hard to control since I didn't have a good grip on him. He was swinging again, and this time it was aimed squarely at Eva. Pastor Morgan saw it coming, but the best he could do was move so that the blow caught him in the back of the head. I heard him grunt at the punch, and I could hear shouts of surprise and exclamations of fright from the women and children.

I slipped behind Max and grabbed up and under his arm and got him into a half-nelson. He tried to throw himself backward, and we fell. As we fell, I twisted, so he took the brunt of the fall.

My other hand grabbed the hand that he'd just struck Pastor Morgan with, and I twisted it without thinking. That forced him to roll over onto his stomach. I heard a cry of pain from Max as I winched the arm up and behind his back. I pushed up with my legs, dragging him up into a sitting position.

"Get up," I growled. I issued the command in what I called my cop voice. The voice I reserved for criminals. I drug him into a standing position.

"What the hell is wrong with you?" I yelled at him as I pulled him up. I started pushing and carrying him to the door.

"Let me go, damn it," he shouted.

"You come into my home as a guest, and you try to assault your wife in front of me! I think you've worn out your welcome, Max!"

"You're throwing me out!" he cried in surprise. "You're my friend!"

That didn't carry a lot of weight right then and there.

"You bet I am. But, if there's one thing I've zero use for is a man who beats a woman!" I shouted. I was starting to wonder what to do with him. Maybe a night in jail would do him some good.

He decided for me.

"Let me go. I'll leave," he said.

I pushed him away and went instantly into a defensive crouch.

"Jewell," I said, not taking my eyes off him. "Toss him his coat."

Jewell went into the bedroom, brought it out a second later, and handed it to him. Jewell had made a tactical mistake, and I was ready if he tried to grab her. I moved my leg back slightly, ready to use it to spring into an attack if he did anything except take the coat.

He grabbed the coat and started to put it on.

"Come on," he said angrily to Eva. "We're leaving!"

I noticed out of the corner of my eye that Eva hesitated, moved like she was going to go, then stopped again.

"Eva is a woman in my house and under my protection. She's free to stay," I said, not taking my eyes off him.

"Eva," Jewell said, an edge to her voice. I felt, rather than saw that Pastor Morgan, Carol, and Jewell had formed a battle line slightly behind me, but in front of Eva. "You don't have to go with him."

"Where the hell's she going to sleep?" Max growled as if that was a major problem. "She's my wife."

"We've got a couch," I said. "Now, get the hell out." The last was said with a growl to my voice.

He stood looking at me, a mix of anger, hate, and pain on his face. And then he said, "Sarge! I never thought it would be you who stabbed me in the back."

He turned, opened the door, and left, slamming the door so hard behind him that the glass shook. I heard him run to his truck.

"Eva," I said. "Does he have a gun in the truck?"

"Rifle," she said.

"Shit," I whispered. Quickly I locked the door and killed the lights. My pistol was upstairs in our bedroom. What a time to be away from your weapon.

Max got into the truck and started it. He slammed it into reverse, and with a roar, the truck went spinning out of the driveway, slinging snow and rock. He pulled rapidly out onto the road, kicked it into drive and floored it. The tires screamed as they fought to find some traction, and the truck fishtailed down the road.

I stepped out and watched the tail lights recede. It was several seconds before I realized that Pastor Morgan was next to me.

"You okay," I asked, my eyes still watching the receding taillights.

"I'm okay," he answered.

We went back into the warmth of the house. Gerry had picked up the chair, and everyone was still standing around, shock on their faces.

"Apologies," I said as if this happened every day. "Please. Let's sit and eat."

And surprisingly, everyone did. Once they'd begun eating, I excused myself and went upstairs. I got the 45 out of my holster and stuck it in the small of my back. I also grabbed a snub nose 38, which I passed under the table to Pastor Morgan. He took it, secreted it away, and nodded like nothing had happened.

Jewell looked at me across the table, and then at Pastor Morgan. She knew we were both focused on listening for anything outside.

The Morgan's left about 10 PM, and we all went to bed. I tucked the pistol under my pillow. It had been a long time since I'd done that.

"All in all," Jewell said, "not one of the better Christmases I've had."

I slept on a hair-trigger that night, looking outside often, but all I ever saw was the snow.

EPILOGUE

I gave Max a couple of days to simmer down before I called him. I really shouldn't have been surprised that my call went to his tape machine. I left him a message asking him to call me.

Several days went by, and still no call.

This time I dropped by his apartment. My knock on his door went unanswered. I walked out of his apartment building and noticed that his pickup wasn't there. I guess I'd missed that, and decided he just wasn't home.

Over the next several days, I tried calling. I left him a couple of messages and dropped in at different hours. He was never home.

Eva was ecstatic that he wasn't bothering her. We'd gotten a Sheriff's Restraining Order on Max. Basically, it's an order to leave someone the heck alone. It's a temporary thing, and they have to run it through the courts for it to become permanent. We couldn't find Max to serve the order. And he was nowhere to be found when the matter went to court. Judge Gordan looked at the evidence and issued the order.

The Sheriff told Eva that if Max showed, to let us know right away.

Eva promised she would, and went back to work. A few days later, she got herself a lawyer and started the process of driving a stake through the heart of her marriage.

The problem was, no one knew where Max was, and I was getting a little concerned. The La Jara cops hadn't seen him. Neither had the guys and girls who worked the markets and gas stations around town. I even called Jonesy and Terri, figuring they might have heard something from him.

Neither had.

A few weeks went by before I asked his landlord if she knew where he was. She told me that he'd come in, paid four months rent in advance, and said he was going to Mexico.

"Good," I said. "Maybe he can sort out his life down there."

I figured he was on some beach down there, a bottle of Tequila in one hand, and his arm wrapped around some brown-skinned beauty.

I figured I might never see him again.

I was wrong, of course.

About the Author

William Ablan is the pen name of Richard L. Muniz.

The son of a rancher, Richard, left the ranch to work in police work. He studied Astronomy and Physics but soon realized he was pursuing a degree he couldn't get work in.

One night he did a ride-along with Alamosa Police Department. That night convinced him that he just might have a future in law enforcement. He applied and spent the next twenty years working as a police officer.

He's also a veteran of the United States Army and served as a Military Policeman. He worked undercover narcotics, VIP security, and Military Police Investigations while stationed at Ft. Riley, Kansas, with the 1st Infantry Division.

He saw action in the Gulf War as a member of the 1st Armored Division.

Muniz has also worked in Disaster Planning and Recovery Operations.

Today, he resides in Greeley, Colorado, with his wife, Julie.

He works in Information Technology and is considered an expert in Virtualization and Cloud Technologies.

Like his central character, he's an active member of his church and community.

Check out and follow him at the website below:

https://williamablan.wordpress.com.

William R. Ablan

COMING SOON

The sequel to "The Cross and the Badge" . . .

Against Flesh and Blood . . .

Watch for it November 2019

Made in the USA
Columbia, SC
11 June 2020